A Life
—Worth Living—

A.J. Hughes

Anicale Publishing—Madison, WI
ISBN: 978-0-9998967-0-9
Library of Congress Control Number: 2022904704
Title: A Life: Worth Living
Author: A.J. Hughes
Digital distribution | 2022
Paperback | 2022

This is a work of fiction. The characters, names, incidents, places, and dialogue are products of the author's imagination, and are not to be construed as real.

Also by A.J. Hughes

A Walk on the Other Side

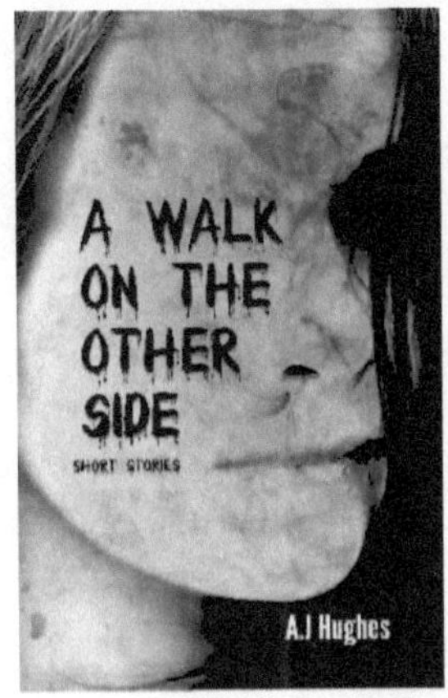

Are you ready to take a walk on the other side? Be prepared for the supernatural, thrillers, fantasies, and tales of ghosts, fairies, and even death. These creepy stories are surely to die for, but not before getting weird or just weirded out.

A Day of Rain

A Day of Rain is a collection of LGBT short stories about romance, heartbreak, loss, rejection and acceptance on rainy days and nights.

DEDICATION

To my mother for all her help and support.
To my Grandmother Renee.
To my family.

Thanks to everyone that helped me in the process of this book.

CHAPTER ONE

I have never been in love. I've had crushes but I've never felt butterflies in my stomach, the sweaty palms, or that yearning to see him. I always wanted to know what it was like to be in love, but I gave up. No matter what I did, love seemed impossible. I've gone on dates, but none of the men were the "one". I wondered if I could even fall in love. Was it the guys I was around or was it me?

I was lonely. I wanted to experience love and epic romances like the heroines in movies, books, and video games. I lived through the books I read, the anime and cringe-worthy movies I watched. When I read or watched romance novels and movies, it allowed me to live vicariously through the characters.

But those stories made me feel even more empty inside. Why do I even bother? Love stories allowed me to see what love was like through the eyes of others.

After a while, I was done. I was over trying to feel it. What could I possibly do to fall in love? Most of the people I spoke with said I was depressed and the others, I was cold-hearted. Was I depressed? Was my inability to find "the one" depressing? Yeah, a little. I already knew the truth, I just had to admit it to myself. It wasn't for lack of potential suitors out there in the world. I was the problem. I was cold-hearted.

That was the revelation that led me to the ledge of the Brooklyn bridge, looking into the depths, facing the inevitable. My heart hurt. I was tired of being alone. What life could I possibly live when I couldn't even feel a simple human emotion like love?

I looked down at the dark calming waves. The city lights sparkled against the rippling waves. I heard the numerous sirens around the city, the honking cars behind me. No one was coming for me. I was in an inconspicuous space. Just out of the blind spot of passing cars.

The breeze was gentle and cold. Chills traveled down my spine as I wondered what would happen to me. What was death like? Where would I go? I was religious but doubt still crept in my mind when I thought about death. I inhaled and closed my eyes. My heart was racing. Pounding hard against my chest. This was it. I positioned myself and started sliding off of the edge.

"This isn't the way to fix your problems," a low voice said. I opened my eyes and looked to my left. A hand gently reached out to me.

I turned around to see a man in his mid-twenties. His gray eyes panicked. He was handsome, his jaw line was smooth, but curved perfectly, not sharp but not too soft. His hair was light brown and shaggy, neatly parted to the side and cut at the nape of his neck. He was nicely dressed, maybe returning from a business meeting, he wore black dress slacks, a white dress shirt so clean it looked like it was glowing in the dark, and the top button unbuttoned. His jacket matched his pants, he wore a long coat that stopped at his knees and black dress shoes.

"What's it to you?" I asked, turning back to the water.

"I can't let you kill yourself. If I can do something…"

"So it's out of obligation?" I asked.

"N-no." He shook his head. "Life is hard. I'm going through a lot right now too. Please, you're not alone."

"Yes I am." I blinked slowly to hold back my tears.

"You're not. I'm here, and what about your family? Do you know how much they'll be hurt when they find out you're dead?"

"I was a foster kid. I was given away when I was 5. I was never adopted, and my foster family only took 'care' of me because of the paycheck. I'm by myself," I said, looking away. Tears filled my eyes I couldn't hold them back any longer.

My father died in a car accident when I was 3 and my mother was never the same. She was distant. When she came home from work, she would go to her room and cry. Leaving me to eat whatever I could find. When I was 5 my grandmother came and took me away. My mother was happy to see me go. She cried and thanked her for taking me off her hands.

The differences between my mother and my grandmother were vast. I was loved, and I got to play. I would eat the cookies she baked. I slept in a warm bed.

But life with my grandma was short lived. My grandmother died a year later. It was only when she didn't show up for her weekly physical therapy that her doctors decided to check on her. Which was when I was found. Child Protective Services couldn't find any living relatives. My grandmother had cut all ties to my mother, and I didn't know of any uncles or aunts. So I was placed in foster care. I watched as my foster siblings were adopted one by one, while I remained in the horrible home of the Rogers family.

Margaret Rogers, a divorced mother of three, became a foster parent solely for the money. My foster siblings and I were abused and treated like second class citizens. We ate last, after her sons. We were only allowed showers when we had doctor's appointments, or when our case workers visited. We were rarely bought clothes, and when my sisters' and I did something wrong, she shaved our hair. She called us good for nothing little whores. And my brothers? They were forced to sleep in the garage, in a tent, or on the porch. We were there when she and her husband divorced. She blamed us for "tempting him". He fell for my oldest foster sister, and they ran away together. They left with his son I never spoke to and moved far away. No one else bothered to run away because we all had to pay for it. But each one of my siblings were set free except me. I stayed with that horrendous woman and her miscreant sons until I was 18.

After a certain age, it's harder for foster children to be adopted. We're considered "emotionally damaged" or at least, that's what Margaret told us. And maybe I was, but could you blame me for being aloof, rude, and mean to her and her sons? I was abused. They broke things and blamed it on us. She didn't resort to violence, but she did little things you wouldn't notice looking at us, like not feeding us. The only happiness I had was when I was reading romance novels. I sat in the attic all day and read books. I was envious of the lives the women had and their luck falling in love so quickly. Why was I any different from them? Did I do something in a past life to receive such a horrible flaw? I had a few crushes, like the football coach who was 23, and the soccer coach who was 27. I wasn't interested in guys my age. They were immature and rude. The feelings I had for them never lasted more than a few months and my feelings were as if they never happened at all.

When I was 18, Margaret threw me out. I had nowhere to go, but I saved money from the job I kept secret from her. I was able to get a hotel for the night. I came across an ad for New York City, which stated moving there would be the "highlight of my life" and was gullible enough to fall for it. I flew there immediately. It was only when I came to New York that I accepted my fate as an ugly, heartless person, not worth living. I crossed the Brooklyn bridge daily for almost a year. I looked over the ocean. If I had to die, I wanted to fall in there. It was so peaceful. Which is where I would have been if that guy hadn't stopped me.

"I'm sorry to hear about that, but surely there was a mistake?" he asked. He stepped onto the beam, his legs shaking. I could tell he wanted to sit next to me, but fear possessed him. "I don't think your mother would have given you away."

"You're a fool," I scoffed. He must have grown up in a happy loving home. "Not everyone is an honest or good person."

"It doesn't hurt to believe."

I stared at him. "What's your name?"

"Daniel," he said. "Daniel Rogers."

"You have the same name as my foster family," I said, standing up. "Are you related to a Margaret Rogers?"

He shook his head. "First I've heard of her."

"Good," I said, looking him closely in the eyes.

"Would you like to talk about your troubles?" he asked gently, a smile on his face.

"Not with you," I replied, as I walked past him.

"Where are you going?"

"That's none of your business."

I walked along the side of the bridge towards Brooklyn, strangers stared at me like I was crazy. I had a cheap apartment, in a decent area, but I needed a job at some point before my money ran out. As I walked on the bridge, I could hear someone behind me. I turned to see Daniel.

"What do you want?" I asked.

"Nothing, just making sure you don't jump."

"I won't, damn." I fastened my pace.

He followed me for blocks. I couldn't escape him.

"Please stop following me."

"I live over here."

"Then walk ahead of me," I said.

"Fine by me," he said, shrugging his shoulders, a smug look on his face.

We walked into the same apartment building.

"What are you, my stalker?" I asked.

"Not at all," he said. "Pretty sure I lived here first."

He was my neighbor. I lived in apartment 6B, and he lived in 6A. My luck was perfect. This guy with the same last name as the people I wanted to avoid, was living in close proximity. I needed to move soon. Last thing I needed was Margaret popping up at my doorstep, her shrill voice, pasted on tan foundation and poorly dyed blonde hair asking for Daniel.

I flopped on my bed and looked at the ceiling. What was my life becoming? I closed my eyes. I was exhausted.

I can't believe I almost died, I thought. *If he hadn't been there...* I trembled as reality sunk in. I covered my mouth stifling my cry.

What came over me? I wasn't originally suicidal, it was just at that moment, my body moved on its own. I was angry at first, but I was thankful he stopped me. Deep down, I didn't want to die. I made my resolve, but I knew that was taking the easy way out. And I didn't want to die without ever experiencing love.

The next day, I pretended like nothing happened. It was only me and Daniel that knew about that incident. And, I probably wasn't going to see him again, so good riddance. It was nice getting some of it off my chest. Even just to him. It was the first time in a long time I had a conversation with someone aside from employees at stores despite the circumstance. I didn't have friends. Not since moving to Brooklyn. I didn't have a job yet and I wasn't social enough to walk up to people and talk. I just spent most of my time going to different libraries and touring the city.

I didn't feel like going out, I was too mentally drained. By 7 PM, I was starving. I hated cooking but I also couldn't waste money on take out. I survived on canned goods and frozen meals. That night however, I just wasn't up for anything and decided to treat myself to take out. I got dressed. I didn't know what to eat. Eventually I chose a Chinese restaurant that wasn't too far away. When I opened the door, exiting the elevator, was Daniel. He looked as handsome as ever.

Shit, I thought my face flushed. I receded inside my back against the door as I waited until I couldn't hear anything in the hall.

"Is it really worth it? I could just settle for a TV dinner."

I walked away from the door and placed one in the microwave. After eating, I walked to my room and plopped on my bed. I closed my eyes and let out a huge sigh. I was so tired, I dozed off.

Minutes later, I heard light tapping coming from the other room. I opened my eyes and sluggishly answered the door. I had a feeling who it was. Who else could it be? I peered through the peephole and watched him. He stood there fixing his hair. He shook his head and fussed with his bangs. I contemplated whether it was a good idea to deal with him.

"Yes?" I asked, opening the door.

"I just wanted to give you a housewarming gift." He smiled and handed me a box of chocolates, plate of brownies, and a vase of flowers.

"No thank you," I said, handing it back to him. He was attractive, but I knew this would end up like all the other crushes I had, pointless. I wasn't going to go back down that spiral, not on my watch. In fact, I wanted him to dislike me. I drove everyone away with my personality. And what other way to push someone away than to be rude? He could get hurt or offended, but he would get over it in no time and forget I ever existed.

"What?" he asked, surprised. I met his puzzled dark gray eyes. "It's rude to reject a gift."

"I don't want it," I said, closing the door.

I wished all memories of last night washed from existence. Why couldn't he just move on?

"Why?" He placed a foot in the door. "Are you upset with me?"

"No."

"Then why are you being rude?"

"Because of your name." Which was partially true. He looked speechless, rather offended by what I said. I didn't really care but I was a little taken aback by his reaction.

"My name?" He looked confused and squinted his eyes. "What's wrong with Daniel?"

"Not your first name. It reminds me of my foster family."

"Then call me something else."

"Goodnight," I said, trying to force the door closed.

"Wait," Daniel said. He forced his body halfway through the door, placed his arm above my head on the wall and rested his head on his arm. He towered over me. He had to be 5'11 or 6 ft. Oh gosh! He was so attractive, it was intimidating. "Give me a shot."

"Why?" My face was hot. He was too close for comfort. His gray eyes studied me. A sort of flirtatious look in them.

"I want to be your friend."

"You're just saying that because I tried to commit suicide." I stepped back into my apartment.

"That's not true," he said, walking in completely. "I saw you when you moved in, then again on the bridge. I wanted to be your friend from the beginning."

"What, don't have any other friends?"

"I also just moved here. I don't know anyone."

"Why not ask another neighbor?"

"Because it has to be you," he said. His smile said one thing, but Daniel's eyes told otherwise. Serious and intense. Recognition hit his face and his eyes softened.

"That came out wrong," he continued, holding composure. "I meant…I want to be friends with you. That's why I said it has to be you."

It was looking more and more like a scene out of a romance book, but I knew I wasn't lucky enough or pretty enough to experience it in real life, so I disregarded it as him wanting to be *just* friends. I took a minute to think before finally accepting his proposal. I would just have to be annoying or something, make him regret his decision.

"Fine," I said. "But if you say anything about your last name, or suicide, it's over."

"Gotcha."

I ushered him out of my apartment, he was still insistent on me taking his "house-warming" gift. I grabbed it and closed my door. I felt kind of stupid agreeing to be his friend. But I also thought about it logically. Him wanting to be my friend was friend zoning me. I just had to keep that in mind when being around him.

Maybe he was trying to be my friend out of pity? I spilled my guts to him, spewing all kinds of nonsense. Saying I was lonely… yeah, it was *definitely* a pity offer. I didn't want to be friends with someone out of pity. That was worse than being alone. What would he even get out of being friends with me?

I looked at the gifts in my arms. He went all out on it. The brownies looked handmade. If he really did make those himself, it was impressive. Any woman would be lucky to have a guy like him baking desserts.

Was he even dating someone? There was no way someone as handsome as Daniel was still single. He was most likely taken, he only wanted to be friends out of pity, I had nothing to worry about if I remembered those two little things.

The next morning, Daniel knocked on my door.

"Do you know what time it is?" I asked, opening the door.

"Yep. 7 AM. I wanted to say good morning before I went to work."

"Good morning. Just fyi, I don't wake up before 11, so no more of this please."

"That's not a good time to wake up. You miss most of the day."

"Not 'most of the day'. Besides, I don't have a lot to do. I'm just going to relax all day or walk around. I'm not missing anything."

"We can change that. Want to have dinner with me?"

"No thanks. Have fun at work. I won't be answering my door for a while. Need some me time, so you shouldn't waste your time coming back."

He looked at me, smiling. I did everything in my power to refrain from returning his look. I slowly closed the door. Would being his friend make me feel that overwhelmed by his presence? I hoped sooner rather than later he found someone else to ride the pity train. I certainly didn't need a ticket. I spent my entire life dealing with it, I didn't need it now as an adult.

"I don't know about that," he said, sliding inside my apartment.

"Who said you can come in?"

"We're friends now. I think we should be able do that to each other. I also think I should have a spare key to your apartment, you can have a key to mine."

"Not happening," I responded, quickly.

"I just…" Daniel paused. He was choosing his next words carefully. "I think…it would be best since you're suicidal, that I have a key…to be safe…" he trailed off.

There he was, pitying me. Shoving that suicide in my face. I understood he was trying to be considerate, but it just made me feel worse. "We just met. I can't give you a key."

"Maybe in a few weeks, or days, you'll know me well enough to feel comfortable giving me one."

I sighed. I didn't respond and walked to the couch.

Daniel walked into the kitchen and asked, "Have you had breakfast?"

"Considering you woke me up not even 5 minutes ago, I haven't."

"Great, I'll make us something to eat."

"I appreciate it, but I don't eat breakfast."

"Breakfast is the most important meal of the day, you gotta start eating."

"I'm fine."

"If you say so." Daniel looked disapproving but didn't push it any further. He was judging me. It was so obvious. He saw a few of my pantries, practically empty. Maybe he thought I was so poor I couldn't afford food. Or that I was anorexic. Well, I mean, he wouldn't be far off. I could only afford what I could, but I didn't have an eating disorder. Even if I did, that didn't warrant any kind of ill-thoughts.

"What time do you work?" I asked.

"7:30."

"Don't you think you should be hurrying to work?"

"Nope. I work 10 minutes away by bus, 20 minutes walking."

"You probably already missed the bus."

"I can jog. My boss won't say anything if I'm a few minutes late." Daniel smiled then sat next to me. "If we can't hang out for a while, might as well enjoy the time we do have together."

Daniel stayed another 10 minutes before leaving for work.

I sighed. "Finally some peace and quiet."

I wondered if he really didn't have other friends. Why was he so hung up on trying to talk to me of all people? If he really was lonely, there were other people to converse with. He clearly had no problems talking to me. So clearly he was an extrovert. Unless there was something wrong with him that I wouldn't find out until it was too late. I mean there had to be something. Why would he want to talk to me?

A few days passed and no word from Daniel. I hit my head at some point. When, I couldn't remember. But I was thinking about him too much. Was I paranoid he would knock on my door and bother me or did I want him to come?

No matter what I read, I couldn't stop thinking about him. I needed to take my mind off him.

I texted my sister Anna. Well, she wasn't my biological sister, she was my foster sister. Anna was one of the only siblings I kept in contact with, everyone else either forgot about us, or didn't want to be associated with us. It hurt of course, but I understood where they came from. A shitty upbringing with terrifying memories. I was fine with them forgetting me. I wanted to forget mine as well, but not my foster siblings.

I told Anna where I was moving and ever since, she randomly visited me from time to time. She was a year younger, so she could never stay long.

"Do you have anything planned?" I asked.

I waited a bit before she responded, "No, why?"

"No reason, just miss you. Plus I want to get my mind off things. Can you come over?"

"I'd have to ask Jane," she responded.

"Okay," I replied.

We texted for a bit longer before Anna went back to class. I guess Daniel was right, I didn't think of it at the time, but Anna would have been the only person who missed me. If I had jumped, she wouldn't have anyone to vent to. I added that to my mental notes of things to be grateful to Daniel for.

Anna only took him off my mind temporarily, then I was back to thinking about him.

That's it, I thought, jumping out of bed. The only way to get him out off my mind was to say hi, I would thank him for the housewarming gift and wipe my hands clean of any lingering thoughts.

I got dressed in a navy-blue hoodie and shorts, put on a pair of black socks and left my apartment. I stood outside of his door for 2 minutes trying to will myself to knock. I was nervous, I wanted to see him, but I also knew that I was admitting something I wasn't supposed to feel.

"We're only friends," I reassured myself. "Friends say hello all the time. There's nothing more to it. He has a girlfriend. You don't feel anything."

I knocked on his door. No response. *Guess he's not home…oh what a shame,* I thought, turning away from his door.

"Maya?" a voice called, as the elevator doors opened.

Shit, I thought. I turned around.

"Did you need something?" Daniel asked, smiling. He wore a grocery store uniform and carried bags.

"Uh…sugar…" Not the best excuse.

I stepped back as he went to his apartment.

"You're in luck," he said, smiling and sitting his bags down. "I just got some today."

Why is he always winking? I thought. Did he think that was attractive or something?

"You wanna come in and wait?"

I shook my head. "No, it's fine, I don't mind waiting here."

"Okay," he chuckled, as he went inside, the door closing behind him.

I waited not even 30 seconds before Daniel came out with a measuring cup full of sugar. "Take your time returning the measuring cup."

"I can pour it into something else and give it back to you. You bake right? You need it more than I do."

"I do bake, and I have two measuring cups. There's no rush."

"It's fine, I can give it back right away."

He leaned on his door and smiled. "Take it."

I sighed. "You win."

"Good. You have any plans tonight?"

"Kind of."

"Oh? What are you up to?"

"Stuff. Thanks for the sugar. I better go…." I backed away and opened my door. "Oh and thanks for the gifts…"

I awkwardly waved and closed the door. I inhaled deeply. I looked at the measuring cup. He literally filled it to the top. I didn't have sugar, but I didn't cook, so what was I going to use it for? I grabbed some Ziplock bags and filled them with sugar.

"I could try to make cake," I mumbled.

I didn't even need sugar for cake. I would just buy the cake mix. I put the sugar away, grabbed a book and sat on the couch. I read everything on my bookshelves. As much as I loved these books, I was tired of reading them. I didn't have enough money to splurge on new books and I'd already read most of the books I was interested in at the library.

I read for maybe 20 minutes before someone knocked on my door.

"Yes?" I asked.

"I'm here to get my measuring cup," he said, trying his best to hold his laughter in.

"You literally fought with me on keeping it, now you want it back? I could've given it to you earlier."

"I didn't want it, now I do." Daniel stepped through my doorway. "Can I wait inside while you get it?"

I stepped aside and he walked in. Thankfully I had already washed it. I handed him the measuring cup. We stood in silence for what felt like 10 *very* awkward minutes.

"Well, are you gonna leave now…or…"

"No, I hadn't planned on it." He shook his head. "We're friends now, I think we should spend this time to get better acquainted."

I rolled my eyes and said, "Do whatever you want, I'm going back to reading."

He grabbed my hand and led me to the couch. "You can't do that."

"Let's watch some scary movies," he continued. "What do you want to watch first?"

"I don't like scary movies."

"Why?"

"Just not my style." It wasn't like I was scared to watch them. I just didn't like the violence or unnecessarily gruesome scenes. I could never understand why some people liked watching others get harmed. Seeing gore made my stomach churn.

"What kind of movies do you watch?"

"Romance."

"So, chick flicks?"

"If romance movies are considered chick flicks, then yeah."

"Okay, then you probably have a few, right?"

I nodded and pointed to a box labelled "movies/anime." I still had packed boxes. I didn't have the motivation to finish unpacking.

"Alright, then I get to choose which one."

Daniel walked to the box and shuffled through the stacks. "How about, 'The Forest Within'? Or there's an anime called 'Say You Love Me,' wanna watch that?"

"You like anime?"

"A little. A sorta 'roommate' of mine loved watching this. I didn't watch it with her, but I checked it out myself."

"A 'sorta roommate?' What's that?"

"My family also had foster children. My stepmother was like the wicked stepmother from Cinderella to me and them. I never spoke with the foster kids much. I always wanted to but because of her horrible children, they hated me by default. I refer to them as 'sorta roommates' because we lived under the same roof, but they never considered me part of their family. Eventually, my dad divorced her, and I never saw them again." He looked sad. He gazed at the box as he spoke, a small smile on his face. A look of nostalgia. "This may sound funny or weird, but I actually fell in love with my foster sister. She was a loner who liked to read. Sometimes, when she had the chance, she would watch anime. I tried to make things easier for her. You know, staying off the TV when she was home, cleaning the attic where she hung out. But…I could never talk to her. I was too nervous to look her in the eye. I still love her… but she doesn't remember me."

"You never know, she might."

"I doubt it. I'm 3 years older. No way she would remember me," Daniel chuckled awkwardly. I hadn't noticed that he had dimples. They were faint.

He already likes someone. I guess I don't have to worry about a relationship with him, I thought. That was the wake-up call needed. My chest was tight and I felt like crying but that was what I wanted. Something that would keep me from liking him. He was unavailable.

He didn't respond. He rummaged through the box once more and grabbed *The Forest Within.* He walked to the DVD player and put it in.

As we watched *The Forest Within*, I wondered what it was like to feel the way the characters felt for their crushes. At the end, as I watched the main heroine confess her feelings, the way her love interest smiled when he was finally able to be with the girl he liked, I wondered what it must have felt like to finally have requited love. Tears fell from my eyes. I was reminded of the fact that I could never experience that and my heart hurt. I never should have watched that, because as I cried, Daniel watched me.

"You must really love romances huh?" Daniel asked, softly.

"Be quiet, please."

"Alright. Do you feel like watching something else?"

I shook my head. "I really do need to go to sleep. Could you go home please?"

"Sure," he said, standing up. "See you later."

Daniel left and I locked the door behind him. I walked to my room and fell on my bed. The sadness came back, and I cried. I needed to stop watching those films, but I was lonelier without them. I'd rather experience something than nothing. I closed my eyes and fell asleep.

A week went by. I hadn't run into Daniel and life continued like normal.

…Then one day, Daniel knocked on the door. The knocks growing louder each minute. "Wake up! It's 11 AM. Time to get up!"

I swung open the door. "Would you be quiet? Not everyone is up this early."

"True, but you really shouldn't sleep so late," he said, walking in.

"That's none of your business," I said.

"You're pretty grumpy when you wake up huh?"

"I'm not 'grumpy', I just hate that you banged on my door."

"I'm sorry. But I waited 'til 11 to say good morning." He smiled.

I exhaled. "You're right. Thanks for that part."

"You wanna go out for lunch?"

"I have plans."

"Real plans or are you just saying that because you don't want to be with me?"

"Real plans."

"Damn, that sucks. Haven't seen you in a week, missed hanging out with you."

"We only hung out like once or twice, how can you miss me already?"

"Because I told you, I don't have any friends. So I'm bored most of the time or I'm working long hours."

He continued, "Well, if you're available tonight, wanna have dinner?"

"I doubt I'll be, but I'll let you know."

"I'll take that."

This time Daniel didn't slide into my apartment. He went back to his own, "reminding" me about joining him for dinner.

And I really did have plans. Anna was coming to visit. I decided we should go sightseeing. I took the bus over the bridge.

If only I was there, I thought.

If it weren't for him, I would have been at rest. Even though I wanted to die in that moment, I was relieved. Deep down, I still had a little hope. I sighed and looked at my phone. I had a message from Anna, she was in New York and was waiting for a meetup spot. She was only staying one day and leaving in the morning. She had school and could only skip one day.

I smiled and texted that I was heading to Times Square to shop. I sent her the address to a café I loved and that we should meet there before shopping.

Mama was a cute, beautifully decorated café on 73 St. I happened to cross it while sightseeing and I've loved it ever since. I didn't go there as often as I wanted but it was a good way to treat myself. It was small, only 10 tables fit. Two high tables lined in front of both windows, the door in between them, from there, two tables to the wall on both sides, and three taller tables in the middle, separated slightly by walking space required for the door. On each table was a small little potted plant, and plants hung from the ceiling. The walls were pastel blue, the counter natural, light wood, a cash register to the right of the counter and a to-go area on the left. Behind the register was an ice cream counter, desserts next to it. You could see the small kitchen in the back, but even that was nicely decorated. Stoves placed to the right just out of view, ovens and toaster ovens in the middle with cute little decals on the side like cartoon plants, kittens, etc. Expresso, coffee, soda machines to the left of the oven, close enough for the barista to reach but far enough to not block the path.

I entered Mama, the smell of coffee and desserts filled the air. It was always peaceful. My favorite barista Makayla was there. She was very beautiful. Her hair was braided, she had the perfect umber skin tone. She was stylish. Under her apron she wore a white short-sleeve blouse and black skinny jeans. She had crystal-like earrings and a necklace that said "Love". Her smile was so bright, it changed everyone's mood. She was the older sister of your friend that you admired.

I ordered my usual meal, a small, caramel frappe with lots of whipped cream, and an avocado sandwich with tomatoes, red onion, cucumber slices, baby spinach, and clover sprouts on wheat bread toasted to perfection. I felt like I was in heaven with every bite. I would never grow tired of it. Makayla struck up conversation as she took my order. She wondered what plans I had for the day.

"I'm meeting my sister."

"Nice! I wish my siblings would visit me," she said. "I can barely get them to watch my plays on Facebook."

I laughed and sat by the window. Anna wasn't hard to miss, she was very pretty. She had long curly brown hair with blonde highlights, beautiful brown eyes, and she only wore dresses and skirts. She was the most popular out of all of us. Guys asked her out daily. And she dated all of them. I always wondered how she could just say yes to anyone, but she would say it wasn't serious, she was young and didn't want to be tied down.

As I looked out the window, I saw her. At first, I didn't recognize her. Her hair was cut in a pixie style, platinum blonde hair, she wore black leggings, and a black crop top. I was stunned. She hated leggings. She would say they were tacky, lazy, and un-ladylike. But there she was, wearing the exact thing she contested since she was 10.

Anna noticed the look on my face. "I know, I know. I decided to give these a try. They're surprisingly comfy. Ever since wearing them, even more guys have been hitting on me."

"You look amazing," I said, my mouth agape. "I thought you hated guys hitting on you?"

"I did, but the new school has a bunch of jealous bitches. They keep bothering me. So I got hotter, now more guys like me."

"Alright, if that's what you want. Just be careful."

"I will," Anna said. Anna grew silent, her face serious as she continued, "Hey, when I graduate, can I live with you?"

"I don't mind but what's wrong?"

"Nothing. Just… Max, my 'dad' seems to like me a little too much."

"What do you mean?"

"He…touches me a little differently than how a parent should."

"What do you mean he touches you? Like—"

Before I could finish Anna interrupted, "Oh god no. Not like that. He hasn't touched me sexually, but it's very sensual. Like he caresses, and touches my hands, shoulders, lower back, and thighs."

"That's so inappropriate. Did you tell Jane?"

"No, she wouldn't believe me. Jane and Max adopted another daughter, she was 14 years old. After only a few days living with us, she said to me and Jane that he 'touched her in a naughty place.' Jane yelled at her and told her not to lie. She sent her back, saying she didn't think she was in the right environment."

"That's fucked up. That girl probably distrusts people even more."

"Maybe. But yeah, I wanna get out, and if something happens before I graduate, I need a place to fall back on."

"You always have me."

Anna smiled. "Thanks."

Makayla walked over with my order. "Here you go. This must be your sister."

"Yeah, Makayla, Anna. Anna, Makayla."

"Hi, it's nice to meet you," Anna said.

"Nice to meet you too."

We finished lunch and I took Anna on a tour of the city. I didn't know where anything was. But when you show someone else around, you always have to front so they think you know everything. Anna thought I did, and I needed to keep it that way.

After getting lost numerous times, we went back to my apartment. When we reached the 6th floor, Daniel waited at my doorstep. It looked like he was about to return to his own apartment before seeing us. Our eyes met and my heart skipped a beat.

Not good, I thought.

"What took you so long?"

"I didn't tell you to wait." I scurried past him to my door and put the key in. My side, the side that Daniel stood on burned. My muscles tensed.

"No, you didn't."

Daniel paused and looked at Anna.

"Who's your friend?" he asked. "I thought I was your one and only friend."

"This is my sister. And when did I say that?"

"After you cried during—"

I lunged at Daniel and put my hand on his mouth. "Shut it!"

While we argued Anna stare at us.

"Sorry about this, he's leaving."

"I'm not."

"Bye," I said, opening the door.

Anna stayed still and asked, "Hey, aren't you—"

"It's nice meeting you. Let's go inside. We should get to know each other," Daniel said.

"You're so right." Anna nodded. "My bad. Nice to meet you, I'm Anna."

"Ignore him," I complained.

"Daniel. Maya, you told her I'm your boyfriend huh?"

Anna shot a glance towards me, a devious look in her eyes. "You didn't tell me you had a boyfriend!"

"I don't!" I turned to Daniel. "Stop making things up."

"I'm not. I said I wanted to be your friend."

"Whatever," I said, grabbing Anna's arm. "Let's go."

"Wait for me," Daniel said, coming in before I could close the door.

"Please leave."

"Let him stay," Anna said. "If you guys are friends, you should be nice to him."

"Annaaa," I groaned.

"Thank you," Daniel said, walking to the couch.

I sighed, "I'll make some food. You…just sit there."

As I cooked, and by cooked, I meant boiling macaroni in a pot, before placing it in the oven to bake. I grabbed whatever canned food I could pass as handmade and microwaved it. I checked every so often on Anna and Daniel. He was too flirtatious, so I couldn't trust him not to attempt wooing Anna. She was definitely hot enough to catch his eye. But they appeared to be comfortable around each other. No awkward conversation like I would have had. As I was finishing up, I checked one last time, I was going to announce what I made when I overheard their conversation.

"Did you tell her yet?" Anna asked.

"No, why would I? I can't be like 'hey, remember me? I'm in love with you.'"

"Why not? The fact that you guys met again, *and* you live close to each other, means it's meant to be."

He shook his head. He mustered an amused tone, "I don't know about that. She always mad."

"Just tell her!"

Daniel lifted his bangs. "Ugh, it's even harder now than back then."

"Only because you're making it that way."

"You wouldn't understand," Daniel said.

"Nope, I don't believe in love. It's a waste of time. I mean, look at you, you're a mess."

"Yeah, but love is nice. It's just, I have the unfortunate luck of loving someone who hates my guts," he chuckled. "I'll more than likely say nothing. If I do, it'll be the Daniel she knows now, not the one from the past."

"Good idea…I guess. But she's a pretty girl in New York, you better hurry before someone snatches her from you."

"That's a horrible thing to say," Daniel said.

"Horrible but true."

"I know, but it's harder than you think."

Anna made a face and said, "I'm gonna check on Maya. You should calm down. Your face has been red since we came earlier."

"No shot," he said, sitting up straight and covering his cheeks.

Guess he figured he wasn't acting as cool as he thought he was, I quietly scoffed.

I ran back into the kitchen and took the dish out of the oven. It was kind of burnt. Anna knew I wasn't a good cook.

"Just in time," Anna said.

"Yeah, just in time to help."

"I don't know about all of that, but I'll give my support."

"Gee, thanks."

"Hey," Anna whispered, her tone more serious yet playful. "What do you think about Daniel?"

"What do you mean?"

"I mean, like, do you think he's cute?"

"Why do you ask?"

"I was just wondering. Usually, you're very reserved. But you let a stranger in."

"I don't know." I shrugged. It was hard for me to express my feelings, sometimes even to Anna. "He kept asking so I eventually gave in. I can't explain it, but I trust him a little…I guess."

"That's not what I'm asking. Do you like him like him?" she asked.

I tried to avoid the subject. "Here, can you take these into the living room?"

Anna grabbed the plate and said, "Sure, but what do you think about him?"

"I barely know him."

"So?"

"I don't know, not really. He's attractive but you know it's impossible for me to fall in love. I don't feel anything."

"You will someday," Anna said. "Daniel could be the one for you."

"Doubt it. I heard you two talking. He already likes someone, so what does it matter if I do like him?"

"That doesn't mean anything. Just steal him from her."

"It's fine, I don't want to stir anything up if it's not there to begin with."

"If you say so, but I give it a week."

"Sure," I said. "You won't even be here to find out."

"I have my ways."

We walked back to the living room, when I looked at Daniel, he was smacking his face.

"What are you doing?" I asked.

"Oh nothing." He jumped. His face was as red as a tomato.

"Shit, you really did some damage." Anna laughed taking out her phone.

Daniel looked in the camera to see his face was red ear to ear.

"Whoa," he said. "I still look good, don't I Maya?"

"Not in the least."

"You're so mean," he mumbled.

I rolled my eyes and handed him a plate.

"For me?" he asked.

"Well yeah," I said, bashfully.

"That's sweet," Anna said, mockingly. "Hey why don't we watch some movies?"

"Okay, no romance movies," Daniel said.

I shot him a look. "Romance movies are fine. Anna you should pick one you like since you're leaving tomorrow."

"Okay," she said, going through my collection.

She put on Pride and Prejudice and sat on the other side of Daniel.

"She has no choice but to talk to you," she whispered.

"Thanks," Daniel said.

She was so obvious. I knew she was trying to make me steal Daniel from whoever he liked. It wasn't going to happen. I scooched away from Daniel and placed my legs in-between us. I rested my head on the arm of the couch. It was a little chilly, but I tried to pretend it wasn't.

"Are you cold?" he asked.

"I'm fine."

"I am," Anna said. "I'll get some covers."

She jumped up and ran into the bedroom. As we waited, it was kind of awkward. I really didn't want to talk to him after figuring out Anna's plan. But he was all for it, oblivious to the true motives behind Anna's disappearance.

"Are you sure you're not cold?" Daniel asked. "I can grab my jacket in the meantime?"

"No, I'm fine really," I said, curling into a ball.

"You certainly look cold," he said. "I'm wearing more layers than you, and I'm still freezing."

"That's you," I mumbled. "People have different tolerance levels."

"But I can feel you trembling," he laughed. "Or is the movie getting to you already?"

"Shut up," I said. I kicked him softly.

"I'm just messing with you," he said, holding my foot. "It was an honor to see you cry."

I didn't respond.

"I'll let you finish the movie in silence…for 5 minutes. Then you'll be begging to cuddle because it's too cold."

"In your dreams," I said.

"I know."

Anna didn't return until over halfway through the movie.

"What took you so long?" I asked.

"I fell asleep."

I laughed, "Just like before."

Anna stuck her tongue out and tossed over a blanket.

"What are you guys going to use?" I asked.

"We'll share," Anna said. "Or…at least you two will."

Anna smiled and wrapped herself in another blanket and with perfect timing, Daniel said, "Man, I sure am cold."

I rolled my eyes and pushed out part of the covers.

"Thank you," he said.

The rest of the night was fine. We watched a few more movies before falling asleep on the couch.

The next morning, Anna and Daniel were gone. I looked at my phone, it was 8 AM. I plopped my arm back down and stared at the ceiling. Alone again. As usual. Accompanied by the silence that no longer bothered me. I sighed, got off the couch, my back ached, went into my bedroom and crawled into bed. It was serene.

Not even 5 minutes had passed before Daniel knocked on the front door. I heard the door swing open. "You didn't lock the door? That's dangerous. Any creep could just waltz in here," Daniel said. He tapped on my bedroom door. "You wake? I'm coming in."

Daniel walked into my room and sat on the bed.

"Get off," I demanded.

"You need to wake up," he said. "You already missed Anna's goodbye. You can't miss the rest of the day too."

"And who says I can't?"

"I do, you're not supposed to sleep for so long. You actually gain weight."

"Please leave."

"No can do," he said, in a matter-of-fact tone. "I have today off. I'm spending it with my bestest friend."

"Then you should probably meet them now."

"I'm talking about you."

"Oh, silly me," I said, sarcastically.

"Let's go," he said, pulling off the covers. "Get dressed."

"Give me back the covers," I said, shooting up.

"Nope, we're going out. I guarantee you'll have fun."

"And if I don't?"

"I'll do *almost* anything you want for a day."

I paused, "Make it two days."

"Deal," he said, grabbing my hand.

We shook hands and I got dressed.

For some reason, I thought. *I feel like I just got duped...*

Daniel and I walked around Manhattan. We saw the empire state building, the Museum of Metropolitan Art, and the Museum of Modern Art. It was fantastic, I knew they existed of course, but I never thought I'd see them in person. All the while, I had great conversations with Daniel, he was more charming than usual, less annoying and I could tell he was trying his hardest not to be. We walked to Mama and Makayla was working.

She was cutting the roses for the day's décor.

"Hey Makayla," I said, running to the register.

"You're visiting so many times lately, I feel so honored," she said, placing her hand on her chest and batting her eyelashes.

We laughed and she looked over at Daniel.

"And who might this be?" Makayla gave me a look and extended her hand to Daniel. "I'm Makayla."

"Daniel, I'm Maya's boy friend."

Makayla looked at me. "You didn't tell me you had a boyfriend."

"I don't, he's just a friend."

"*Just a friend?*'" Daniel repeated, offended. "Is that all I am to you?"

"Yes."

Daniel straightened and blinked his eyes quickly. "Why I never."

So much for being charming. Hello annoying, I thought.

"I'm his 'bestest friend,'" I sighed.

"Oh ok." Makayla winked. "Gotcha."

I rolled my eyes and ordered a drink. We sat at a table by the window. Daniel was quiet and avoided eye contact.

"For someone that's quick to annoy me every chance, you're certainly quiet."

"I need time to reboot. It takes a lot of energy to be annoying."

"Uh huh." I nodded.

I looked at my phone and played games. Every so often, when I took a sip of soda, or a bite of my food, I caught Daniel staring. When I looked at the door when someone came in or left, Daniel stared. I knew he wanted to say something, but he probably didn't know how to say it or when to say it. After lunch, we walked around the city, just looking at monuments, buildings, and whatever else interested us.

Hanging out was great. I had to admit, I was having fun. A little too much for someone like me to have. How can I stay depressed if I was just going to cheat on my feelings? So un-loyal. We walked to a carnival just off the edge of New York City by the coast. From the looks of it, not many people knew about it. But that was a nice feeling, not having to deal with the intense crowds and long lines. We bought tickets and entered the carnival. I was decent at the games. I won a few prizes, but just little mini toys. We played games like dunk tank, Whack-a-Mole, darts, Ring Toss, etc. I was grateful for bringing a tote. It was convenient for our prizes. As we walked through the carnival, I saw the cutest bear hanging on a rack. It was blue, fuzzy and half my size. I always wanted a big bear. But if Margaret had seen it, she would have thrown it away or her sons would have destroyed it. I stopped and looked at the game, *Strongman*. There was no way I could hit it high enough.

Daniel placed his arm on my waist, leaned close to me and asked, "Did you want to try this one?"

"Yeah, but I wouldn't win anyway."

"Which prize did you want?"

"That one." I pointed to the bear.

"Oof, that's a high prize…"

"Yeah, I know. I could probably find it at another, easier booth."

"Nope," the game master interrupted. "All prizes here only."

Daniel took his wallet out and handed the man $5. Daniel winked and said, "Here goes nothing."

He rolled up his sleeves, muscles flexing. He wasn't buff but he still had toned muscles. He lifted the mallet above his head, his muscles tensing. I couldn't help staring at them. And he swung it down. The alarms went off and the game master said unenthusiastically, "Winner."

"Whew," he said. He grabbed the bear and handed it to me. "Just barely reached it. Would've been embarrassing if I hadn't gotten it on the first try."

We both laughed.

I took the bear and hugged it. "Thank you. I love it."

"My pleasure." Daniel smiled.

We continued to walk. I looked at the sky, the sun was going down. I was surprised that time went by so quickly.

"It's crazy, the day went by quickly," Daniel said, as if reading my mind.

"Yeah," I said. "I have to admit, this was really fun. You know how to show your friends a good time."

"Yeah," he let out. "I…was actually meaning to ask you today…"

He paused for a while and pulled me to stop.

"What is it?" I asked.

We stared into each other's eyes. As I waited for him to say it, I started to think of the similarities from romances. My heart pounded. I could hear it in my ears. For a moment, I was experiencing a romantic scene, though I knew that wasn't the case. More like a romantic comedy between the love interest and his friend. Daniel looked away.

"Never mind," he said. "I'll tell you another time."

"Wait, you can't do that," I whined. "You can't start something, build up suspense, then leave it at that. That's actually a really huge pet peeve of mine."

He laughed and cupped my cheeks. "Sorry, I guess I'll have to do that for today. I promise I will tell you eventually."

"That was mean," I said, walking again.

Daniel caught up with me and asked, "Do you want to go on the Ferris wheel?"

"Why?"

"Because they're fun, and I haven't been on one."

"Really?" I asked looking at him. "It's not as great as you think."

"That's what everyone says," he said. "But when you haven't done something before, it'll always be a bigger deal than what it actually is."

"I guess," I muttered. "I can relate."

I thought about Anna and my other sisters saying liking someone wasn't as great as it appeared in the movies. When you haven't felt that, you can't help but want what they had.

"So you understand, then let's go."

Daniel grabbed my hand and led me to the Ferris wheel. I didn't have the mental fortitude to protest. I was more focused on the warm hand that held mine firmly. Our fingers entangled. We gave our tickets and went inside a booth. It was tight packed, with a roof giving us privacy. I sat on one side and Daniel on the other. The Ferris wheel went slower than the ones back in my hometown, they were more like rollercoaster rides than a leisurely one. The dimly lit booth gave a sort of romantic atmosphere, of course to something that wasn't there. I looked out the window, and I could see buildings on one side and the ocean from the other. I was mesmerized. I really loved the view.

"This is kinda romantic huh?" Daniel asked. He looked out the window.

"What do you mean?" I asked, looking at him.

Daniel smiled and leaned over me. I struggled to process what was happening. Daniel was kissing me, and not just a teasing peck but a passionate one. I succumbed to him. My hands gripped his shirt. His lips were soft, his body was warm as he pressed against mine. My mind grew hazy. It was surreal. Daniel pulled away and looked me in the eyes. His eyes were so alluring I could get lost in them. "Romantic like that."

He sat back down and glanced out the window. I was too dumbfounded to yell at him or ask what that was. I just stared at him. My face burned like I had stuck my head in the oven.

"W-what was that?" I managed to ask.

"What?"

"That, what was that?!"

"I don't see what you're looking at," he said, searching out the window.

"You kissing me," I said.

"Oh, that." He smiled. "Don't worry about it. I just wanted to kiss someone in here."

"Yeah, but you need to ask first."

"My bad, I was in the moment. Besides, you would have said no."

"And?!"

"And I wanted to kiss you. No big deal."

"It is for me, considering that was my first kiss."

Daniel's mouth dropped. "Seriously?"

I nodded.

"Wow," he stuttered. "I…feel so honored."

"Good for you," I said. "Apologize."

"No, I don't believe in apologizing when I'm not honest about it or feel like I have to."

"Don't you like your neighbor? Shouldn't you be kissing her?"

"What gave you the impression I liked my neighbor?"

"I heard you and Anna talking last night."

"That… wasn't about our neighbors. You're the only woman on the floor… that I know."

"So you're…"

"No," Daniel exclaimed, catching on to what I was going to say. "I'm not gay!"

"Then who do you like?"

Daniel sighed, "I guess I have no choice."

Daniel moved next to me, and I leaned away preparing to dodge his next kiss. I held my bear tightly.

"I…like you," he said. "I have for a while now. It's a long story and I really care about you."

"You like me?" I asked, in disbelief. No way this hot guy liked me. There had to be a loose screw, or he was fucking with me.

"Yeah, I wouldn't have pleaded to be your friend if I didn't. I wouldn't do that to just any girl."

And be that persistent…

"So you really are my stalker."

"I'm not a stalker," he said, exhausted. "Whenever I see you, I can't take my eyes off you and that night, I saw you get off the bus and walk to the edge. I needed to stop you."

I was silent.

"I know this is a lot to take in, but please bear with me."

"I understand. It's a little weird for you to like me of all people but I get it."

"I'm not a creep or a stalker, please don't think that."

"I'm not, I just want to know what you planned to do after telling me this."

"I don't know, usually in this situation the girl likes the guy back and he just asks her to date. But I'm a bit hesitant, I know you don't see me in that way...."

As he spoke, I began to tune him out. I was deep in thought. *I could easily turn him down and be done with it. I mean, that's what you wanted from the beginning and a broken heart keeps anyone away. But...if I give him a shot, I could see what a relationship was like. Who knows when I'll get another chance? He is attractive, charming, and passionate.*

I nodded as Daniel examined me silently. "I'll date you."

"Seriously? You're not joking right? This isn't payback for my annoying behavior all the time?"

I shook my head. "No, I just want to give you a shot. Just make me fall for you."

Daniel smiled widely. "You won't regret it."

As he smiled, I thought about the same depressing things. There it was again the look of sheer happiness when the woman he "liked" agreed to date him. I couldn't understand why this was happening.

"Can I kiss you again," he asked.

"Now you ask?" I complained. Flushed I said, "Yeah it's fine."

Daniel smiled and leaned over to kiss me. This time he was more delicate. I felt my heart flutter. I pulled away and looked out the window.

"Was that bad?" he asked.

"No, it was fine. I just want to look out one last time before we reach the bottom."

"I understand."

Daniel gazed out the other side and I glanced over. He was trying to hold back his smile, he bit his bottom lip and stared into the distance.

Daniel and I walked home unhurriedly, our hands intertwined. We didn't say much. I looked at the ground and he looked at the sky.

"Man," Daniel said, breaking the silence. "If this is a dream, I don't want to wake up."

"What makes you think it's a dream?"

"I never imagined I'd date you."

"Oh," I said, looking down again.

We returned to my apartment and watched movies. I remember saying goodnight and falling asleep.

CHAPTER TWO

I woke up, my alarm was blaring. I thought maybe the night before was a dream. A nightmare to be exact. That was not how I planned my first relationship to happen. I was supposed to love him unconditionally. Every little thing he did was supposed to move me. Even make me swoon. Daniel was handsome yes, but aside from dream Daniel's kiss, he didn't do that for me. I sluggishly got out of bed and walked to the bathroom. I looked in the mirror, my curly hair standing up and messy. I brushed my teeth and washed my face. I didn't feel like taking a shower. I walked into the living room. The dream I had was bugging me. It felt so real. But there was no chance I would experience something like that, it was even more rare to dream about it. But there I was, dreaming about kissing Daniel. Him of all people. And agreeing to date him. I shivered. I saw the blankets from the night Anna was there still on the couch and figured it was better to clean up then instead of later.

I pulled the blankets up and underneath Daniel slept peacefully. Flushed, reality sank in, and I yelled, "Get up! What are you doing in my house?!"

"Don't you remember last night? Before you went to bed, I asked if I could crash here and you said, 'sure whatever,' so I slept on the couch. I didn't want to go home," he said, his voice was deep and croaked.

"You shouldn't ask someone that when they're tired."

"I'm sorry, but I do have one comment," Daniel said, intensely. "You're cute when you wake up."

"Get out!" I stormed into my room and slammed the door. What was I thinking? Why would I say yes to him? It was spur of the moment, but it must have been the setting. I was stupid for falling for his "charm." What would dating someone entail? Would we have to hold hands and hug? Would we HAVE to kiss? The thought of kissing Daniel had my body conflicted, on one hand it sent chills down my spine, and I shivered. On the other, I remembered how I felt last night. His warmth, his passion…I was going to have to break it off. I grabbed the doorknob and stopped. I couldn't. I felt bad. I said yes, then I was going to end it 12 hours later. I decided to stick with him for a few months then break up with him, that way he got his illogical fill of dating me and I wouldn't look like such an asshole for breaking up with him not even 24 hours later.

Daniel knocked on the door 10 minutes later. He walked in with a tray.

"What's that?" I asked, sitting up.

"What it looks like," he replied. "Breakfast."

"You didn't have to…" I mumbled.

"Nonsense," he said, setting it down in front of me. "As your boyfriend, it's my duty to make sure you eat properly."

On the tray were scrambled eggs, the mini blueberry pancakes I had in my freezer for two months, and canned fruit cocktail.

"Thanks," I said, grabbing a fork and going for the scrambled eggs.

"I'm a pretty good cook if I do say so myself."

I looked at Daniel and took a bite. It wasn't bad, I bit an eggshell but otherwise it was seasoned well.

I nodded my head. "It's good. Where did you learn how to cook?"

"From my foster sister," he said. "She taught me how to cook. Said that's what girls like in a guy. Is it?"

"I mean sorta." I looked down. "I never really thought about what I find attractive in a potential boyfriend."

"Ok, but I'm not a 'potential boyfriend,' I'm your actual boyfriend."

"…yeah…"

Daniel laughed. "You don't sound so happy."

"No, I'm just not an energetic person. I don't jump up with excitement."

"I understand, I don't expect that much from you… No offense!"

"None taken."

Daniel smiled and rested his head on my shoulder. "If it's alright, can I keep my head here?"

"Yeah, that's fine."

We sat there for a few minutes, Daniel's arm wrapped around my side and my head rested on his, my eyes closed. I liked how warm he was…not that I liked him…. The food was getting cold, but I didn't mind. Suddenly, I felt something touch my thigh. Daniel's hand crept up my inner thigh until he reached the hem of my shorts.

"Uh no," I said, moving away from him. "It's waaay too early for that."

Daniel looked down disappointed. "I'm sorry. I started to get in the mood."

"I can tell, but just…don't try it for a few months. Try to restrain your…urges…."

"Yeah, you're right. I'm a bit impulsive. It's such a bad quality. I don't want you to hate me."

"I don't," I said, giving him a gentle smile.

"Okay. Thank you. Can I kiss you?"

"I think maybe you should cool off." I laughed and pointed to the door. "You should go to the bathroom."

"Yeah…" Daniel chuckled and stood up.

"I'll finish eating," I said. "Then you can go home."

"What?"

"I need some time to relax alone," I said. "I spent the past two days with you."

"Yes, but this is the first day of us as a couple."

"And? I need a break from socializing with people. Even boyfriends."

Daniel looked disappointed. "But if I can't see you for the day, I really do need a kiss. I might as well just handle my business in my own apartment."

I contemplated whether I should, I didn't want to, considering what he was going through. But I remembered my second oldest foster sister. She was always fixated on finding me a boyfriend. She said everyone needed companionship, and that me not feeling anything was psychological. She asked me what would happen if my boyfriend wanted children. I told her it sucked for him because I didn't want children. She responded disappointingly that "a relationship takes two people" and that "it can't always be about what you wanted and never what your partner wants." I took that a little to heart, not because she was always badgering me about relationships but because out of all of my siblings, she always had the longest and most successful relationships. I heard before I moved out, 5 years ago, she married her college boyfriend, had 3 children and was living "happily ever after." Something the majority of us never thought we could ever achieve.

I sighed. "Just one kiss. A peck."

Daniel leaned over the bed and kissed me. "I'll see you tomorrow."

Daniel smiled and walked out the room. I could hear the front door shut. I felt a little bad, but I really did need a break from everyone. I wasn't much for socializing. If I were rich, I would never leave my apartment. Only because I needed money and food, I interacted with people.

I locked the door. Anna understood me the most out of my siblings. She knew when I was in my "I don't feel like talking," state and left me alone. Whereas my other siblings would get annoyed and try to force me to talk. I felt like that was what made my bond with Anna the strongest and why we kept in touch. We understood each other's feelings. And knew when the other was upset and wanted to be alone, but also knew when to butt in and make each other feel better.

I thought about her current situation, I really hoped everything was going to be okay with Anna, and that she could make it through with her adoptive parents and graduate this year.

Anna was attractive, she was drop-dead gorgeous, and she was always the magnet of creepy old men. That was how she came into foster care. Her mother would let men molest her. When Anna first told me, I thought her mom was just unaware of it, who would suspect a mother would let her boyfriends do that to her child? But Anna told me the incident that placed her in foster care.

Her mother had recently broken up with her boyfriend and began sleeping with an older man, he was 57. She slept with him so he would pay her bills. The day Anna was found, her mother was watching TV, it was 10 in the morning on a Saturday. Her mother's friend came over to see her, but she told him she wasn't in the mood. He was pissed off. Anna said he argued with her mom, that he lied to his wife and drove an hour away from their family reunion to see her. He wasn't going to leave until he had sex.

Anna's mother refused and instead of telling him to go away, she told him to "have some fun with Anna." Anna said she could still remember the look on his face as he assessed her. He agreed and to thank Anna's mother, he gave her a diamond necklace. Anna said she screamed as loud as she could when he carried her to her room. The mailman heard her and called the cops.

It was a terrible story, especially since she joined our "family" at 9 years old. I could still remember how quiet she was. She didn't trust our brothers until she was 11. I was the only one she would talk to before then. I couldn't shake the feeling something would happen with her adoptive parents.

I lay in bed and looked at my phone.

"I'm a day late, lol, but did you make it home safe? Also, Anna please let me know if anything happens. You can come here any time," I texted her.

As I waited for her response, another text came in.

"I already miss you"

I smiled. Daniel was clingy. I didn't mind, though it was a little embarrassing. I didn't know how to respond to him. I didn't want to say something stupid, but I didn't want him to think I was falling for him.

I responded, "Haha already? It's only been 20 mins. I miss you too."

I set my phone down and rested my head on my arms. My phone buzzed right away.

"You don't know how happy that just made me. ♥ Can I come over?"

"No. lol I need a day by myself."

"Can I come by later tonight? I don't care how late."

"Maybe."

"☺ I love you. ♥"

"Love you too. Bye."

I sat my phone on my nightstand and took a nap.

I looked at my phone. "What time is it?"

It was 5 PM. I stretched and got up. I was heading to the bathroom when Daniel called.

"Hello?" I answered.

"Thank goodness you picked up," he said. He sounded really exhausted. "I left my work shoes in my apartment. Can you bring them over to Loue's grocery? It's in Brooklyn, not far from where we live. I can't come back and grab them. He's only going to let me continue work if I have someone bring them over."

"Yeah, I could, but I don't have a key to your apartment."

"I know, I have a spare under the mat."

"That's pretty cliché. Don't you worry about someone finding it and stealing all your stuff?"

"No, not at all. I don't have anything worth stealing, plus our building has cameras, and you have to have a key to get into the first doors."

"That's true. Okay, I'll be over there soon."

"Thanks, I'll see you soon," Daniel said, and hung up.

"Guess I can say I did something productive today," I muttered, walking to my closet.

I didn't have much to wear, I was quite the "tomboy." I barely had skirts or dresses, just jogging pants, hoodies, and leggings, some t-shirts. I grabbed my favorite hoodie and a pair of leggings. I brushed my hair quickly and left out.

I walked into Daniel's apartment. It was very neat, not what I was expecting. I looked around the living room and saw a pair of black shoes on the coffee table.

"That must be it," I said, grabbing them.

I shopped at Loue's Grocery every now and then. It really wasn't far. Thinking about it now, I wonder if that's where Daniel first saw me? It was a twenty-minute walk, so I got my day's exercise in too.

I walked into Loue's and pulled out my phone.

"Maya!"

I turned around and saw Daniel jogging over to me.

"Thank you so much." Daniel hugged me. "Sorry to have you come all the way here."

"It's no problem."

"Still, it's inconvenient to have you leave, walk like twenty minutes, only to leave right away. A whole forty minutes of your time wasted."

"It's not that big a deal. I wasn't doing anything anyways."

"Well, can I come over tonight?"

"You're really pushing it huh?"

"If you don't want me to, I understand."

"Maybe, let me think about it, I'll text you when I decide."

"Who's this," a voice said, behind Daniel.

I leaned over and saw a woman. She was taller than me, almost Daniel's height. She was a brunette and very skinny. She was pretty, but she wore a lot of makeup.

"Oh Jessica, this is my girlfriend, Maya."

"Hi," she said. Her voice was loud, and deep. "I'm Jessica. Nice to meet you."

"Nice to meet you too," I said. I didn't want to talk to her. My introverted side pulled me in.

"You didn't tell me you had a girlfriend."

"Well you never asked."

"Hmm, I feel bad for Maya, you don't talk about her. Ever."

"That's fine, I wouldn't want him to…" I smiled. "Well I better head home. I'll see you tonight."

Daniel's eyes lit up. "Alright, see you then."

I walked over to Daniel and kissed him on the cheek, with a parting glance at Jessica before I left. I was overthinking what Jessica said. I didn't know how to deal with the catty girl talk especially since I was never in any love triangles. But what she said seemed like she wanted me to feel bad about Daniel. Like I wasn't a thought when he was anywhere else.

I looked at my phone, Anna responded while I was talking to Daniel and Jessica.

"Thanks! So far it's okay. I got back yesterday afternoon. Max picked me up… and it was just as uncomfortable as ever. I used to want to sit in the front seat. But with him always touching my leg, or just being close to him makes me uncomfortable, I sat in the back seat. Of course he teased me, trying to coerce me into sitting up front."

"That's so creepy, I'm sorry you have to go through that," I responded. "I really do think you should tell Jane."

Anna called me. "I would if I could. But you know how the shit works, they'll take their husband's side 85% of the time. I told you what happened to the little girl right? She had the same background as me, and what happened when she reached out for help? Jane got offended, said she was lying and sent her back. People already chastise women when they report rape incidents, imagine how it is when you're raped or molested at a young age. Some of these adoptive mothers won't believe a thing you say. They probably feel like we lied about the first situation and want to do it again. As if we didn't suffer enough."

"It's really sickening. I can't believe people are like that. My thing is, I get some women lie about rape, but the majority of rape cases are real. Do people really think women should have to prove they were raped just on the small chance the man who raped her is innocent?" I mean think about the children who are molested or raped. They become too afraid to say anything because they're scared no one would believe them.

"Well, that's how the world is I guess." Anna sighed. "Maybe it will change in the future. I don't want to risk anything, not until I graduate."

"I know and totally understand. I just don't want anything to happen just because Max thinks he can get away with it. Could you at least tell your case manager?"

"No, I don't have one anymore. Felt I was okay enough to be a 'normal kid.'"

"That's good in a sense, but I just worry, you know. Maybe you could start shipping your things here. You have a little over two months left. That way after graduation, you just hop on a plane with your last suitcase and be free of him."

"Yeah, I might do that. Only thing is I don't know how much it costs. And I don't have money. I know Jane wouldn't mind but I think if Max found out, he would be scary."

"What do you mean by that?"

"I don't know. Whenever we talk about my plans for the future, he always argues with Jane, that I shouldn't move out and should stay with them. It looks like he's being a doting father, but I pick up on his creepy side saying that. Like, he has some plan. Kind of like when Rebecca ran off with Margaret's ex-husband?"

"Yeah."

"Like he plans for us to run away or something, or like, have an affair behind Jane's back."

"Ew, aren't they in their late 40s?"

"Yep, well, Jane is. Max is 52."

"That's even more gross."

"I feel like I'm overthinking things, but I just can't shake that feeling."

"Well, I'm planning to get a job, so I can help pay for you to move. Are you able to get a job?"

"Sort of, Jane and Max want me to focus on school and keep my grades up. I think at this point, it should be okay."

"Alright, that's our goal then. We'll both work hard so we can move your stuff."

"Okay, thank you Maya."

"Of course, and in any case, you're not overthinking anything. Your safety and wellbeing come first. Don't question yourself, okay?"

"Okay."

"I gotta go, I'm gonna start looking for a job."

"Hey Maya?"

"What's up?"

"…nothing. Don't worry about it."

"If you say so. Don't hesitate to tell me anything okay?"

"Okay, I'll talk to you later."

"Bye."

It seemed like she wanted to tell me something important. Her tone was enough to key me in on it, but it was not something to push her about. She would tell me when she was ready.

I couldn't think of where to get a job. I somewhat knew New York, but I really only stayed in Brooklyn. I got to my apartment and went on my laptop. Most of the jobs I looked at required more than a high school diploma. It was going to be tougher than I thought.

After searching for hours, I took a break. It was 11 PM. Daniel was late. I was beginning to think he forgot when I heard a knock on the door.

"Sorry I'm late," he said, rushing in as soon as I opened the door.

"That's okay, we didn't really set a time."

"Yeah, but I wanted to get here right after my shift but I ended up working overtime."

"It's okay. Work is work. Besides, I was busy too."

"With what?"

"I'm trying to find a job."

"Aww." Daniel reacted holding my cheeks. "You don't need one, I'll provide for the both of us."

"Very funny." I rolled my eyes.

"I'm serious. I would. You would just have to move in with me though."

"It's too soon for that. Besides, Anna's moving in. I'm saving up for getting all of her things here before she graduates."

"Why?"

"Because it'll make her move here easier if we do it along the way, rather than all at once."

"That makes sense. Do you have an idea where you want to work?"

"No, everything I've looked at requires a college degree."

Daniel walked over to the couch and looked at my laptop. "Nursing, paralegal, paraeducator, a regional manager for a travel company? Well obviously, you'll need some sort of degree for these."

"Those are the only places hiring."

"No there are more, you just need to broaden your search," he said, sitting down. "This would be your first job, right?"

"No, I was a waitress in high school."

"How?"

"What do you mean?"

"Wouldn't Mar—uh wouldn't it be hard since you were in high school?"

"Not really. My foster mom didn't look at anything we brought her to sign if it involved school. And I went to the farthest place from where she would go."

"Ok."

"Yeah, but you don't get paid much as a waitress, that's why I want something else."

"If you're interested, you could work at Loue's. We're always hiring."

"Wouldn't it be weird working with your girlfriend?"

"Not at all. The opposite in fact. I'd be with you all the time. Which would be amazing."

"Well, I guess. So long as I can make enough money."

"It pays my bills. Fill out this application," Daniel said, typing. "And before you submit it, make sure you put me as the person who referred you. He'll hire you immediately."

"Okay, can you hand me the laptop?"

"No."

"Then how am I supposed to fill out the application?"

Daniel patted his legs.

"No way. I am not sitting on your lap."

"Why not?" Daniel asked, pouting.

"Because…" I couldn't tell him it would be awkward and embarrassing.

"Please," he asked, smiling. "You don't have to sit on me. Just here." He patted part of the couch.

"Between your legs."

"That way I can hug you while you work." Daniel smiled.

I sighed, I guess it wasn't all that bad, especially if I want to date properly. And if I needed help, he would be right there. I sat in Daniel's lap and began typing. Daniel wrapped his arms around me and rested his head over my shoulder.

"I missed you," Daniel said, kissing my shoulder.

I was blushing. I didn't understand why I was so shy. Maybe because I never did that before, or because I was so close to a man. I don't know. But I wasn't going to let him see me like that. I quickly finished my application and sent it in. I stood up and went to my room. I locked the door and told him he could spend the night in the living room if he wanted to. He didn't mind as much, "as long as he was close enough to me." I lay in bed, staring at the wall, confused. Why did I feel so weird around Daniel?

A week went by, and I finally got a call from Daniel's boss Loue. We did an interview over the phone, and I got the job. I was starting the next day. It was weird I didn't need an in-person interview. But I guess because Daniel convinced him to hire me or something. Daniel was more excited than I was. He came to my apartment an hour early. "Are you excited?" he asked.

"Not really."

"Why? We get to work together. And I'm pretty confident I'll be the one training you."

"I guess it'll be fun. I'm gonna see how you act around me when you work and teach me."

"You're so cute," Daniel said, as he pulled me close.

We got to Loue's about 30 minutes before our shifts started.

"Welcome," a man shouted. "Oh, hey Daniel. This must be Maya. Loue, it's a pleasure to meet you."

He extended his hand, grabbing it I responded, "Nice to meet you too."

"Daniel mentioned you were his girlfriend, but I didn't think you'd be this cute."

"Oh…thank you…" I replied. I wasn't used to compliments, so I didn't know how to respond.

"I told you she was."

"Yeah well, considering it's you…I wasn't expecting much. No offense Maya."

I laughed. "None taken."

"What's that supposed to mean?"

"Whatever you think it means."

I liked Loue. He was a funny older man. He looked like he was in his sixties. And liked to get under Daniel's skin but all in good fun.

"Good morning, everyone," a voice said.

I turned around to see Jessica. She was wearing more make up than the last time I saw her. She wore a tight pencil skirt and the uniform shirt.

"Morning," Loue said. "I guess we're allowed to wear tight skirts at work now. So long as we wear part of the uniform."

"Sorry, I forgot. I was running late and forgot I left my pants in the dryer. I grabbed whatever I could."

Maybe if she didn't put on so much makeup, she would've had time to grab her pants.

"Morning, Jessica," Daniel said. "You remember Maya?"

"No, but I guess she's new here?"

"Yeah, you met her last week when she brought over my shoes."

"Oh yeah, I remember. Wanna work with your boyfriend huh?"

"Yeah, but mostly because it's a twenty-minute walk from my apartment."

Jessica smirked. "I see."

Changing the subject, Loue said, "Well, Daniel you're in grocery and Jessica, since Maria is on maternity leave, you'll be training Maya."

"What? Why can't I?" Daniel protested.

"Well for one, I highly doubt you'll be able to focus on actually training her. Secondly, Jessica isn't dressed appropriately to do stocking. And I know how far she travels to get here, so I'm not sending her home to change."

Daniel smacked his lips and mumbled under his breath as he walked away.

"You'll be in good hands," Loue said. "Start with the cash register for today."

"Roger that," Jessica said, saluting Loue as he left. "How much experience do you have with a register?"

"None, I used to work as a waitress but that was my only job."

"This is gonna be tough." Jessica said, rolling her eyes. She walked to a register. "Come on over."

Jessica showed me how to use the register. It was easier than she made it seem. By the end of my shift I had already mastered it.

"Nice going," Loue said. "I might just have you only working cashier, you're better and faster than those two."

"Uh, don't forget who taught her."

"Guess the pupil already passed the master." Loue shrugged.

Jessica sneered and walked away.

"I swear sometimes she's quite the handful. If my brother hadn't asked me to give her a job…" Loue shook his head and threw his thumb over his shoulder.

"She's your niece?"

"Unfortunately so," Loue said, rolling his eyes.

I smiled. "Well thank you for the opportunity to work here."

"No thank you, it's tough here. We're always understaffed. Now that my assistant manager is on maternity leave, it's been rough. So I really appreciate you applying," Loue said. "We're like family here. You won't have to watch your tongue around me or anyone else here. Relax."

"I will," I said. "Have a great evening."

I walked out the store and Daniel was waiting for me.

"You didn't have to wait you know."

"That's okay, I don't mind. I just wished I could have worked with you at least once today," Daniel said, kicking a rock. "But I guess tomorrow will be better. You have to learn every department or almost every department. Maybe he'll let me teach you when you're stocking."

"He said he might keep me only on register because I was better than all of you."

"Seriously? That's good that you did well, but that would mean I would never get to work with you."

"That's ok. We can have our breaks together."

"True."

I smiled at Daniel. We reached the apartment complex and went into the elevator.

"I take it after a long day, you want to be alone?"

"Hmm, possibly. You could still come over though."

"You sure?" Daniel asked. "Well, maybe you could hang out at my place."

"Uh, I guess. Let me change clothes first, then I'll come over."

"Deal," Daniel said, holding the elevator doors for me.

"I'll wait for you out here."

"Okay," I said, walking into my apartment.

I took off my uniform and looked in my closet. I didn't want to overdress, but I also didn't want to look sloppy. I grabbed my blue tank top, an oversized black t-shirt and my black leggings and got dressed. I looked in the mirror. I looked okay. The oversized t-shirt hung off my shoulders and looked kind of as if I was wearing a dress. I pulled my hair in a ponytail and shrugged. That was as good as someone with my looks was gonna get. I wasn't planning on spending the night, so I grabbed my phone and keys and locked the door.

"You took pretty long," Daniel said.

"Really? Seemed like only 5 minutes."

"Nope. Try 15," Daniel said, checking the time. He smiled and examined my outfit. "And it took only 15 minutes for you to look so cute."

"I'm not cute."

"You're right," he said. "You're beautiful."

I blushed. "We should go inside."

Daniel unlocked the door and said, "Welcome to my lovely abode."

I had already been in his apartment, but I played along. "I like it, I wasn't expecting your place to be so neat."

"Yeah, no one does." Daniel laughed. He wrapped his arm around my waist and pushed me in. "Don't be shy come all the way in."

I looked around as I walked into the living room. I didn't get to fully look because he needed his shoes. Daniel's apartment was the opposite of mine. His layout was on the other side. Meaning his and my living rooms were next to each other, and bedrooms and kitchens were on the opposite sides. It was kind of weird. Daniel had a white couch and love seat, and a light brown coffee table. In the corner he had a large flat-screen TV on a light brown stand. Everything matched. No random colored furniture anywhere. He also had a minimalist design. He actually took time to make his apartment look nice. I just bought whatever was cheap and comfy.

"You can sit down," he said. "Do you want anything to drink?"

"Do you have any soda?"

"Just 7up and Coke."

"Can I have a Coke?"

"Coming right up milady." Daniel bowed and went into the kitchen. I smiled and shook my head. "Are those the only sodas you drink?"

"No, I drink a few others. I just prefer those."

"We like the same drinks," I said.

"Really? Guess that means we're meant to be," Daniel said, emerging from the kitchen with a Coke. He plopped on the couch next me and put his arm over me. "Did you want anything to eat?"

"I'm good, I'll eat when I go home."

"Oh…" Daniel paused. "You don't plan on sleeping over?"

"We work tomorrow."

"We can go together. We work the same shift. You can grab your uniform tonight that way you don't have to get up earlier to get ready."

"Let me think about it," I said.

I didn't have any desire to sleepover. I rarely slept at anyone's place. I figured I wouldn't ruin the mood by being a stickler. I planned to tell him when I was ready to leave.

The night went by fast. I kept an open-mind and ended up enjoying myself. He made it so fun. We ordered a pizza. One peperoni pizza and one pineapple and olive. Of course, pineapple belonged on every pizza. Daniel didn't agree. That was honestly grounds for break up. We watched movies and criticized the characters. We played video games. In only a few hours, I was more comfortable around him.

It was 10 PM and I figured it was time I headed home. I wanted to spend the night, but I wasn't totally sure he still wanted me to. Daniel was sitting by the corner of the couch, and I leaned on his shoulder.

"I had so much fun," I said sitting up. "It's getting late. I should probably head home."

"Why don't you want to spend the night?" He sat up and hugged me.

"Is it okay for me to stay?"

"Yes. That's what I've been trying to have you do all night."

"Alright, let me grab my pajamas, uniform and a few other things and I'll be back."

Daniel smiled his dimples fully showed this time. I smiled back and went to my apartment. When I came back, Daniel was in his room.

"Do you have an extra blanket for me?"

"No," Daniel responded. "Are you still cold with just one?"

"So you do have another one for me?"

"Just the one we'll be sharing."

"I was planning to sleep on the couch…"

"Why? We're dating," Daniel replied, laughing. "It's okay for us to share a bed. Besides, there's no way I would let you sleep on the couch. Are you uncomfortable sharing?"

"It's not that," I said, quietly.

"Then what is it? You can tell me."

"I…I never shared a bed with a man before…" I paused. "It's kind of embarrassing."

"Well, there's always a first for everything. It'll stay that way until you give it a try."

"I guess…"

Daniel smiled and held out his hand. "Then let's get ready for bed."

I took Daniel's hand. Daniel was ready before me and was already in bed. I lay down and faced the other direction. I was too nervous to look at him. I felt Daniel's arm wrap around my waist as he drew his body closer. He was so close. My heart was beating faster and faster, as if it was going to burst out of my chest any moment. My face was hot.

"Goodnight," Daniel said, his head now above mine as he spooned me.

I flinched as he said it. It was hard to speak, I managed to say in a quiet and raspy voice, "Night."

Daniel laughed softly but it was loud enough for me to hear. I was so embarrassed and nervous. I couldn't wrap my head around why I felt this way about him. Was it because he was a guy? Or was it because I was sharing a bed with him?

Then it hit me like a wrecking ball, I liked Daniel.

What came over me? When and why did I start liking him? Us dating was only supposed to be temporary. This wasn't supposed to happen. Or at least not like this. I wanted it to be something grand. Like how it happened in movies. I would see him for the first time moving in slow motion, the world stopping around us, maybe cherry blossoms, I would take any flower petals honestly, blowing in the wind. A gasp of fresh air returning my breath. But not like that, no. Not just hitting me out of nowhere. I looked up at Daniel. He was already asleep. I couldn't remember him being so handsome. It was like his facial features intensified. He was a quiet sleeper. Kind of cute when he slept. I stared for a while. He must have been in a deep sleep.

I paused for a moment. I wanted to hug him. I was nervous but he was asleep. He wouldn't even notice. I slowly and gently turned around making sure he wouldn't wake. I was awkward. Hugging a guy was hard as is and now adding on to that, me liking him. I took a deep breath, reached my trembling arms out and hugged Daniel.

I dug my face deep into his chest and closed my eyes. He smelled so good. Enraptured by his scent, I felt so comfortable I dozed off. Daniel tightened his arms around me and snuggled close.

CHAPTER THREE

The next morning, I woke to an empty bed. I stretched and lay sprawled out in his bed. Daniel had a king-sized bed. Why he needed it for one person was beyond me. But in that moment, I totally understood. I only had a full-size, so this felt like luxury. I heard a huge laugh and opened my eyes.

"You're so cute, I swear," Daniel said. "I'm glad you like my bed."

I sat up and crossed my legs. "Your bed's really soft. I love how much space you have."

"Yeah? You can sleep in my bed any time you want. Even if I'm not here."

"I might take you up on that."

Daniel smiled. "Come on, I made breakfast."

"But I don—"

Before I could finish Daniel said, "Nope, today is always our busiest day. You need to eat."

I stayed quiet then got out of bed.

"That's what I'm talking about," Daniel said.

Daniel cooked a big meal. He made sautéed vegetables, an omelet, bacon, scrambled eggs, sausages, biscuits, chopped fruits, and pancakes.

"Wow," I said. "You made a lot."

"Yeah, I know. I wanted to make the perfect breakfast for you. I went a little overboard."

"It's okay. Thank you for breakfast."

"Enjoy," he said pulling my chair out.

After breakfast, we got dressed and headed to work. We decided to walk. It was early enough, and it was a nice day. I was still nervous around Daniel. Just being close to him made me tremble and lose footing. Oh gosh, the last thing I needed was to faceplant into the concrete. Daniel talked my ear off, not noticing, or at least I hoped he didn't, the number of times I stumbled behind him. All I could do was give short answers like 'yeah', 'no', and 'I guess'. It was so hard to focus.

"You don't seem very excited today," Daniel said, slowing his pace.

"I never act excited," I mumbled.

"True." Daniel nodded. "But maybe every now and then, give me a little encouragement?"

I looked down, hiding any semblance of blushing. "I'll try but I'm not an energetic person."

"It's okay. It takes time. I just hope one day you'll open up to me."

"Yeah…It'll happen."

Daniel leaned over and kissed my forehead. We reached Loue's and waiting outside was Jessica. Her face lit up when she saw Daniel.

"Hey Daniel." She waved. "You're early. Loue isn't even here yet. Oh, hey Maya."

"Yeah, I got up early to make us breakfast. It's actually rarer for you to not be late."

"You went to his house for food?" Jessica asked.

"No, I stayed the night…at his place."

"Hmph," Jessica scoffed. She turned her attention back to Daniel. "I didn't know you could cook. Maybe you can make me something."

"Nah, I don't like cooking."

"You cooked for Maya," Jessica snapped.

"Because I'm his girlfriend," I said, quietly.

"Exactly." Daniel agreed with me.

"That doesn't mean anything," she fussed. "I've known you for so long, yet you never cooked for me."

"Didn't think I had too." Daniel scoffed awkwardly.

"You don't," I said.

Before Jessica could continue, Loue arrived. He walked to the door. His collar wrinkled. He wasn't much of a morning person.

"You all are early," Loue grumbled.

"Yeah, me and Maya had such a good date night, and wonderful breakfast, we came early."

"Yeah," Jessica whined. "He made Maya breakfast, but he's never even made me a piece of toast!"

I rolled my eyes slightly.

"Because they're dating and correct me if I'm wrong," Loue said. He stopped and looked Jessica in the eyes. "You and Daniel have never dated. Now stop complaining and punch in."

Jessica smacked her lips.

"She can be quite the handful," Loue said. "She thinks what someone else has, she also deserves. She's never once cared about if he made breakfast until you said so. So don't mind her."

"I can see that now," I said, uncomfortably. "And I won't."

Later, during my break, Jessica went into the break room and sat down at my table. I stopped chewing my food and stared at her. She sat quietly for a moment glaring at me.

"I want to apologize," she said, breaking the silence.

"For what?" I asked.

"For how I've been acting. I can get pretty toxic in the morning. I was just annoyed and took it out on you two. Also, I'm overprotective of Daniel. He's one of my closest friends. I don't want him to get hurt. I shouldn't have been defensive around you."

"It's okay," I said. I didn't really believe her, nevertheless I decided to forgive her. Taking whatever she said with a grain of salt.

"I would also like for us to become best friends. I don't have many girl friends and we're both close to Daniel. It wouldn't hurt for us to be friends, right?"

"I don't mind," I said, cautiously. "We should get to know each other despite you being friends with him and me being his girlfriend."

"You're absolutely right," she said, nodding. "It's going take some time, but I would like the end result of us being close too."

"I agree."

I wanted to finish eating before my break was over, but she just kept talking. Repeating the same thing over and over again. It was getting obnoxious at that point. Daniel walked into the break room and looked at me and Jessica.

"Well isn't this nice," he said, walking to his locker. "I haven't seen you two talking before. Or at least not without me."

"We're friends now," Jessica said.

"Becoming friends," I corrected her. I wanted to change the subject, "Are you on break too?"

"Yeah," he said, pulling up a chair next to me. "When are you done?"

"In like 20 minutes," I said. "But if we're all back here, who's on the floor?"

"Oh, I'm not on break," Jessica said. "I just wanted to talk to Maya."

"Well, you better get back out there," Daniel said. "Before Loue gets mad."

"I don't care," she laughed. "The worst he could do is fire me. If he does, my dad will have something to say about it."

"Still," I joined in. "He's nice enough to keep letting you work here. You should at least care enough to be on the floor."

Jessica looked at me unamused. "You're right I suppose. I'll let you two love birds enjoy your breaks."

Jessica left and closed the door. Daniel sighed. "I swear, she's just ridiculous sometimes."

"Yeah…" I agreed. "I don't know her very well, but she comes off as self-entitled and mean."

"You're not wrong," Daniel said. "Are you two really friends?"

I shook my head. "That's what she came in here for. She said because we were both close to you, we should become best friends. To be honest, I'm not very excited about it either. She was way too rude to me since we met. I don't really trust it."

"I don't blame you," Daniel said. "But…I wonder where she got the impression we were close?"

"You're not?" I asked.

"Nope, she's just a work friend. I didn't think we were closer than that."

I laughed. "That's so unfortunate for her."

"Right?"

The rest of the day was productive, Daniel wasn't lying when he said it would be busy. Ever so often, I needed to call Daniel and Jessica to the front to help. And when the rush ended, Jessica wouldn't go back to stocking. She would stay up front to talk to me. She was so bad, I only called Daniel to the front, and she would still come. I was physically and mentally drained from work AND Jessica. We left the store as the closing team came and Jessica followed after us.

"Do you have any plans for tonight?" she asked.

"Not really," Daniel said.

"Great, do you guys want to go out for dinner?"

I looked at Daniel, he knew what my answer was, but still said, "Sure. It's nice to get out sometimes, right?"

I didn't say anything and rolled my eyes.

Jessica turned around. "Great, I heard there's a really good Chinese restaurant in Brooklyn worth trying."

"Do you remember what it was called?" Daniel asked.

"Nope, not a clue. I just know where it's located."

I mentally sighed. I already regretted going, but something told me to go with them.

We arrived at the restaurant roughly 30 minutes later. It wasn't too far from Loue's by bus. I looked at the name, "Panda Express" and sighed deeply.

"You've never heard of Panda Express?" I asked.

"What, is this a popular restaurant?"

"Very," I said.

Daniel exploded into laughter. "Typical."

"What," Jessica said.

"You must've really grown up privileged if you've never been here." Daniel shook his head.

"My family doesn't eat fast food, so I didn't know. We only eat at 5-star restaurants, 4-stars if we want to switch it up a bit."

"This probably tastes better," I mumbled.

"Maybe." Jessica nodded slowly. "Until you've had the finer things in life, I guess you'll never know."

I scoffed quietly and rolled my eyes.

Feeling the tension, Daniel changed the subject. "Well, are we going inside? I'm starving."

"Sure," Jessica said, opening the door. "Otherwise this would have been a waste of time, right Maya?"

"Right," I said, walking in.

I ordered the eggplant tofu with chow mein, Daniel ordered the broccoli beef with chow mein, and Jessica being her snobby self, ordered the firecracker shrimp after making numerous inappropriate comments to the employees about what they were serving. I was mortified. And Daniel most likely was too. Embarrassed, I rushed to a seat in the corner and put my head down.

"Why are we sitting so far in the corner?" Jessica asked.

"I don't like people looking at me while I eat. I always make eye contact with random people."

"Yeah, that does seem awkward."

After we finished eating, I asked, "Well, what do you think?"
"I've had better," Jessica said.
"I liked mine," I responded.
"Different pallets I guess," Jessica said.
"I liked what I ate too," Daniel agreed.
"You have great tastes, that's why," Jessica said.
I didn't bother responding.
"I know," he said quietly, locking eyes with me.
"Well anyways," Jessica interrupted. "I'll try what you had next time."
Assuming there will be a next time, I thought.
"You should. It's good." Daniel looked at his watch. "It's kinda late, we should head home. Jessica, I'm pretty sure you won't be comfortable going home in the dark. So let's call it a night?"
"It's only 6 PM…" Jessica complained.
"Yeah, but you should go home before it gets dark. You always said you were nervous to go home when we had to work overtime or closing shift."
"But that was just so I wouldn't have to work late."
"I would like to relax for the rest of the day. Maya most likely does too."
I nodded.
Jessica rolled her eyes and stood up, "Alright. I'll see you guys tomorrow I guess."
"We're off tomorrow," I said.
"You guys don't even work and you're complaining about resting?" Jessica complained. She threw her arms up. She turned to me and said, "And you just started how do you already have a day off?"
"I'm part-time. I would rather just relax after our busiest day."
"Nothing wrong with that," Daniel said, cutting Jessica off before she could protest.
"That's too bad, I wanted to hang out with you guys," she pouted, walking away from the table.
"Maybe another time," I said, grabbing her tray.
"Sure, whatever," Jessica said.
"Bye," I said.
Jessica stormed out of the restaurant.

I looked at Daniel, who shrugged his shoulders.

After clearing the table, we left the restaurant. Jessica was outside, softly hopping in place and looking at her feet. "Took you guys long enough."

"I thought you left already," Daniel responded.

"I wouldn't just leave without saying bye. What do you take me for?" she laughed.

Mean, rude, tacky, ignorant…. There were so many answers I could have given but I bit my tongue.

"Well, thanks for hanging out with me even if it wasn't for that long."

"Yep," Daniel said.

Jessica reached over and hugged Daniel. We were both taken aback. It was so bold. Jessica kept her arms around Daniel's neck for about a minute. Daniel just looked at me wide-eyed and awkward. He showed me his palms, making sure I saw his arms weren't around her. I tried my best to not look pissed.

After Jessica let go, she waved at me and walked the other way. Quietly, we watched her walking off in the distance. I turned around not saying anything and walked in the direction of our apartment building.

"Okay, I know you're probably pissed but that wasn't my fault." Daniel jogged to catch up to me.

"Yeah, but you let her hug you…for a *long* time."

"I didn't know what to do, I didn't want to be rude. At least I didn't hug her back, right?"

I didn't say anything and kept walking.

"Maya, please talk to me. I know you're upset. Just talk to me." He grabbed me by the elbow, turning me around. "Instead of giving me the silent treatment."

"You already know why I'm mad. What else needs to be said?"

"If you're mad at me or her."

"Both of you."

"I didn't do anything," he said. "I was the victim in it."

"I get it already," I shouted. I snatched my arm from him and continued to walk. "I don't want to keep talking about it."

"It's better to vent than bottle it inside."

"I get it. I just… would like to not talk about it *right* this second."

Daniel didn't say anything and walked behind me.

I wasn't necessarily angry at Daniel. I was just upset that she hugged him, and he didn't do anything to stop her. I was also jealous of how causally she did it. I couldn't even stand a foot away from him without my knees quivering. And the more he talked about it, the more upset I became.

We didn't talk on the bus ride or the walk to our apartment building. When we reached the 6th floor, I got off the elevator still not speaking to him. Daniel leaned on the wall between our doors and watched as I unlocked my door. "I take it you don't want to hang out tonight?"

"I don't mind. If you want to come over, you can," I said. I was still salty over the ordeal but there was no point harping on the hug. Daniel didn't do anything worth giving him the silent treatment.

Daniel smiled. "Let me change and I'll be over."

"Okay," I said, walking in and closing the door.

I took a quick shower and slid into my pajamas at record speed and waited for Daniel. He was taking too long. I tilted over falling onto my side and rested my head in my arms. Just as I got cozy, someone tapped lightly on the door.

"Come in," I said, sitting up on the couch.

"Sorry that took so long. It's just that—" Daniel paused.

"What?" I asked. I glanced at Daniel lying back down.

"I was talking to Jessica. I told her what she did wasn't appropriate, especially in front of my girlfriend."

"Yeah, and I think what took the cake was that after she hugged you, she just waved at me and left."

"I talked to her about that too."

"Did she say why she did it?"

"At first, she said she hugs everyone, so I asked, 'why didn't you hug Maya?' and she said, she thought you were being rude all day, especially at the restaurant…. And that she felt closer to me."

"She said *I* was rude first?"

"Well, I mean… you kind of were…" Daniel said, nervously.

"How was I rude?" I sat up, facing Daniel. "She made snide comments all day and on the way to Panda Express. On top of that, you saw how she treated the employees there. How would I not be annoyed or angry with her?"

"Yeah, but you come off as mean all the time. Even when it's just you and me. You're *pretty* nasty to me."

"I don't mean to," I said, timidly. "You're my first boyfriend so I just don't know how to act. And with Jessica, she's always rude to me first so of course I'm not going to be nice back."

Tears filled my eyes. I looked down. I did my best to keep my tears from showing. The truth hurt. I was rude to him at first, but I didn't think I was still mean.

"All I'm saying is, I think you need to try and be nicer to others."

"I'm always nice," I said, forcefully. My throat was tightening. I wasn't going to back down. I understood what he felt, but it wasn't true. "I'm nice to Loue, I'm nice to Makayla, strangers, *restaurant staff*. I'm not going to be nice to her if she makes me uncomfortable or says rude remarks about my relationship with you or anything involving me for that matter. I don't think she deserves that."

"She doesn't. But it doesn't help if you do the same thing."

I rolled my eyes and grabbed my phone.

"That's what I'm talking about."

I looked back at him. "It's better I don't say anything."

"You need to be more expressive instead of doing shit like this and rolling your eyes 24/7."

"Why are you even sticking up for her?"

"I'm not, I let her have it too. I'm just saying that I also think you can be mean."

"Then why didn't you say anything before? Why now after standing up for her?"

"I'm not standing up for anyone," he said, ignoring my question.

"Exactly. You didn't *defend* me, even when she was clearly in the wrong."

"I care for you Maya, I really do," his tone softened as he spoke. "But I'm not going to let you manipulate situations just to make you happy. I can get over your rudeness towards me every once in a while, but I'm just telling you the truth. Whether you like it or not. I don't care who you're nice to if you aren't nice to me. You don't have to be 'buddy-buddy' with Jessica, but you can at least be civil."

"I'll try to be nicer," I mumbled. I didn't want to keep arguing. I didn't want to hear anything more hurtful and cry. "But if she does anything else that I don't like, I'm not going to let it slide."

Daniel sat on the couch and hugged me. "If she says or does something you don't like, I'll say something next time. Okay?"

I didn't look at him or say anything. I scrolled through random apps on my phone.

"I'm sorry," he said. "I'm quite the mood killer huh?"

I didn't respond and continued looking at my phone.

"I didn't mean to hurt you," he said, leaning over, trying to look me in my eyes. "And you know I will always have your back over hers or anyone else's right?"

I nodded.

"You don't seem convinced," he said, leaning on my shoulder.

"Well…" I paused, I bit my lip and thought, *You didn't just now, so…*

"I'm sorry."

"It's fine. You're entitled to an opinion just like I am."

"I know. I wasn't planning on hurting your feelings or make you feel attacked."

"I know, sometimes it's best to hear what people really think," I said, practically whispering. "What I find acceptable, won't be to someone else and might make me come off as being a jerk. I'm sorry for how I treated you. I'll be nicer and I'll try to be better at expressing how I feel."

"You don't always have to. I think it's cute the way you act when you're embarrassed."

"Make up your mind," I snorted, smiling faintly.

"Oh, there's my smile. Feel better?"

"It's nothing to stay too worked up about."

Daniel kissed my cheek.

"And…I'll try to be civil with her."

"Good, it gets awkward being in the middle of your spats."

I laughed and sat my phone down. I wiggled to turn around and looked at Daniel. His arms loosened a bit and he looked down at me.

"What?"

"Nothing," I said, shaking my head.

I lay down on the couch and looked at Daniel. I waited, wondering if he would take the hint to lie next to me. His eyes met mine, his face slowly turning red. He gulped, then leaning over our lips meshed, and we kissed passionately for what felt like an eternity. I closed my eyes, and I slid my arms around him, as he slid Daniel a hand under my shirt. His fingertips gently traced along my skin, his touch was delicate, as if I were a flower whose petals were close to falling off.

Daniel's legs slid between mine carefully, one by one, until the length of his body covered mine. His weight was comforting, I could feel his warmth, the caress of his warm hand under my shirt felt amazing. Daniel moved down, kissing my neck. And in one slight movement of his hand, I moaned. Daniel gazed wantingly in my eyes.

"Before I go any further," he said, his breaths jagged. "I need to know if you're ready for this."

"Ready for what?" I asked, eyes wide.

Daniel flinched as though I slapped him in the face. He dropped his head and said, "Guess not."

"You won't know if I'm ready until you actually hear my answer."

"But the fact you haven't caught on means it's too early."

Daniel laid his head on my chest and took a deep breath.

"I'm gonna go back to my apartment for the night."

"Why? Did I do something wrong?"

"No," Daniel said, his eyes closed. "Nothing at all, it's just a me problem."

"Okay," I said disappointed.

Daniel stayed a few more minutes then sat up. He tenderly adjusted my pajama top, putting it back in place. I realized how disheveled I must have looked. He stood, his face flushed with what looked like embarrassment

He averted his eyes as he walked to the door. "I'll see you tomorrow."

"Okay, goodnight."

"Night," he mumbled as he closed the door.

Why couldn't he just tell me what it was? I thought, locking the door behind him.

I sat back on the couch. I was racking my brain trying to figure out what he was talking about. Then it hit me.

"I'm so stupid," I said, aloud burying my head in my hands.

I was so stupid and oblivious to his question, and it wasn't like that was the first time we had been in that position or the first time he made a move on me. So why didn't I catch on that time? I reached over and grabbed my phone off the coffee table.

"I'm sorry," I texted him. "I realized what you meant. I'm so stupid."

"Lol. It's okay, like I said, you aren't ready yet. So don't worry about it."

"Yeah but I feel so embarrassed. >.<|||"

"It's okay, really. Don't be. I obviously took whatever you were doing the wrong way. Btw, what was that stare for?"

"WDYM?" (What do you mean)

"When you laid beside me and were looking at me."

"It was signal. For you to lay next to me..."

"Yeah, I definitely misunderstood. You shouldn't feel embarrassed at all. I should be for acting like a lechorous wolf."

"Lol. Well thank you for being a such gentleman. I don't think I'm ready for that. Not yet."

"I know. And I respect that. 😊 Eventually I would like for us to go a step further, but I can wait."

"Do you want to do anything tomorrow?"

"It's up to you."

"Not really, I just want to read a bit. Have some alone time."

"Alright. I hope to see you later tomorrow. If not, I'll see you in two days..."

"Ok. I'm gonna head to bed. Goodnight."

"Goodnight."

The next day was peaceful. I hadn't heard a peep out of Daniel. He really listened to what I was said. I slept in until 12 PM, I didn't have to eat anything when I woke up, and I binged a new manga I found a while ago. It was about a woman that wanted to get married but the man she fell in love with didn't. It was so good and sweet. I kind of sided with her love interest on marriage, but our experiences were different. After finishing the last volume, I lay sprawled out on my bed.

"I wonder if Daniel would be ______ and me ____?" I mumbled out loud. Thinking, I continued, *He would definitely be the one to want to get married first.*

I turned over and looked at my phone, it was 3 PM and still no texts from Daniel. Maybe I was so used to seeing him every day and him not listening to me when I wanted to be alone, that it just felt weird. Like something was wrong.

"How are you?" I texted him.

He didn't respond. *Maybe he found something to do*? I sighed and rolled over.

"I'm good. Are you having a great break?" he replied.

"Yeah I am. It feels kinda weird without you."

"lol I can come over now so it's not weird."

"Yeah, you can."

"Ok. Give me a sec"

I got up and hurried to my closet. Daniel always showed up in 30 seconds, if that, after asking to come over. I wasn't expecting to see him today, so I looked like a wild woman. I hadn't even showered yet.

I grabbed a random pair of leggings and a blue sweater and ran into the bathroom. I set my clothes on the counter and realized he needed to get in. I ran out, unlocked the door, and sprinted into the bathroom. I had different kinds of soap, but I made sure to use the one that smelled the most "girly."

As I showered, I could hear him shouting, "Hello?"

"I'm in the shower," I yelled.

"O-okay," he said.

He said something else, but I couldn't hear him over the water. I quickly got out and dressed. I opened the door and peeked out. *He must be on the couch.* I sighed and walked into the living room.

"Sorry to keep you waiting," I said.

"It's alright," he replied. "It gave me time to set this up."

I looked at my coffee table and spread across it was takeout and some desserts.

He continued awkwardly, "I actually was gonna text you first. I know you didn't eat. You almost never do. So I got Japanese food and stopped by Loue's for some cakes."

I smiled, that was really sweet. Even though I said I wanted to be alone, he still thought ahead to make sure I was eating properly.

"Thank you," I said, sitting down next to him.

He cleared his throat then slid over a bit.

I giggled, *What the heck?*

He noticed and said, "Sorry, it's just you smell really nice, and you're fresh out the shower. My mind was gonna go places it shouldn't."

I…didn't know how to respond.

"Sorry, I made it awkward, didn't I?" he scratched his head, smiling awkwardly.

"It's okay. It's flattering, I guess."

We sat in silence eating our food. I knew he was embarrassed by what he said, but I had no idea how to break the ice.

"You…don't have to be embarrassed about what you said. It's natural to—for that to happen you know?"

He nodded and smiled.

"How was your day?" I asked. "…besides getting food for me."

"Hmm," he finally spoke. "Uneventful. Woke up, showered, lounged around thinking of what to do, then got you food."

"You weren't kidding when you said uneventful. You don't have anything to do?"

"I do, just didn't feel like doing them. And what did you do miss busy day."

"Read. I finished an entire series in 3 hours, all 9 volumes. I broke my record."

"Well look at you miss record breaker. Should I contact Guinness for your photo?"

"That's not how it works, besides, I'm sure someone's read faster than that."

"Then you should read faster." He smirked. He looked at the bookshelves in the corner of my living room. Overfilled with books and the other 20 'neatly' placed books on the floor to the sides of each bookshelf. "You really love to read huh?"

"Uh-huh. I love it. There's nothing better than reading."

"Not even me?"

"Well, last I checked you weren't a hobby."

"I could be. I'll write all over my body and you can read every inch."

I laughed hard. "You pervert. That sounds so dirty."

"I think you're the pervert. I didn't mean it that way."

"Yeah, sure, if you say so."

Daniel wrapped his arm around my shoulder. "Would you rather read in the rain or in the snow?"

"You mean like while it's raining outside or literally standing outside in the rain?"

"Um, let's go with while it's raining, or snowing, outside."

"I think reading when it's raining outside is amazing. Curling up on the sofa, warmly embraced by a blanket, listening to the pitter patter of raindrops pelting the roof." I sighed, my thoughts drifting to a faraway place. "The ambiance of reading in the rain sounds so amazing right now."

Daniel smiled. He didn't utter a word as I continued rhapsodize about reading in the rain.

"My dream is to move somewhere in the woods where it rains a lot, live in a little cabin and just read for the rest of my life." I snapped out of it and said, "I'm sorry, I'm rambling."

"No, don't be. I like seeing you so passionate. Maybe when we're older, I'll buy a cabin and we can live there together. You wouldn't have to work for the rest of your life."

"I mean, that sounds nice, assuming we're still dating years from now."

Daniel flicked my forehead and said, "Don't say that."

I covered my forehead. "It's true though. I'm just thinking realistically."

"Well, I have no plans to break up with you any time in the future."

"Me neither."

"Then what I said works."

"Since you heard my dream, what's yours?"

"I don't have one."

"You have to. There's no way you haven't dreamt of something."

"I already achieved my dream."

"Well what was your dream?"

Daniel smiled. "Something special."

"Well there has to be something else right? Even something minor."

"To live with you in that cabin."

"You can't piggyback off my dream."

"I think I just did."

"Fine, that'll be the only dream we share."

"Deal…I mean until you tell me one even better than that."

"I'm not telling you any more dreams." I laughed.

"We'll see about that." He winked.

We spent the rest of the evening talking before heading to bed for work. Daniel insisted on sleeping in my apartment. My room was an embarrassment. It was horrible compared to his. There were clothes all over the floor and plushies randomly placed on the floor. My bed barely fit us, my bedding was mismatched, I had only two pillows, my blanket was significantly thinner, and my bed was nowhere near as soft as his. Surprisingly, he didn't complain or tease me. We cuddled until I fell asleep.

At work, I was the bigger person and apologized to Jessica. I explained to her what Daniel told me, except our argument of course, and that I didn't mean to come off as rude. She was taken aback but apologized as well. Her apology felt half-assed, but I couldn't say much. I didn't really mean mine as well. I just wanted to squash whatever she had against me and that from that moment on, any aggression that came from her, couldn't be blamed on my personality.

A week went by, and Jessica was slightly more respectful. She wasn't as mean to me, her snide comments lessened to maybe 5 times a shift, and she stopped pushing for us to be friends. I didn't mind that part as much. "Changed" personality or not, I didn't think we would be compatible. She acted indifferent to the job like usual and slacked off every chance she got.

She still clung to Daniel. I trusted him and he already said he liked me, so I wasn't worried. But sometimes her hugging him flashed in my mind and I felt uncomfortable.

But I reminded myself every time, that I was dating him, not her and that he didn't even hug her back. Jessica also stated she thought of him as a close friend, one-sided or not. I had nothing to worry about.

It was my off day, Daniel worked so I had peace and quiet most of the day. I missed him…to an extent, but I loved getting the chance to binge my romance movies and read more. Since meeting him, I barely touched my movies. I missed my daily ritual. Starting with a few movies then finishing the night reading two or three novels.

While I watched *The Forest Within,* I didn't feel sad. Something was off. At first, I thought maybe I had grown accustomed to the movie after bawling my eyes out that last time with Daniel. Yet every movie I watched I didn't feel like I was missing something. I wasn't sad, I wasn't lonely. Was that because I had Daniel, or had I overcome whatever was holding me down?

I didn't think it was because of Daniel. I hadn't experienced the same things I wanted in romance. Like how I fell in love. I didn't fall in love at first sight. I didn't meet him on some weird…well, we did meet under dire circumstances, so that was one point. But I wasn't swept away, there was no magic, it was basic. He didn't have any talents, to my knowledge, that drew us together or made our relationship romantic.

I felt bad thinking these things, but it was true. I was stubborn when I first met him, refusing to like him. I pushed him away. None of the movies I watched or books I read, had a heroine like that. So I ruled out my relationship with Daniel as the cause for me watching movies like a normal person. I wondered if I'd ever figure out why I wasn't upset watching them. And I was happy that I could enjoy them without my heart crushing into millions of pieces, but at the same time, I enjoyed that feeling. I wasn't a masochist, but the heartbreak made me feel alive.

Daniel helped me feel less lonely. Sometimes a little too much. I was gradually enjoying the time we had together and hating our time apart.

But I wondered how long my feelings would remain. Prior crushes lasted no longer than 3 months. We were approaching a month in our relationship, and I was dreading the outcome. Just thinking about it, made me quiver. I would see if dating changed anything. I desperately wanted it to. I wanted to like him for years to come. But I was terrified I would regress. I was scared I would stand over the bridge again, facing my end. I was scared of hurting Daniel. Tears filled my eyes as I reclined on the couch. I didn't want to feel that way again.

Would it be better if I break up with Daniel before it happens? I thought. I rubbed my face before covering it with my hands, my eyes peering between my middle and index fingers. I couldn't, I didn't want to hurt him and there was nothing I could use as an excuse to end it. I knew I wouldn't even be able to muster the words.

I looked at the time. Daniel wouldn't be done with work for 2 hours. He unknowingly took my mind off those thoughts. I sighed. I was stuck with them until he came home. Was it normal to miss him so much?

I opened my patio door. I hadn't been out there since the first week I moved into my apartment. The lawn chair I left outside was dirty, remnants of snow nuzzled its arms and the seat.

Why is there snow here? I thought, running inside and grabbing paper towels. Most of the snow around the city had melted yet chilling on my balcony was a pile of snow. I used the snow to clean the dirt off the chair, dried it and sat down.

The weather was so bipolar. Sometimes 40s and 50s during the day, 20s and 30s at night. And unfortunately that night, it was outrageously cold. I looked at the relatively nice view seeing part of Manhattan in the distance. The night breeze caressed my cheeks. I pulled the chair to the railing and looked down. I stared at the people walking past. I did the same when I moved there. People watching was a good time passer. You never knew what they were going to do or say. My eyes followed every person that passed.

One man looked up, why I didn't know, and we made eye-contact. He shouted, "The fuck is you lookin' at?"

I quickly moved from the banister and leaned back in the chair. I erupted into laughter. I wished I had that "New York vitriol" like that guy. I would've yelled funny things back. That was enough people watching. It was colder anyways, so I went inside.

I pulled the throw from behind the couch and wrapped myself into a burrito. I knew it wasn't a good idea to watch anymore movies, but honestly, it was one of the only things I did. I put on something light-hearted and watched until I fell asleep.

I woke to knocking on my door. I got up, my eyes still closed and peeked through the peephole. Daniel stood on the other side and looked down at his phone. I heard my phone chime and unlocked the door.

"Can I help you?" I teased.

"Yeah, I have a special delivery."

"What is it?"

Daniel stepped to the side and carried a bookshelf back to my door. I moved to the side, holding my door open as he carried it in. He mimicked the voice in those infomercials, "But wait, there's more!"

He jogged back out and grabbed a box.

"You didn't have to do this," I said, smiling.

"I know, but just think of it as a late birthday present."

"My birthday was in January…wait how did you know it was recent?"

"Don't worry about." He smiled. "And this isn't a birthday gift, I said think of it as one. That reading corner of yours has been driving me crazy."

"Guess your neat-freak side is coming out huh?"

"I'm not a neat-freak. I just want you to have a nicer arrangement."

"Well thank you." I hugged him.

"No problem. I also got you these," he said, handing me the box. Inside was the complete series for *My Immortal* by Rain in mint condition.

"No way," I squealed, hugging him. "I loved this series when I was a kid. It went out of print years ago. These were being sold for over $200. How did you find them?"

"I have my ways." He smiled.

"Wow, I love it. Thank you." I hugged him even tighter. "I have to get you something even better."

"No, I don't need anything," he said. "This was spur of the moment. That corner bothers me. Your gift can be making it a little more…organized."

"Does the rest of my apartment bother you?"

Daniel laughed, neither confirming nor denying it. I knew my disorderliness bothered him. Just one look at his apartment and I knew he preferred organization. Not even a thread on his couch pillows could be out of place. He really was thoughtful of my feelings. Suffering through my messes. I decided from then on, I would clean up more…before he came over.

Daniel stayed and helped me tidy up my bookshelves. He moved all the big stuff while I put everything on the new shelves. When we were done, everything looked new. Those rundown Goodwill bookshelves looked newly assembled and it made my apartment look a little more "elegant."

We reached our "1 month anniversary". Daniel was more ecstatic about it than I was. He planned to spend the day with me, we requested the day off. Loue was pissed because that meant him, Jessica, and someone else was working. I felt bad for them, but Daniel wanted our anniversary to be special and I wanted to make him happy.

I wanted to wear something cute, but I didn't have much. And I also thought about how I wouldn't look good in it. Last thing I needed was to look stupid. I sat in front of my closet. Daniel said it was casual and I didn't need to worry about being fancy. But that also meant not looking bad either.

Daniel was supposed to arrive at my place at 12 PM and we would just relax in my apartment. I had 30 minutes to find something decent. I saw pushed to the far wall was a light pink and white letterman jacket I wore once a year ago. It was more of a collector's item than something I would ever wear. It was an official jacket from a band I loved. I only wore it once to the store so I wouldn't feel bad spending $80 on a jacket I'd never wear.

It was the only pink item I had. I grabbed that and black leggings and tossed them on the bathroom counter. I was going to take a shower, but I remembered to tidy up before he came. I cleaned up all the clothes I had strewn about my room, I folded the throw on the back of the couch, swept the floor and put away the dishes in the sink. After feeling good about my cleanup, I hopped in the shower.

Daniel came at exactly 12 PM, not a second later. He wore a blue hoodie and jeans. I was glad he didn't wear anything dressy. I would've felt bad about my outfit. He had a lot planned. He rented 3 rom-coms, bought lunch and supplies for dinner. He went all out.

He brought another gift for me. I protested that time. He was giving me so much and I hadn't even given him a stick of gum. He said he would "forgive me" for not getting him a gift on our anniversary but expected one on our 2nd. Was it normal to have monthly anniversaries? I wasn't complaining, I did owe him a gift.

We set up lunch on my coffee table. Daniel bought desserts from Mama's, strawberry shortcake, and their signature brownie cookie crumble cake. And takeout from a Chinese restaurant. He ordered beef fried rice, vegetable egg foo young, orange chicken, General Tso chicken and there was a side of white rice. Before we ate, I opened his gift. It was a silver necklace with a crescent moon and a small star.

Small diamonds were engraved along the shape of the moon and the middle of the star.

"It's beautiful," I said. "Thank you."

"Mm-hm. You know, woulda been nice if I had a gift too…" he teased. He took the necklace and put it around my neck.

"I'll give you one later, I promise."

"I'm just messing with you. I don't need anything. Just spending today with you is the greatest gift."

That's so cheesy, I thought. Out loud I said, "Well, you're welcome."

Half-way through our meal, Daniel grew silent. He tried his best not to show whatever problem he had on his face.

"What's wrong?" I asked.

"I…" he started before pausing. "I've been thinking about this for a while, and I don't know how to bring it up. And I'm sorry if it makes you uncomfortable."

"It's alright. Go on."

"Do… Do you find me attractive?"

"Yeah… I mean, I-I guess." I looked away from him.

"'Guess'?" he repeated. "Do you not know if you find me attractive?"

"It's not that," I said, my sentence trailing off. "It's just, it was so random. Why do you want to know?"

"Well… Actually first, I wanna say this, if this conversation makes you uneasy just let me know, okay?"

I nodded motioning for him to spit it out.

"We've been dating for a month now, right?"

I nodded impatiently.

"I myself, am ready to take things a step further."

Oh no, I thought. *What happened to him being patient and waiting until I said I was ready?*

"That's why I asked if you found me attractive. Like physically attractive," he continued. "You've rejected all of my advances. And I just feel like it could be because you don't like me physically."

"I'm just not ready. And I think you're moving too fast for me. It's only been a month since we started dating."

"I know, I just really like you," he said leaning his head on my shoulder. "It's something I've always thought about."

"'Always?'" I repeated. "How long is 'always?'"

Daniel sucked his lips in, as if he said something he didn't mean.

"What do you mean by you've 'always thought about'?"

Daniel sighed. "I feel like I shouldn't tell you, but I guess you should know."

"Okay?"

"I've known you since we were younger," Daniel mumbled. Sarcastically he said, "'The stepbrother you never talked to.'"

"Wait so when I asked you if you knew Margaret, you lied?"

"Yeah…."

"Why?"

"Who wouldn't?" he said sitting up. "I don't know about you, but I don't want to be associated with that woman. It sucks enough she never changed her name back."

"How come you waited so long to tell me?"

"I was never going to."

"Why?"

"…I see that house as a nightmare for all of us. And since I was a part of that family, I knew you would hate me."

"You're not wrong," I said, taking a bite of orange chicken. "But I'm moving towards that being in my past. I'm not gonna blame you for your stepmom's actions."

"Ex…" he corrected me.

"You know what I mean. Thinking back on it, was that what you and Anna were talking about when she came to visit?"

"When?"

"When you, me, and Anna all hung out. Before we were dating."

"You heard that?" He rubbed his hand through his hair. "Well yeah, Anna's the only one that talked to me back then and she even remembered me now."

"Wait you guys talked to each other? But she hated boys."

"She did." He nodded. "But one time when you were gone to see your case worker, she was scared and wouldn't leave her room. Margaret made me bring her some food. She wouldn't talk to me or open the door. So I had to go out and buy her that extremely expensive dollhouse she wanted. Then like after 20 minutes she started talking to me. Ever since, we were friends. But we only talked if she didn't have you. Then I moved, and lost contact with you guys."

"So you basically bribed her into liking you?"

"Kinda, all that matters was that she warmed up to me."

"I always wondered how she got that. I thought Margaret or your dad bought it."

"Nope, all from my allowance."

"That was sweet."

Daniel shrugged. He tried to play it off like it wasn't a big deal.

"Anna's been my right-hand man for a long time. Kept me updated on you. But then after she was adopted, her parents made her change numbers or got her a new phone, whatever happened, and we stopped talking."

"Yeah, Jane spoiled Anna. She got adopted by a rich family."

"Damn that's lucky."

I didn't say anything. In theory it was the dream life, but with her adopted father being a huge creep, it was the last place she wanted to be. Sometimes what looks good on the outside, isn't as great on the inside. I sighed and leaned on Daniel.

"What's wrong?"

"Nothing." I shook my head. "I just can't believe you really are my stalker."

Daniel smacked his lips and slid away from me, making me fall on the couch. "I'm not your stalker. I lived here first."

"Is what you say."

Daniel stayed silent. As I sat up, Daniel "tackled" me onto my back, hugging me and squeezed hard.

"Ouch." I laughed. "Get off!"

"It's punishment for calling me a stalker. We're gonna be here a while."

I tried pushing him off, but I gave up and hugged him back. "Was this the 'lifelong dream' you accomplished?"

"Hm?"

"Dating me."

Daniel laughed. "You're so confident."

"Well you said you liked me for years."

"It is," he said loosening his hug a little bit. Daniel kissed my forehead. "Never imagined this would happen."

We embraced for a long time. Our food was getting cold, but we didn't care. It was just nice holding him. I definitely liked Daniel. Was it okay to care for someone that much? That I was content just holding him?

When I opened my eyes, I was in my bed. Daniel slept next to me.

"What time is it?" I mumbled. I picked up my phone. It was midnight. "No way I just slept 10 hours...."

I rolled over to Daniel who slept peacefully. I delicately ran my hand through his hair. He really was handsome.

Where would I have been if I hadn't met him? I thought.

He was a life saver, literally. He changed me in so many ways, I was open to trying things. I met more people through him than I did one year living in New York. I owed him a lot of thanks. It was crazy. I realize at that moment how much he'd done for me.

Daniel smiled and said drowsily as he opened his eyes, "Why are you awake?"

"Because we slept like 10 hours." I smiled.

"What time is it?"

"Midnight."

Daniel moved closer to me and said, "Well go back to sleep we gotta work bright and early."

"I don't think I can," I said as I hugged him. "But you can. I'll hold you until you fall asleep. Then maybe I'll fall asleep too."

"Hmm... I'll take you up on that."

My heart was racing. I really wanted to let Daniel know how much I cared for him. I learned from romance novels and movies, saying "I love you," made people feel better and I did like him. I didn't know if "love" was too strong a word, but I was going for it.

"Daniel?" I paused.

"Hm?" he asked his eyes closed.

"I—I love you...."

Daniels eyes opened. He looked down at me and said, "Are you sure?"

I nodded. "Sorry. Too soon?"

"Don't be." He smiled. "I'm just a little shocked. That made me really happy. So happy you don't even kno—. I can't sleep now either."

"You're overreacting." I laughed.

"Nah, I can't sleep now." He shook his head. "That's the first time you said you loved me."

I shrugged. I was a little embarrassed.

"You're gonna have to take responsibility and stay up with me."

"What? We need to go to sleep."

"We could…." he started. "But I think I'll need you to say you love me a few more times before I can."

"You're too much." I laughed.

"You think I'm joking? I'll make enough noise to keep the whole building awake if I can't sleep."

"Over me saying I love you?"

"Yeah." He nodded. "I'll literally start screaming."

"You wouldn't dare." I giggled. "I'm not saying it again."

Daniel took a deep breath and yelled, "Maya from 6B said she loved me! Maya from 6B said she loved me!"

"Stop," I shouted covering his mouth. "I love you, Daniel. I love you, love you, love you. Stop screaming."

Daniel kissed the palm of my hand. "I love you too Maya."

Daniel leaned over and kissed me. He placed his arm gently on my lower back. His kiss was so passionate, I lost all senses and was enveloped in ecstasy. Daniel moved away.

"Better stop there," he whispered softly. "Thank you for loving me."

I shook my head. "Thank you. I wouldn't be here if it weren't for you. You changed my life in so many ways. How can I not love you?"

Daniel smiled. "I feel the same way."

My face was hot. I didn't know if it was from the kiss or not, but I didn't want him to see me blushing. I buried my face in his chest and hugged him tightly.

"Are you getting tired?" he asked.

"Yeah."

"I'll hold you until you fall asleep."

"Okay, goodnight," I whispered.

"Goodnight, Maya."

CHAPTER FOUR

I couldn't sleep last night. I lay there pretending to sleep. Daniel also couldn't sleep and scrolled through his phone. He didn't let go of me except once to go to the bathroom. I eventually fell asleep at 5 AM.

"Morning," Daniel said groggily as I opened my eyes.

"Morning, did you go to sleep?"

"Yeah…."

"What time?"

"2 AM."

I snickered. "No you didn't. I saw you on your phone."

"Oops, busted."

"Did you even go to sleep?"

Daniel shook his head.

"You're gonna fall asleep at work," I said.

"I'll be fine if I get some coffee."

"Wanna leave early to get some?"

Daniel shrugged. "Sure. I don't mind. I gotta get dressed first."

"Obviously. I do too."

Everything between me and Daniel seemed normal. He didn't talk about me saying the "L" word on the walk to get coffee or on the way to work.

I, however, could barely focus on work. What happened the night before kept flashing in my mind. I couldn't believe I actually told him I loved him. I was proud of myself for being bold and expressive like he said. But I was still embarrassed. My face turned red every time I thought about it. Customers asked if I was sick because I was, "as red as a tomato." I couldn't ignore that I said something I knew I would regret. That day was kind of slow, so thankfully I didn't have to see Daniel.

After work, I waited for Daniel outside. The warm breeze tickled my cheeks. I couldn't believe it was already April. The time I spent with Daniel and working at Loue's really made my days fly by. Reminiscing in thought, I hadn't noticed Jessica standing beside me.

"Hi," she said as I looked over.

"Hey, sorry I was spacing out," I said, fully standing up.

"It's cool, that happens to me."

I nodded.

"Anyways, Loue asked Daniel to work a little later just until second shift came. They're all apparently going to be late," Jessica said cynically. "Daniel wanted me to let you know to go home without him."

"Oh…ok," I said. "Thanks for letting me know."

As I turned to walk to the bus stop, Jessica shouted, "Wait! I'm going the same way. Wanna walk together?"

"Did you have something to do in Brooklyn?" I asked. The way I was going took you deeper into Brooklyn. And Jessica didn't peg me as the type to be in this area. It wasn't a bad area or anything, she was just… snobby.

"Yeah," she said. "I…wanted…to…check out some stores down here."

"Ok," I nodded. "Well I have to hurry, or I'll miss the bus."

"Oh ok." Jessica hopped and rushed to my side.

We didn't talk for a block before Jessica broke the silence.

"Actually Maya," she said. "I don't really have anything to do over here."

No really? I thought sarcastically.

"The reason I wanted to walk with you, was because I want us to have a fresh start," she said. "Let all anger or hate we have for each other just be gone."

I bit my lip, I needed to speak my mind. "Well Jessica. The reason I don't really like you is because of how rude you've been to me from get go."

"You were rude to me too though."

"After how you treated me," I cut her off. "The first day we met, that was all you. I just came to drop something off for Daniel."

"And I apologized, 'cause I'm a little protective of him."

"He never asked for your protection, especially not from his girlfriend."

"You're right." She nodded. "But let's just squash this. I want a girl friend for once."

"I don't mind Jessica," I said.

"Great, this is going to be cheesy but I'm Jessica." She stuck her hand out.

I laughed shaking her hand. "Maya."

We talked for a long time while I waited for the next bus. Surprisingly, we had a lot in common. The same likes and dislikes, people talking loudly, romantic movies, you name it. I judged her too harshly. She wasn't as bad of a person as I thought she was. We exchanged numbers as the bus came. I said goodbye and got on.

Later that evening, Daniel *finally* got off work and came over. When I opened the door, Daniel kissed my forehead and said, "I heard you and Jessica are friends."

"She texted you?" I asked.

"Yep," Daniel paused and smiled. "I'm glad you kept an open mind."

"Yeah." I smiled.

Daniel sat on the couch and hugged me. "As long as she doesn't take you from me, I'm all for this."

"How can she take me from you?"

"She can take away my alone time with you."

"I doubt that," I said. "I don't think I'll be hanging out with her here. I wanna be kinda like you are with her. Work friends."

"Okay, I prefer that anyways."

The next day, Jessica was all over me. I wasn't annoyed though. After talking it out with her, I wasn't on edge. I figured she wouldn't make rude comments anymore, and she didn't. She even complimented me in the morning. We had a break together, she spent most of her shift just leaning on the register.

"Maya! Jessica!" Loue hollered. "It's nice you're all buddy-buddy now, but Jessica you need to help Daniel with the new load!"

Jessica rolled her eyes. "Let's talk after work Maya."

"Ok." I waved.

"Don't let her bad work ethic rub off on you," Loue said.

"I won't, I promise."

"I'm curious." He walked closer. "Weren't you two sworn enemies or something? I'm all for good relationships but when?"

I chuckled. Loue rarely meddled in our personal affairs, it was the first time I saw him so nosy. "The past few days Jessica's been asking me to be her friend. We talked about how we felt and decided to start over."

"Wow." Loue nodded slowly. "That's not as exciting as I thought it would be...."

"It's really not."

"Well I'm glad there won't be any more disputes between you two."

"Hopefully. I mean, that all depends on one person."

"Keep up the good work Maya," Loue said. As he walked away, Daniel walked towards me. Loue rolled his eyes. "Now Daniel is slacking off. Maya, you might be my only good employee."

Daniel lifted his hands in defense. "What? I just did most of the load by myself, and I'm on break."

"Hmm..." Loue grunted then walked off.

"Are you really on break?"

"Yes," he said annoyed. "Unfortunately, because you two 'best friends' took your break together, I had to wait for mine."

"Sorry."

"It's not your fault. I'm only blaming Jessica."

"Why her?"

"'Cause, not even a day after burying the hatchet, she took my break with you," Daniel ranted. "I told you, as long as she didn't take away my time with you, I was fine with this."

"It's okay," I said. "It's only during work. You have me all evening."

"I better."

Daniel stayed with me until his break was done.

Over the week, Jessica took most of my time at work. And after work, stayed with me and Daniel until the bus came. It was stifling. Was it normal to feel this way with a "friend"? I spent way more time with Anna and my siblings, and I never got tired of being around them. Maybe it was because we were siblings? Daniel didn't complain, that much. But I could tell he was getting angry with Jessica. It was kind of cute to see him jealous.

Friday slowly rolled around. I was happy we both had the weekend off. Two days without her was going to be a blessing. I felt like a mom that sent her kid off to grandma's for the weekend. To reiterate, I didn't mind having her as a friend, but she was moving way too fast. She was also very pushy when me and Daniel tried to be alone. After work, Daniel rushed out of the store pulling me along.

"Why are you in such a rush?" I complained.

"You know exactly why." He didn't look back. "If we don't leave now, I guarantee she would follow us to the bus stop then ask to hang out at your place."

"I can see that happening." I laughed.

Practically running, we made it to the bus stop just as the bus pulled off.

"Damn," Daniel said. "I don't want to talk to her right now."

"I mean, we could walk. We've done it before right?"

Daniel thought about it for a minute before saying, "You know what, it is a nice day to walk."

Daniel held my hand and we walked back to our apartment. Along the way, I got a text from Jessica.

Daniel looked over and asked, "Is that Jessica?"

"Yeah, she's wondering if we left or not."

He rolled his eyes. "She's obsessed with you."

I didn't respond to him and replied to Jessica.

"Yeah, sorry. We decided we were gonna walk home so we left right away."

"Really? Damn, I wanted to talk to you since I wasn't gonna see you this weekend."

"Sorry." Trying to not make it awkward I wrote, "We can still text and I'll see you Monday."

"She's not obsessed," I said continuing the conversation. "I just think she's happy to have a girl friend."

"Nah, I don't think so. She's obsessed."

"Whatever you say." I shrugged.

Daniel spent all day holding me on the couch. He said he didn't want to waste the only time he might have with me. Even though Jessica didn't know where I lived, he still felt like she would show up unannounced. I didn't hold it against him or get angry. It was more of a compliment than anything else. And I definitely couldn't deny that she was unnervingly clingy.

The next morning was relaxing. Daniel rested in my bedroom, and I relaxed on the couch listening to music while I read. That was the quietest it'd been in over a week. I read for a few hours when I got a call from Jessica. She was in tears.

"Maya," she sobbed.

"What's wrong? Are you okay?"

"No. The guy I liked rejected me."

"Oh no," I said. *She likes someone already. I was worried over nothing.*

"Yeah. He said I was too stuck up and self-centered."

He wasn't wrong, I thought. Out loud I said, "You're not even close to…self-centered."

"Thank you, Maya. But he might be right. I only think about myself."

"Noo," I said, humoring her.

"Yeah, I'm sorry," she paused. "If it's alright, can I come over to your place? I need someone to talk to, and you're my only friend."

"Didn't you work today?"

"Yeah, I called in," she sniffled. "I'm not emotionally ready to go in. Can I come over?"

"Sure…" I rolled my eyes. So much for a quiet day. "I'll text you my address. If you can come in like an hour, that's enough time for me to get ready."

"Okay Maya, thank you. Sorry to bother you on your day off."

"It's okay Jessica."

I hung up and sighed. I knew Daniel would be pissed when he found out she was coming over. I thought about waking him up and telling him to go home, but at the same time, Jessica already had eyes on someone else. It would have been even luckier if he slept through the day.

As I got my hopes up, Daniel walked into the room yawning.

"Morning babe."

"M-morning," I said, startled.

Daniel looked at me confused. "What's wrong?"

"Nothing…" I chuckled nervously. "Just uh, have some plans for today is all."

"What are you going to do?"

"Well, Jessica—"

Before I could finish Daniel rolled his eyes. "Come on, it hasn't even been 24 hours yet and she's already all over you."

"It can't be helped. She just got rejected and is crying. I kinda have to cheer her up."

"Yeah, but I wanted to have a day alone with you."

"We can do that tomorrow. I already promised her."

"And you promised me."

"I know, I'm really sorry. You can hang out at your place if you don't want to see her. She won't be here that lo—"

"She's coming here?" Daniel interrupted. "So she's going to know where you live and me by default."

"Kinda, I mean she won't know which apartment you live in."

Daniel looked so done with it. He shook his head and walked back in the room. Was I being inconsiderate of his feelings or was he overreacting? I didn't want to put Jessica's feelings over his, I just felt like she needed me. I understood Daniel's frustration, but was it too much?

I texted Jessica my address. I told her I would be ready in an hour and thirty minutes. I had to talk with Daniel, and I knew she would come over as quickly as she could if I didn't give a time.

I walked into my room. Daniel was dressed and sitting on my bed.

"Going home?"

"Yep."

"You don't have to go right away. She won't be here for like an hour."

Daniel stayed quiet.

"You can't be mad at me. I mean, if you did this for your friends, I wouldn't be mad."

"None of my friends live in New York, so they wouldn't get in the way. Like I said, I'm not mad at you, I'm mad at Jessica. She's way too clingy."

"She's not clingy…" I trailed off. She was undeniably clingy. "She just needs some support. She said I was her only friend. She probably wants another woman's input or something."

"I wouldn't be surprised if she was lying," he mumbled. "Just promise me I'll have you all to myself tomorrow."

"I promise. You can hang out with us too."

"I'm good," he quickly refused. "One, I know I'm going to be shitty towards her. Two, I'm sure she wants just you and no men, considering she got dumped. And three, I don't want her knowing where I live, so I'm leaving before she gets here, and if I stayed, I don't want her to see when I do leave."

"So you're leaving now?"

"Yeah." Daniel kissed my forehead. "I'll see you tonight or in the morning."

"Okay…" I pouted.

"You're so cute." He kissed again. "Just hope she doesn't overstay her welcome. The faster she leaves the better."

I walked Daniel to the door and waved bye. I really didn't feel like doing anything today. I was completely unmotivated. However, I would never leave someone who's hurt alone.

I sat staring in space until I heard a knock on the door.

"Hi," Jessica said, all smiles.

For someone that was heartbroken and needed some cheering up, she was very giddy.

"Are you feeling better?"

"I cheered myself up waiting."

"You bounce back pretty quick."

"Yeah well, why waste away on a man that doesn't want me." Jessica shrugged and walked past me. "I still came 'cause I would have felt bad if I didn't show knowing you were expecting me."

"No it's okay."

"So is it just you?"

"Yep."

"Where's Daniel? Isn't he always over?"

"No. Not today."

"Aw shoot, I was hoping we all could hang together."

"Sorry, he's busy today." I wasn't going to tell her he intentionally left *because* of her. It would crush her.

"That's okay. We can talk shit about the guy who rejected me."

"Alright, rant away."

"Well for starters, who the fuck does he think he is calling me a snob? Like the fuck?"

"He had no business saying that."

"He didn't. And it's not even true, right?"

"…Right."

Jessica talked my ear off for hours. She told me a lot of personal things and secrets. Like how she's afraid of dying alone, has insecurities and self-esteem issues. She was scared of poor people… and other things I promised to never tell…. Except for just now. She really trusted me. I couldn't do the same, but I did feel closer to her. Maybe in time, I could confide in her like I did Makayla and Anna.

It was getting late, and I knew Daniel was being impatient in his apartment. In a way, it was fun hanging out with her. I felt bad thinking about how if this was fun, hanging out with Makayla would be better. But I kept it to myself, so I didn't have to worry that much.

"Hey Jessica?"

"What is it Maya?"

"It's getting kinda late—"

"Say no more," Jessica interrupted. "I better hurry while there's still light out. Unlessss, you and Daniel walk me home?"

"Um, I don't think Daniel is home yet, and I don't feel comfortable walking back alone in the dark," I said. I noticed Jessica rolling her eyes when she turned to look at her phone. "I can walk you to the bus stop now though."

"Yeah, I was…just checking the bus schedule. Next one's coming soon."

"Okay, we better get going."

I grabbed a jacket and put on my shoes. I could feel Jessica judging me for going out in my pajamas. But that was okay. Why get dressed just to go two blocks away for 5 minutes?

As we walked down the hall to the elevator, Jessica looked around and said, "Which one of these is Daniel's apartment?"

"I, don't think he would be comfortable if I gave away his address."

"But it is this floor, right?"

"No it's not."

I didn't want to lie, but it was weird for her to be so set on figuring out his place. I just hoped he didn't tell her any time soon.

"Hm, I thought you said you lived next to each other."

"Yeah, in the same complex. Not like same floor."

"Ah ok. So then you aren't NEXT to each other."

"Yes…"

We didn't say anything in the elevator. She was probably pissed I didn't give her his address. I didn't care though, it's an invasion of his privacy. I wouldn't betray him for her. Especially over something like that.

"Well, there it is." Jessica took coins out of her bag. "I normally refuse to take the bus, but it's the closest thing to getting to the station."

"Uh huh."

I waved as the bus drove away. My phone buzzed in my pocket.

"She's gone right?" Daniel asked.

"Yeah, how did you know though?"

"I could hear you guys in the hall. By the way, thank you for not giving in to her pestering."

"It's no problem."

"I know but it's weird. Maybe she's trying to off me so she can have you all to herself."

I laughed. "No I don't think that's it. Are you still in your apartment or are you waiting at mine?"

"Neither," he said. He hung up the phone and shouted, "I'm right here."

"You actually walked to the bus stop?"

"Yeah. I don't want you walking home in the dark."

"It's not that dark."

"It kinda is."

"Well I appreciate you coming here."

"Of course. Now I have you all to myself. She better not be here tomorrow."

"No, she called in today, so I bet Loue's going to make her work tomorrow."

"Only fitting she does."

The rest of the night was peaceful. Just me and Daniel relaxing and watching movies. Sunday, I didn't hear a peep from Jessica.

CHAPTER FIVE

Giving Jessica my address was the worst decision *ever*. She was worse than when I first met Daniel. She showed up unannounced at random times of the day. It was hard to detect a pattern in her visits. Daniel was unlucky half the time. Over time though, Daniel and Jessica became good friends, he wasn't rude to her when she came over nor at work. He most likely got used to her. But whenever Daniel was there, Jessica was all over him. You would think she was there for him and not me. But I knew she still had feelings for "Paul" the guy that rejected her a few weeks ago. I trusted her, but I… I felt like I was paranoid. Maybe she lied about Paul. Her story conflicted with what she told me about being over him. However, I acknowledged that people lied to themselves. So I gave her the benefit of doubt. Was I right to do so?

Her random visits weren't always useless. Sometimes she gave me, unwanted, advice on my relationship with Daniel and it was more helpful than I thought. She just seemed a little too fixated. Maybe she wanted to help? She knew I was inexperienced.

"Maya, Maya, Maya," Jessica slowly called in the break room, disappointment in her voice.

"What?" I asked, taking a sip of soda.

"Daniel told me you *still* haven't had sex yet."

I choked on my drink.

"Don't die in the break room." She rolled her eyes.

"It would be your fault," I said, gasping for air, my eyes teary.

"Yeaah…no." She sat down next to me. "Is it true though? You haven't?"

"No. I'm still a virgin."

"Okay and? It takes two for a relationship. If you're not going to devote yourself to him and his happiness, you should just break up now."

"So not having sex means I don't care about him?"

"Pretty much. Did you think to ask what he thought about it?"

"We had that conversation."

"What'd you say?"

"That's private."

"I'm trying to help you. If your discussion was just, 'I'm not ready,' then it wasn't a discussion."

"That's not how it went, there are more things to a relationship than just sex."

"Says the virgin in her first relationship."

"I'm not ready to lose my virginity. Daniel understands that and that's all that matters. No matter what you say."

I stood up and gathered my trash. I was done eating and didn't want to spend the rest of my break listening to her.

"You're just going to leave?"

"Yep, I'm not talking about this with you."

"I'm just trying to help you."

"That's not helpful at all."

"Whatever you say, I just won't help you anymore."

"That's fine."

I left the breakroom and looked for Daniel. I was, of course, going to give him shit for telling her.

"Hey babe," he said.

"Don't 'hey babe' me."

"What's wrong?"

"You telling Jessica we haven't," I paused and whispered, "had sex."

"Uh. She kinda pressured me into saying it. But I told her I was cool with it."

"Yeah, she didn't care. She just berated me in the break room about how important it is to have sex with you for your happiness, regardless of my comfortability. And if I can't, I should break up with you."

"It's not that important. Well, it is important to me but there's no rush. I want you to be ready and not feel pressured, you know? Don't listen to Jessica. That's not something to break up for. Our relationship is based off love not sex."

"Okay. It just kinda annoyed me. I didn't even finish my break."

"I'm sorry, I should've ignored her."

"It's okay. It's not your fault she went overboard."

"In time." He kissed my forehead. "I gotta get the next pallet out."

"Okay, have fun."

I punched back in and went to the register, waiting was Jessica. I sighed and walked up.

"I'm sorry Maya. I didn't mean to come off like I did. Remember, I care about Daniel, as a friend obviously, and I want to see him happy. But you're also my friend and I care about you too. I won't pressure you to break up with him. That was too far."

"It's fine," I mumbled. "Log out, I'm done with my break."

"Are you sure you're not mad."

"Nope. It's not that big a deal."

"Alright Maya."

I wasn't mad at her for long. She just overstepped boundaries, that was her personality, I didn't hold it against her. She was the type to sleep with guys on the first date and that was totally fine. I didn't like her not respecting my choices. There was nothing wrong with being a virgin, especially as young as I was. There was no need to rush it. And not sleeping with him didn't mean I didn't love him. He knew I did and there were always other ways to show him.

I will say, Jessica did influence me a little. She had me wondering, *was Daniel really fine with it*? It slipped my mind that we'd had that conversation about a month ago, him feeling insecure. He thought I didn't find him attractive. So for him to easily "rant," well I assumed he did, meant he really was bothered by us not taking that next step. He said it was important but how long could he wait?

That Saturday I went to Mama. I needed to get an unbiased opinion and I trusted Makayla, she would be straightforward and wouldn't steer me wrong. I leaned on the counter explaining everything.

"Well, if I'm honest, your friend should stay out of your business. There's a difference between giving advice and just being annoying. Sex isn't necessary to have a healthy relationship. There are people that wait longer than you have with Daniel. I'm talking like over half a year and you guys are what 1, 2 months in? It's not a race. And if Daniel is impatient or unwilling to understand you, then you might have to find another boyfriend."

"Daniel said he was cool with waiting. It's just, I don't know if he really thinks that. I mean, he clearly had something to say to my friend for her to feel the need to tell me, 'Have sex or break up.'"

"True, but you just need to sit down with him and discuss it."

"We already did."

"And how long ago was that?"

"A month I think."

"Well have it again, it doesn't hurt right? And it helps you not get crazy ideas."

"I guess, I just feel like it's gonna be awkward."

"Why?"

I shrugged. "Just is."

"I think you should step out of your comfort zone just to know where you both stand. That way you're not wasting each other's time."

I nodded.

"Just think about it. Conversation is key."

I searched online later that night. I tried everything to dodge having another talk. Maybe someone online had another way of looking at it. There were a lot of articles explaining that it depended on the person. There were studies on the benefits of having sex. Emotional benefits like self-confidence, relieving stress, and bonding on a deeper level with your partner. Physical benefits like a boosted immune system, healthier heart, improved cognitive functioning, soothing headaches, etc. of course, it also mentioned that abstaining from sex didn't mean people would become ill, just that those who were sexually active, would probably have improvements in these areas. And that just because there were pros to having sex, didn't mean a person should hold that against their partner.

The article also said the justifiable reasons why people didn't have sex. Like health conditions and mental health issues. It was best to just have a conversation about it and find common ground or slowly ease your way in. There were other ways of maintaining intimacy without sex, like massages, kissing, cuddling, holding hands, etc. The articles gave me a better understanding about sex and relationships but nothing useful for me and Daniel. The talk was unavoidable. I just didn't know how to bring it up or even what to say. "Hey, I don't want to have sex with you so deal with it?" That wouldn't be helpful considering I wanted to know what he was thinking. Even if we did sleep together would anything change?

I wasn't going to have the talk. He said he was okay with waiting, which was enough. If he felt differently, he would tell me. Whatever he told Jessica was told in confidence. I was not meant to hear it. It bothered me but that was just how it was. I wasn't going to badger him to tell me.

Over the next week, I couldn't help but think about if we should have sex. Jessica certainly alluded to it…many times. "Break up with him."

It was annoying. All it did was make me question if I was doing the right thing in the relationship. And I couldn't go to Makayla for advice because she'd know I never talked with him. My mind was filled with Jessica's constant "devote myself to him" like it was the 1800s. Maybe she was right…not completely but in some way correct? She was the type to give her all for her guy, was she the standard or the "ideal" type of woman? She definitely had the ideal body and look down. Maybe I should've listened to her?

I just couldn't wrap my head around having sex. I loved him yeah, but I didn't feel comfortable. If I'm totally honest, I was scared. I had an…impression about how it was supposed to happen because of movies, and I knew I wouldn't live up to it. I didn't want to embarrass myself and/or for Daniel to find me unattractive. I couldn't bear the thought of it.

And I wasn't completely averse to sex. I wanted it to just happen, nothing planned. But I also didn't want an unexpected advance, I was very indecisive.

"Still haven't done anything?" Jessica asked, walking to my register and placed a bottle of water on the belt.

"What makes you say that? Did he tell you?"

"Nope, I just know."

"How can you 'know'?"

"I just do, call it an expert's eye."

I rolled my eyes. "Jessica, can we talk about something else?"

"I know I'm probably annoying you but I'm just trying to help you. The longer you wait, the more impatient he's going to get. And eventually, he's going to find pleasure somewhere…else…if you know what I mean."

"He's not that kind of person." I shook my head. He said he loved me for years, no way he would risk it all for that…right?

"Eh, doesn't matter what his personality is with you. Guys change and they hide a separate side of themselves. He's doing it too."

"I just don't think he would."

"I've been in more relationships than you Maya, and a third of them I was cheated on. Thought I would hold out and they slept with someone else in a week. I wouldn't be surprised if Daniel is already seeing someone."

"Not possible, he's with me almost every day."

"Keyword 'almost' Maya. ALMOST every day. What's he doing on his off days?"

"No…" I paused. "He wouldn't do that."

"Whatever you say. But if I were you, I'd be careful," Jessica said, partially smiling. She grabbed her drink and walked out the store.

"Daniel isn't like that…" I mumbled.

I spent most of my shift thinking about what Jessica said. Why did she have to say that? Was she that obsessed with me sleeping with him? Or did she want me to break up with him that badly? I just couldn't look at Daniel the same. He was very handsome. He could get any woman he wanted. He was a good boyfriend, he was considerate, kind…who wouldn't want him?

"What's wrong?" Daniel asked, on the way home.

"What do you mean?"

"Well, you haven't looked at me once today. Did I do something wrong?"

I shook my head. "No, you didn't do anything."

It was hard to look him in the eyes. I couldn't help but think about the possibility of him cheating on me. I knew I would make a face if I looked at him. Maybe even cry, which was *definitely* a no-go. But could that have been why he was okay waiting? Because he had someone else to "tie him over"? What if Jessica knew something but wasn't going to tell me out right? Was that part of their conversation?

"Then why?" he asked.

"I can't answer that because there's nothing wrong. You're overthinking it."

Daniel stopped and grabbed my arm. "Then look me in my eyes."

"Why?"

"Why not? If I didn't do anything and there's nothing wrong, you wouldn't have a problem looking at me."

"I just don't feel like it. I'm tired and I wanna go home."

"Maya…" Daniel said, softly. "I'm sorry. I don't know what I did, but I don't want you to be mad at me."

"I told you I'm not mad at you," I shouted. "Stop saying it."

Daniel didn't say anything and let go of my arm. We walked in silence the rest of the way home, Daniel trailed behind me. When we reached the apartment building, I rushed inside to beat him to the elevator. Before the doors closed, Daniel reached his arm inside and the doors opened again.

"Made it just in time." Daniel winked.

I didn't say anything and looked down.

"Maya," Daniel said. He hugged me. Whispering he said, "I really am sorry. I don't want you to be angry with me. I'll do anything for you to forgive me. Please tell me what's wrong."

"I told you it's not you."

"You can say that all you want, but I know it involves me. Or else you wouldn't be like this."

"Like what?"

"Standoffish."

"Is it any different than how I usually am?"

"Yes, you think I don't know your personality?"

"I don't want to talk about it." I walked out of the elevator. "You didn't do anything wrong."

"Is there anything I can do to make you feel better?"

I shook my head. "I just want to be alone is all. I'll talk to you later."

"Okay…goodnight."

I didn't respond and went inside.

I lay on the couch and closed my eyes. He wasn't really the type to cheat, or at least I didn't think he was. To be honest, I didn't really know much about Daniel. I couldn't say I knew he wouldn't do that when I didn't even know his favorite color. All I knew was that he was in love with me for years and that was the only reason I could cling to for why he wouldn't cheat.

I felt bad about how I treated him. I just didn't want him to be offended if it were false and I certainly didn't want to hear him confirm it. I needed to think this through before I saw him tomorrow. Otherwise, I couldn't look at him.

I spent an hour racking my brain for a logical excuse and ways to ignore what Jessica said but it was to no avail. Eventually I decided to call Anna. She was rational enough to speak some sense into me. I told her about Jessica and how she acted since we met until then.

"Well first off," she said. "'Jessica' needs to mind her own damn business. She isn't dating him, you are, and you need to make that clear. I wouldn't trust a word she says. If you think she's interested in Daniel, she's clearly trying to get you to break up with him. Don't let that get to you. If Daniel really is cheating, I'll beat the shit out of him. But we both know he wouldn't do that."

"Yeah, thanks. I was thinking the same thing, but hearing it makes sense."

"So why don't you want to have sex with him?"

"I was hoping you wouldn't ask that," I mumbled and snickered. "Um, it's not that I don't want to, I just don't think I'm ready. If it happens, it happens. But I don't know much about Daniel. How could I just sleep with him?"

"I mean, there couldn't be a better person for your first time. Considering he's loved you so long. At least you know he really cares about you."

"I guess. But I think I need to really know him better before that happens."

"And that's your choice. At the end of the day, none of our opinions really matter. It's your body and life, you choose when you're ready."

"Yeah. And I should talk to Daniel or something, 'cause I know he's sacrificing a lot waiting for me."

"Kinda. I mean he doesn't have much of a choice, he has to wait or break up. He's older than you and more experienced. It would be shitty for him to pressure you into it."

"True, but I'll still see where we both stand. Plus, I should rat Jessica out."

"Yep, let Daniel know how toxic she is. He'll probably confront her, and that'll shut her up."

"I hope so. Thanks Anna, you always know what to say."

"Of course. Keep me up to date more often. I love the tea."

I laughed. "Alright. And you need to too."

"I will if anything worth telling actually happens."

"I'll let you go to sleep. Night Anna."

"Night," Anna said, then hung up.

I looked in my text messages and stared at Daniel's last text. I needed to talk to him, but I was nervous. It could go well or horribly wrong. I bit my lip and wrote, "We need to talk."

"Uh oh," he responded. "What about?"

"Well," I typed. I was already embarrassed. "Just everything that's been happening the past 2 weeks."

"Want me to come over?"

"If you want. It can wait until tomorrow."

"It's better to talk now," he replied. "Otherwise, I'll be up all night worrying."

I sighed. I was hoping he would say tomorrow. I got up, unlocked the door, and cracked it a little. I sat on the couch and twirled my thumbs. My heart pummeled the inside of my chest. I hated confrontation.

Daniel opened the door. His hair was messy, a little patch of hair stood up. He had bags under his eyes.

"Were you sleeping?" I asked. "Sorry. We can talk in the morning."

"Don't worry about it." He sat beside me. "What's up?"

"Uh, well... About why I've been kind of moody and distant," I paused and looked down. "As you know, Jessica's been harassing me to have sex with you—"

"Still?" he interrupted.

I nodded. "And lately, she's been telling me all kinds of things."

"Like?"

"You were 'finding pleasure elsewhere'..."

"You don't actually believe that do you?"

I shrugged. "I know you wouldn't, but it still bothered me. That 'what if.'"

"Well, I've never cheated on you. I already told you I was fine with waiting." Daniel was trying to not sound upset, but his tone was clipped. "Why would I cheat on you?"

"I don't know. Jessica was really convincing." I couldn't look at him. I regretted having the talk. I should have just trusted him and went on like nothing happened. Now he was going to look at me weirdly or think there was a lack of trust...which there was....

"From now on, please don't listen to what she says."

"I won't..." I looked at Daniel. "Are you mad?"

"At you?" he asked. He shook his head. "No. I *am* mad at Jessica."

"I just don't understand why she's so obsessed with our love life."

"I don't either."

"Do you think she has feelings for you?"

"Jessica?" He laughed. "No."

"I think she does."

He shook his head. "Nah. But if it'll make you feel better, I'll ask her."

"Just like that?"

"Yep."

I didn't know how to feel about that. I nodded. "Okay."

"And next time something like this comes up, just tell me. Don't go around me, don't ask others. All that does is cause problems."

"I didn't ask anyone else…"

"I bet you called Anna."

"Um, there's something else," I said changing the subject.

"What?"

"Be honest with me, are you *really* okay with not having sex?"

"Yes, really."

"I don't believe you."

"Why? More of what Jessica said?"

"Well, you did tell her stuff. So you clearly aren't as okay with it as you're telling me."

"I do want to make love to you, but I want you to be ready." His hand cupped my chin, slowly lifting my head so that my eyes met his. "Maybe if I rephrased it. I want to sleep with you, but I'm okay with waiting until you're ready. Does that work?"

I turned my head to move his hand and nodded. "If you say so. And…I don't mind having sex, I just want to know more about you."

"What don't you know?"

"Almost everything. I don't know your favorite color, favorite food, your likes and dislikes, hobbies…" I trailed off.

"I'm sorry I never thought about that. I assumed you knew that already."

"No." I shook my head. "I bet you probably know more about me."

"For the most part," he said. "I'm pretty sure some of your interests have changed since we were younger."

"Yeah."

"How about some time soon we just sit down and talk about it?"

"Okay."

Daniel smiled. "I might as well sleep over."

"You can."

"Then let's go to sleep. If you don't have anything else to talk about."

I shook my head. "I'll get you a pillow and blanket."

"For what?"

"The couch," I teased.

"The hell I'm not." Daniel stood up, ran into my room, and closed the door.

I walked to the door and tried to open it. He locked the door.

"Daniel," I yelled banging on the door. "Open up."

"No."

I laughed quietly. He was so annoying. "Open it."

"Promise I won't have to sleep on the couch?"

"Yes, open the door."

Daniel cracked the door and peeked out at me. "You're not tricking me, right?"

I shook my head.

Daniel slowly opened the door then walked to my bed. He plopped on it and stretched as loud as he could.

"Seriously," he yawned. "Please just talk to me before things get out of hand. I don't think I could handle any more suspense when you're upset. Especially when you send me texts with only, 'we need to talk.'"

"Sorry." I sat next to him. "Better late than never."

"Mm-hmm." He nodded, his eyes closed. "And I'll talk to Jessica in the morning. I don't appreciate her telling you that bullshit."

"It's fine," I said. "I don't want any drama."

"There won't be. I'm nipping it in the bud now. She needs to learn her place. She can't just overstep boundaries and try to ruin relationships."

"I agree…"

Daniel yawned once more and fell asleep. He must have been really tired. I pulled the blanket over him and lay beside him. I was glad Jessica was wrong and that Daniel wasn't *that* offended. We didn't talk as long as I hoped or rather, expected, but I was glad I said something. I couldn't wait to see Jessica's reaction after he talked to her. I was curious about how she'd respond to Daniel asking if she liked him. I hoped she didn't, but after how she was acting, it was obvious. I dozed off not too long after.

The next day at work, I anticipated their talk. After our lunch break, Daniel took Jessica to the side. I ran away to avoid the backlash. 3 hours passed and no word from either of them. I assumed they were working. But I wondered if Daniel even talked to her. There was no way Jessica wouldn't've bitched right after it. Then again, she could have been respecting whatever Daniel said and not bothering me.

Regardless, it was bound to come back to me sooner or later. It all depended on whether Jessica was willing to risk her relationship with Daniel.

Jessica slammed a loaf of bread on the belt and startled me. She was aggressively putting her items on the belt.

"Are you done with your shift?"

"No Maya," she said sarcastically. "I'm just shopping in the middle of my shift."

"I was just making conversation, relax," I said, placing her items in the bags.

She rolled her eyes. "What? You going to tell Daniel about this too?"

I didn't respond. I wanted to ring her stuff up as soon as possible. She was very salty over whatever Daniel said. And… she did shop during her shifts. She was yelled at several times for it.

"Next time we have a conversation between us," Jessica said, coming closer. "Keep it between us. No need to run to your knight."

Before I could respond, Jessica grabbed her bags and practically ran out of the store.

"Next time maybe not act like a bitch and stay out someone's relationship…" I mumbled. She was right, I did plan on telling Daniel what she said. But I was more interested in what he told her.

Once our shifts were over, I was going to ask him. I turned the corner to the break room as Daniel was punching out.

"Hey beautiful," he said.

"Hey…" I trailed off. "Uh, what did you tell Jessica?"

"You mean our talk?"

I nodded.

"It was a lot. To summarize, I told her it was inappropriate what she said to you. And that I didn't like her lying behind my back and putting weird thoughts in your head."

"That's it?"

"And I asked if she had feelings for me."

My stomach dropped. I wanted to hear her answer, but I also didn't want to. It would make me more stressed if she actually had feelings for him.

"She…" Daniel paused for dramatic suspense. "Doesn't like me. She actually laughed at me for even asking."

"That's good…I guess. But why was she so fixated. I don't think she was telling the truth. There's no other logical explanation for why she would do that."

"Just take her word for it. Everyone knows I love you. Even if she did like me, it wouldn't matter. I like you and only you. Okay?"

"Okay." I smiled. "Did she say why she lied on you?"

"Mm, not really." He looked away. "Testing us or something like that."

I didn't say anything. I went to my locker and grabbed my bag. They probably had a personal conversation that he didn't feel comfortable sharing. I was fine not knowing. I already had the answers I needed. Even if I didn't trust them.

"Let's go on a date," Daniel said breaking the silence.

"Tonight?" I asked.

"Tonight."

"Uh…" I didn't feel like doing anything after work, but it had also been a long time since we last went on one. Actually, it was the first official date since we started dating. We hung out every day almost, but those didn't count as dates.

"Do you want to? We don't have to. Just thought it would be fun."

"I don't mind, we can go on one."

"Okay." Daniel smiled.

"Can we go home and change first?"

"Of course."

When I went into my apartment, regret hit me. Due to my own protests of clothing, I barely had any "formal" clothing or anything dressy. I had 4 skirts. A black one with skulls, a TB12 skirt—another collector's item, a purple skirt, and a black and white checkered skirt with suspenders. And I'd only recently bought those, so I praised myself for the foresight. But why did I not think to buy clothing for important events? My life choices were finally biting me in the ass. I searched through my closet and dresser once more with a last bit of hope I had a dress or something nice…no use. I didn't want to keep

Daniel waiting any longer, so I grabbed the black and white skirt and a white turtleneck. Once dressed, I put on the crescent moon necklace he got me. I "fluffed" my hair out, so my curls were looser and more like an afro. I looked okay but there wasn't much else to do with my appearance. I didn't wear makeup, and I only had three pairs of shoes. I grabbed the "nicer" pair of white sneakers I wore only once and left my apartment.

"You look cute," Daniel said. He wore a black suit jacket, a white shirt, and black jeans. It looked like the same one he wore on the bridge. "I think I'm a little too dressy…"

"No, I'm underdressed," I said walking to him. "Sorry, I don't have anything better to wear."

"Don't worry about it," he said. He unlocked his apartment door and threw his jacket inside. "There. Now we're equally dressed."

I smiled. Maybe it was because he one-upped me in years of life experience or whatever, but he was a quick "problem" solver. I instantly felt better about my clothes. Though, I needed to go shopping just in case he ever wanted a fancy dinner or something.

"So where are we going?" I asked, as we went into the elevator.

"Hmm, you'll just have to see." He smirked.

"Why not tell me? Not like I know New York that well anyways."

"Just go along with it."

"Fine." I pouted.

We arrived at Azalia, an arcade restaurant in the Bronx. It was a small business. I'd seen flyers around the city. I always wanted to visit but I was too broke. Most of my paychecks went towards my rent and Anna's move. Tonight, I would have to be cheap. We sat down at a table and were handed menus. I'm not kidding when I say my jaw dropped. $15+ for a burger. $10+ for appetizers. What were those prices?! If I wanted to play games, I would have to order a side of fries for $3.

Daniel watched as I pretended to not be fazed by the prices. The corners of his mouth weirdly angled downward, and his dimples were showing. "Don't worry about the price. It's my treat."

"No…I can pay…"

"I want both of us to enjoy tonight. Just let me pay."

"I can't—"

Daniel interrupted me, "How about you let me pay for tonight, and you can pay me back later."

I pursed my lips and looked down. "Okay."

"Atta girl." He smiled. "Get whatever you want. Don't worry about the price."

I nodded. The perks of being older I guess... better finances. I ordered parmesan chicken, a side of jalapeno poppers and root beer. Daniel ordered buffalo wings, fries, nachos, and a beer. He also ordered churros and an ice cream Sunday for us to share. When the order arrived, it was more than what I was expecting. The parmesan chicken came with 2 patties and pasta topped with mozzarella and a huge serving of poppers. Just my order alone was more than I ate in 2 days.

"Do you want some of my food?" I asked Daniel.

He looked unsurprised. He knew I wasn't a big eater. "Sure, whatever you can't finish I'll take." He took a bite from his wings. "It's alright. Just make me feel like a fat ass eating all this food and yours too."

"That's not what I meant..."

"I know." He smiled. "Just messing with you. You can take some of my wings too."

"Okay." Breaking the silence I asked, "What are some hobbies of yours?"

"Hmm?" Daniel looked up from his phone. "Hobbies... well I don't really have many. I play games sometimes, I used to love playing football back in high school. I did tryout for the Missouri Tigers."

"Did you get in?" I asked.

"Nah." He shook his head. "I'm glad though, I had time to do other things."

"Like what?"

"Um, well...stuff college kids do..." he said, awkwardly taking a sip of beer.

"Can you elaborate? I didn't go to college."

"...Things like join clubs. I joined an art club, music appreciation club...I partied..." he mumbled the last part.

"You don't have to be embarrassed about partying. I kinda figured you did."

"I know. It's a little awkward."

"Why 'cause you did naughty things along with it?" I grinned.

"Yeah, pretty much."

"Any other hobbies? You said art club, does that mean you draw?"

He nodded. "Terribly but yes, I draw."

"Do you have any art you can show me?"

"Later. I can look through some sketchbooks when I get home."

"Okay."

"What about you? What are your hobbies?"

"Same thing as always. Reading. I guess watching movies too. I haven't found other hobbies."

"That's fine, plenty of people only read."

"Uh, what kind of music do you listen to?"

"Rap, Rock and some Country. You?"

"K-pop and J-pop mostly."

Daniel gave me a funny look. "'K-pop and J-pop.' Interesting."

"Yep. I love it." I could tell Daniel wanted to say something.

It was most likely the same thing everyone else said when I mentioned I liked both genres. "How can you like it if you can't understand it?" but it was more than just that. I could look up the English translation anytime. But I didn't need to understand the language to connect with the music. It was about the melody, the beat, their voices, the choreographies, the lyrics, etc. The artists I listened to were talented. They never made a bad song. And I planned to learn the languages when I had the time and money.

"That's nice. Maybe you can suggest a few songs to me."

"Really? I can show you some artists later or tomorrow."

We talked for another hour. I learned that he majored in art. His favorite color was green. He hated hot sauce, cauliflower, and macaroni...oops... I felt better knowing more about Daniel. I could spark more conversations. I knew what foods not to make...he no longer felt like a stranger. Neither one of us could finish the food. We put our food in to-go boxes and finished the ice cream. Daniel paid and I went to the bathroom. Once I was done, I headed to the arcade area. Daniel waited by the pay machines. I walked up to the machine to get a card. Before I could start, Daniel slid over a card.

"I got you." He smiled.

"You didn't have to." I took the card.

"I told you this is my treat. I meant the whole date," Daniel said. "You can pay me back later for this too."

"Thank you." I smiled. I held his hand.

"Which one you wanna play first?" he asked.

"Uh, something easy to start with." I looked around. I saw skee-ball in the corner and pointed to it. "How about Skee-ball?"

"Alright. But I should let you know in advance you can't beat me."

"You're on." I ran to the skee-ball machine.

It was fun. Although Daniel was a sweat as promised. But when his score was too far from mine, he would roll 10 pts until I was fairly close to his score. Then he went sweat mode again. After losing… multiple times, I gave up with a score of 600 pts to 410 pts, we moved on to another game. There was a VR zombie game Daniel really wanted to play. Even though I hated zombies, I still tried the game. I was okay at it, but eventually I got off and watched Daniel play solo. Cringing at the "pg13" gore. We played racing games, we played DDR, a game I was better than Daniel at. And then we moved on to other games. We went to a darts game. Daniel was once again challenging me. We made a bet. If Daniel won, I stayed over at his apartment tonight and if I won, he had to buy me a life size teddy bear, and I wanted one that was his height.

Daniel was of course better, he hit more bullseyes than me. I'd say the chances for both of us to hit a bullseye were 4-0. I didn't stand a chance against him. Daniel stood behind me as I aimed. He wrapped his arm around my waist and the other held my hand gently.

"Relax. Take your time." He moved my arm to the right and said, "Okay, throw."

I threw it and hit a bullseye. I jumped up excited. I turned around and hugged Daniel. "Yay! I hit it! You're a good teacher."

"I know I am." He winked. "But…that was your last throw, which means I won." He smiled deviously.

I pouted. I didn't mind staying at his place. He had a comfy bed, but I was disappointed I couldn't get a bear. I would probably buy one later if I saved up. But it was the principle.

"Well Ms. Loser. Guess you're stayin' over."

"Guess so." I smiled.

"Do you wanna play any more games or look over prizes?"

"I wanna look at prizes. What about you?"

"Um, I wanna play a little more. I need a few more tickets."

"How many do you need? You already have a lot."

"Don't worry about it."

"Well, I'm gonna go look at stuff. I'll find you when I'm done."

"Okay," Daniel said, kissing my forehead. "Don't flirt with other guys."

"I'll try not to."

I planned to use my tickets on Daniel. I wanted to look for something he would like. It would be my first present to him. Second technically counting 8 years ago. It was before I hated the Rogers. I gave him a rock I painted. Everyone in the family had a specific color and design. I cringed as I remembered. I wanted his present to be special. Something he liked. I walked along the wall of prizes. What would a 22-year-old grown man like? Would he want a plushy the same way I wanted one? Who knew? He could have liked them, or he would pretend to for my sake. I had a thousand tickets. I could get one small plushie, a football and a mug or shot glass.

I searched the wall of plushies and pulled out a cute gray husky. I walked to the footballs. They were labeled by teams. Only the Giants, Jets and Buffalo Bills were in the bin. Maybe he wouldn't mind a Giants football. I then walked to the glasses. I could afford one shot glass. It was smaller than the others, but the design was prettier. It was emerald green and had the Azalia logo, a pink azalea with a grayed-out arcade machine sprouting from the center. Tinier azaleas were sprinkled around the glass. I asked for a bag and went to find Daniel. I wasn't going to show him until later at his apartment.

Daniel was just getting off the VR zombie game when I found him.

"Hey, just in time," he said.

"Were you only playing this game?"

"Nah, I played that machine a lot." He pointed at a game called Whacko Tally men. I had no idea what the game was, and I didn't want to. Just looking at it stressed me out.

"Does that give the most points?"

"Yep. I thought I'd cool down with VR zombies. It gives a decent number of tickets."

"How much did you make?"

"I gotta check." We walked to the prize area, and he swiped his card. 15,000 tickets. "Way more than I needed."

"Geez how are you so good at games?"

Daniel laughed and shrugged. "I got lucky. I hit a couple jackpots on a few machines."

"What are you going to get?"

"Hmm, I don't know. I gotta think about it." Daniel walked around the walls.

I was nervous every time he looked at the shot glasses and balls. I hoped he didn't pick one of the ones I got him. Eventually he called someone over and pointed to a huge sleeping cat plushie on the top shelf. It was worth 8,000 tickets. I was right that he liked plushies, but why did he have to choose one 10x better than mine? Adding insult to injury, he asked me to hold on to it, while he spent the rest of the tickets. He got a smaller pink Squishmallow octopus for 4,000. He grabbed two green coffee mugs for 850 each, a deck of cards for 1,000 and a small black husky similar to the one I bought and a bear. Maybe I should have grinded more to get him better gifts. But it was too late. He got a bag for the items, and I helped him carry them home. He was curious about what I chose but I kept telling him, "None of your business."

When we arrived at his apartment, we laid out the items he got.

"Okay," he said. "Time to divvy up the prizes."

"What do you mean?" I asked.

He didn't respond. He placed the two mugs, the cards, and the husky in one pile and the cat, the octopus and the bear in the other.

"These are yours," he said. He pointed to the cats.

"Aww." My mood instantly lit up. "I love these."

"I know," he said smugly and smiled. "Even though you're Ms. Loser, I still got you a big plushie."

"I also got you somethings, Mr. Winner." I handed over the bag. As he took the items out, I said, "I guess you have two huskies now."

"Thank you," he said. He took the bear out of my pile and switched it with the black husky. "Now I don't. We're matching."

"That's so cringe." I laughed. "But sweet at the same time."

The rest of the night, we played card games like goldfish, jackass, and two-man solitaire.

Daniel went into his bedroom and returned with a bin full of notepads, sketchpads, and journals. He set the bin on the floor and opened it. He took out a larger sized sketchpad and set it behind him. "You can look at these if you want."

"What's that one?" I asked, pointing to the one he took out.

"It's empty."

"Huh," I said, suspiciously.

I looked through the sketchpads. He was an amazing artist. He drew a lot of popular anime characters and some I think were original ideas. He was incredible at realistic art. He drew a woman with long hair, a cat, flowers, etc. I could tell the journal I was looking at was for an art class. There was a charcoal drawing that had a lot of random objects strewn about. There was a fruit bowl sketch as well. I pulled out a small notepad. It was worn and whatever logo was on the cover was barely visible. I flipped open the first page and laughed. It was a half stick figure half something, it was roughly colored with colored pencils, I flipped through the pages. This was clearly his first-time drawing, and it was mind-blowing how much he practiced from there to where he was now.

Daniel saw me giggling at his original drawings and snatched the notepad from me.

"Hey! I was looking at that."

"You were laughing. You can only look at good pictures."

"Like whatever's in the pad next to you?"

"I told you that was empty."

"If it were, you wouldn't be hiding it from me."

"Don't worry about it."

"I can't not worry about it. You should have taken it out before you came in here. 'Cause now I want to see what's inside."

"I can't… I guarantee you'll call me a creep or something."

"No I won't. Art is expressive right? No judgments, I promise."

Daniel looked at me for a while then said, "Fine."

He pulled the sketchpad from beside him and handed it to me. I was so giddy I opened the first page as fast as possible. It was a poorly drawn woman? lying on a couch. I flipped to the next page. It was the same image but drawn better. It was the same thing on multiple pages, each one better than the first. Then it went on to another image. This time, I could tell it was a girl reading. And the next page was the same image again.

"Is this supposed to be me?" I asked, glancing up at him.

He nodded.

I flipped through the pages faster, skimming them. It was always me on the couch reading. "Did you sit at the table and draw me?"

"Every day," he confirmed.

"Uh-huh." I nodded. I was doing my best to keep my promise on not calling him a weirdo. It was nice I guess that he liked me enough to draw me. Even if it was without my consent… or knowledge. I was halfway through when the pages went blank.

"Is this when you had to move?"

"Yeah," he exhaled.

"Well, overall, I like these. You're an amazing artist and I liked looking at your skill level increase on each page."

"You don't think it's weird that I was drawing you?"

Yes, I thought. Out loud I said, "No, not really. Shows determination."

"If it's alright with you," he said, hopeful. "Can I draw you now. It'll be nice to have a 7-year comeback gap to see how well I've improved on drawing you."

"Uh," I said. I didn't know why he wanted to draw me. I wasn't even that attractive. Was it just to finish his Maya Journal? "Maybe another time."

"I'm gonna hold you to that." He smiled.

I looked through his sketches a little more before we put them away. I showed him a few songs. It was so obvious that he didn't like my music, but he was nice enough to not say anything. We ended the night with Pride and Prejudice, the 2005 version, of course. I forgot to run to my apartment when we got back from Azalia's to grab pajamas. Daniel didn't want me to get any and offered to let me wear one of his shirts and some shorts. We sat in his bed and talked one last time before Daniel leaned over and gave me a goodnight kiss. I kissed him again, it was long, deep, and passionate. We kissed for a long time before Daniel carefully pushed me onto my back and climbed on top of me. He kissed my neck. His hand slid under my shirt and sensually caressed my side. I felt a warm sensation in my stomach. I did my best to stifle a moan.

He stopped kissing me, propped himself on his left arm, his hand rested on my stomach and said, "Before I continue, are you sure about this?"

I nodded. I couldn't speak. I knew if I did, my voice would crack. Daniel kissed me again on the lips. He continued down to my neck. He stopped kissing me and pulled my shirt over my head. I was thankful I wore matching underwear, a black bra, and panties. He unclipped my bra and admired me. He kissed my neck, then down to my chest and stomach.

"U-um," I said my voice cracking. "Can you get undressed too?"

I could feel Daniel chuckle, his breath hitting my stomach with each laugh sending a shockwave through my body.

"Someone's impatient." He sat up and took off his shirt. His body was toned. He tapped my hips for me to lift them up. I pivoted and he pulled my shorts off.

Oh gosh! I covered my face, blushing.

Daniel moved my hands and kissed me. "Don't be embarrassed."

Oh…my…gosh, was all I could think. My heart was racing. It was finally going to happen.

Daniel kissed my neck, he nibbled it softly and surprised me. I let out a moan and heard a loud sound…. I paused, *no way I just did that.* I thought.

Daniel tried holding back his laughter. The smile on his face was huge. I had…passed gas… Ashamed, I pushed Daniel away and flew into the bathroom.

"Maya," he yelled laughing. "It's alright, come out."

"No." I was perfectly fine sleeping in the tub. No way was I going to let him see me after that.

"It happens to all of us. It's not that big a deal. It's natural."

"Not during moments like this."

"Yeah, it can happen. Happened to me once or twice too, it's normal."

"I know you're lying. I completely ruined the mood."

"No you didn't. I promise…. You're too sexy to ruin anything."

"Please don't say that right now." I couldn't face him after farting, and especially one that loud.

"I'm sorry but it's the truth. I really want to with you. If you don't want to continue that's fine but please come out of the bathroom."

I stayed silent for what felt like 5 minutes. Daniel waited outside the door. I was so embarrassed by what I did, but Daniel seemed completely unfazed. I didn't know if he was seriously unaffected by it or if he was just trying to make me feel better. I cracked the bathroom door, one eye peeking out. "You sure you still want to?"

Daniel smiled, pushing the door open. "Of course."

I nodded. "Okay, then we can continue."

Daniel took my hand and led me back to the bed.

"Uh, Daniel?" I asked.

"Yeah?"

"Can we turn the lights off?"

"Sure." Daniel reached over and switched off the lamp. It was still kind of visible. He mounted me again and caressed my thighs. He parted my legs and lifted my knees. He placed his legs between mine, one by one, his lips not parting from my body once.

"Daniel?" I asked again.

"Hmm?" he said kissing my stomach.

"Do we need lube?"

"No."

"Uh, Daniel?" I asked once more.

"Hmm?"

"Do you have a condom? Should we get it?"

Daniel stopped kissing me. He came up to eye level with me and said, "Maya, relax. I haven't even taken my pants off, let alone our underwear. When we get to that step, I'll grab one okay?"

I nodded. Daniel kissed my forehead. Daniel slid his pants and boxers off. He ran his hands along my legs until he reached my panties. "Lift your hips again," he whispered. I raised my hips like he said.

He reached over to his nightstand and opened a drawer. I didn't understand how he was able to see but I guess it was his room, so it made sense. He closed the drawer. I heard him unwrap the condom. He kissed me and whispered in my ear, "Ready?"

I nodded.

Afterwards, I lay in bed my back turned to Daniel, avoiding eye contact. I was mortified, from the moment earlier and shy from how intimate we were.

Daniel pulled me towards him. "I love you, Maya."

"I love you too." I turned around and hugged Daniel.

"Are you okay?" he asked.

"Yes."

"It didn't hurt?"

"A little, but only at the beginning."

Daniel smiled. "Well, we finally made it past that hurdle."

"Mm-hm." I nodded. "Mr. 'I'm fine with waiting.'"

"You initiated it, not me."

"I guess…"

"Unfortunately, we work tomorrow, so we better go to sleep."

"Yeah," I said laying my head on his chest. "I need to shower first."

Daniel made a face and let go of me. After showering, I fell asleep cuddling Daniel.

CHAPTER SIX

I woke up the next morning refreshed. I didn't feel any different than I did before having sex. I think the only difference was that I knew once I saw Daniel, I would be embarrassed, maybe even awkward. I rolled over and Daniel was gone. I checked my phone, it was 10 AM. I wasn't late for work thank goodness. I couldn't remember if Daniel worked earlier than me. I sat up. At the bottom of the bed was a t-shirt. I figured it was for me and put it on. He didn't leave any pants.

The door opened as I went back under the covers and Daniel peeked inside. "Good you're awake."

Daniel walked in with breakfast. He made breakfast sausages, sunny side up eggs, and pancakes topped with whipped cream and strawberries. He had two bowls of chopped fruit, honeydew, strawberries, watermelon, cantaloupe, grapes, and pineapple.

"Did you chop these?"

"Uh huh. I had to go to Loue's to get the melons."

"Thank you," I said, taking a sausage and biting it. "It's good."

"You're welcome." Daniel smiled. "Once you're done, we have to hurry to work."

"Okay," I said. "I have to shower too. So I'll go to my apartment."

"Just shower here. Let's take one together." He winked.

I placed my face in my hands. Why did he have to say that? I was acting normal around him, and he ruined it!

He laughed and continued, "I'm kidding…unless you want to."

"Stoop," I complained. I got up and left the room. "I'll eat the rest after I shower."

"Wait," he shouted. Daniel ran into the living room as I put on my shoes. "Don't leave out like that."

"I have no choice. I don't know where my clothes are." I smiled. "Besides, the chances of someone coming out as I leave is next to none."

"At least wait in here while I open your door."

"Ok." I handed him my keys and he left.

He came back in a minute later and said, "Quickly."

I went inside my apartment and took a shower. I changed into my uniform. When I opened the front door, Daniel was just about to knock. He had my plushies and clothes with him. I took them and sat them on the couch, I would figure out where to put them later. We made it to Loue's a little late. Loue didn't mind me being late but got on Daniel for it.

Jessica was working front end when I walked up to take over. She rolled her eyes, still salty over yesterday and left. Honestly, if it wasn't for Jessica's obsession, I would've never given it any thought and would still be scared to have sex. I owed her for that, though I wouldn't tell her that we did it.

It was a normal day except… Daniel would wink at me and blow kisses. I wasn't going to let him know that bothered me. His teasing wouldn't work anymore. I went on my lunch break and Jessica was sitting at a table eating. She once again rolled her eyes.

"Look Jessica," I said, finally having enough of her attitude. "Don't get mad at me because you tried to fuck with my head. You have only yourself to blame for Daniel being pissed with you. Did you think I would never talk to him about it?"

"No, because those were conversations between me and you. I don't care what I said, you should have kept it that way. I was only trying to look out for you, and you stabbed me in the back."

"I didn't stab you in the back. And I would never keep things that involve Daniel a secret from him. You know this now. So if there's anything you want to say to me without Daniel knowing, I suggest you don't say it."

Jessica stayed silent for a bit and glared at me. "All I said was you needed to have sex with him. That was for the health of your relationship and Daniel."

"A relationship is just as healthy without it, if both partners are okay with."

"And you seriously think Daniel is fine waiting?"

"Yeah," I said. "He wouldn't lie to me."

"Whatever Maya. Just don't expect me to give you any more relationship advice."

"I don't need it. I'll figure it out by myself… with Daniel."

Daniel walked into the break room and Jessica flinched. He went to his locker and said, "No need to argue. Jessica, just accept Maya doesn't want advice. And you know I don't want you saying shit to her that could jeopardize our relationship. Just stay out of our business. And Maya, from now on, what happens between us, stays between us."

He winked and smiled.

I did my best to hide my smile. Jessica saw Daniel wink then looked at me. A look of dread washed over her face. "You guys had sex, didn't you?"

Daniel ignored Jessica and sat next to me. He leaned over and whispered, "Wanna tell her? She'd finally shut up."

"You can if you want to."

He looked at Jessica and nodded.

"Why?" she asked.

"Why not?" Daniel responded, giving her a weird look.

"I was just giving Maya a hard time… I—I didn't want her to actually rush into it."

"I didn't 'rush' into anything," I said. "I did it at my own pace. You had nothing to do with my decision. But I will say, you helped me open up to the idea. So thank you for that."

Jessica didn't say anything. She finished her food and left.

"She always has something to complain about." Daniel rolled his eyes.

"That's okay. Maybe that will teach her not to stick her nose in other people's business."

Daniel kissed me and we finished our lunches.

Over the next week, everything went back to normal. I told Anna that I lost my virginity, and she freaked out. In a good way. Me and Daniel made love once more a few days after our first time. He was more comfortable touching me. It was like his PDA and physical affection was being held captive in a jar that unleashed after having sex. He hugged me more often, smacked my butt, kissed me randomly, he was like a monster let out of a cage.

In terms of our work life, Jessica gave us the silent treatment for half the week, avoided us as much as she could, then she did a complete 360° and was being buddy-buddy with me again. It was weird. I don't care how much Daniel denied it, Jessica had feelings for him. Her reaction last week was enough to confirm it. No one gets that upset when they find out others are intimate unless they loved one of them. And her eyes were set on him. If she really did have feelings for Daniel, I would understand. He was the perfect guy. Considerate, nice, strong, handsome, and respectful. Though, I didn't trust her motives and would look at everything she said as having ulterior motives. But until it reached that point, and I hoped it didn't, I liked having her as a friend.

…But wouldn't it have been easier for her give up on him? He had a girlfriend and showed little interest in her unless I was there. I never understood why some people chose to chase after people in relationships. Why not try to find someone similar to their personality or something. I always hated romantic novels or movies where another woman (or man depending on the genre) would show up and cause problems for the main couple. It always turned me off from a good story.

During my break, Jessica came in with a flyer. "Hey Maya, are you free tomorrow night?"

"I'm not sure, why?" I asked, taking the flyer from her.

"I have this theatre thing going on, it's not that important. But I was hoping you and Daniel could come and hang out."

"I most likely can't," I said. "It depends on the time and what I have planned."

"Ok. Do you think Daniel is going to go if you aren't there?"

"Probably not, but you never know."

"Ok," Jessica said, walking to the door. "I'll ask him. If he says no, please talk to him. I want at least one of you there for support."

"Ok I will." I smiled.

"Thanks Maya dear."

Jessica ran out of the room. I could hear her hopping down the stairs, a slight thud with each landing. I felt bad, I didn't want to go. I looked at her flyer. It was at New York University. I didn't feel like travelling almost an hour. It was from 5:30 to 7:00 PM. I didn't think it was worth it. I worked that morning, and I didn't feel like doing anything afterwards. Only if Daniel forced me, would I go. I was mostly making excuses, I know, but I just didn't want to go.

As I sat the flyer down, Daniel walked into the break room. "I see Jessica already got to you huh?"

"Yep." I nodded. "I'm guessing she already asked you?"

"Unfortunately." Daniel laughed. He sat beside me and kissed my cheek. "Are you going to go?"

"I don't want to…" I mumbled.

"Well, you know if you aren't going, I'm not either."

"She asked me to tell you to go even though I'm not. She said she wants at least one of her friends to go. So that means you."

"Why not you?" Daniel rolled his eyes.

"'Cause I said no first. Plus, she's more fixated on you than me."

"I doubt it," he said. "She knows I have all eyes on you. So what would be the point?"

"I don't know, she just is."

"Nah."

"Well, if you think she isn't interested in you that way, you should go."

"What? Why is that a reason for me to have to go?" he asked, loudly.

"Shh," I said. "You're too loud, she can probably hear you."

"If I have to go," he whispered getting closer. "You're going too."

I laughed. "That's not how it works. Unlike you, I work that day."

"Yeah, but you have the weekend off."

"Doesn't matter. I have to work all week."

"Well, if I go," Daniel said and smiled. "I get a little reward when it's over."

"What kind of reward?" I eyed him suspiciously.

"Some…thing… we've only done twice." Daniel smirked and nudged me.

"You pervert." I laughed.

"Is it a deal? She's more your friend than mine."

"You're friends too."

"Work friends remember. That's different." He rolled his eyes. "But deal?"

"I'll…have to think about it."

"I respect that." Daniel smiled softly.

Loue walked into the break room and said, "One of the second shift workers is going to be late tomorrow, can one of you take the beginning part of their shift?"

"I'll take it," I said, before Daniel could even open his mouth. "I already work, so I'll just stay a little longer. Doesn't make sense for Daniel to come in for a few hours."

"I don't mind." He smirked.

"Nah, it's okay. I can take it. You have that thing with Jessica anyways."

"You're talking about that play thing?" Loue interrupted.

"Yeah," Daniel said.

Loue laughed. "Ha! So that's why you're both fighting for more work…. Well…I don't blame ya. Maya can work longer."

"Yes," I whispered.

Daniel rolled his eyes. "Of course, Maya is your favorite."

"Yep," Loue said, as he left.

"Sorry." I laughed.

"You won fair and square," Daniel said. Whispering he said, "But if it's dog shit, I'm leaving."

"You can't do that."

"Watch me."

When I went back to my register, Jessica came storming up to me. I knew what she was about to say and braced myself for the rant.

"So you took extra hours even though I asked you to go to my play?"

"He needed someone to go, and I know you wanted Daniel to go, so I volunteered. I wouldn't've minded going but if it was Daniel, he would be too tired to go, and I still might have other plans."

Jessica stayed silent for a bit then said, "I guess… I want both of you to go. So I'm a little disappointed, but I guess it's good at least one of you can go."

"Yeah, I hope it goes well. I'll wish you luck tomorrow before you go."

"Thanks," Jessica mumbled, then walked away.

I let out a huge sigh, she was so stressful at times. I felt bad for Daniel, he would have to deal with her for hours. I laughed, it was kind of funny, I imagined him ripping his hair out with how she acted.

After work, Daniel rushed out. I could barely keep up. "Why are you running?"

"I don't want to talk to her, I need a recharge if I'm gonna have to hang out with her alone."

"You're so dramatic."

"I don't wanna go, but I know we wouldn't hear the end of it."

"I mean… she would probably take it out on me more than you."

"Honestly, you might be right. But you don't have to worry about it. I'm taking one for the team."

"Thank you." I hugged his arm.

"You're welcome," he said, flirtatiously. "Staying with you tonight, right?"

"You can, but don't expect anything."

He sighed loudly. "Fine. Cuddling is just as nice… almost."

"Yes, it is."

"Can I draw you tonight? You said you'd let me."

"Uh, you can…"

"What's wrong? If you don't want to, I won't force you."

"It's not that. It's just kind of embarrassing."

"It'll only be seen by you and me."

The problem is you, I thought. Out loud I said, "True. We can go to your apartment then and I'll stay over. This can be your reward for handling Jessica."

"Deal."

I changed and went to his apartment. I didn't want to overdo it on my outfit, so I just wore a hoodie and leggings.

"Looking cute," he said. He must have been sarcastic. "Sit on the couch."

He pulled a chair to the side of the couch.

"Uh, what am I supposed to do?" I asked.

"Just sit there."

"I mean like, should I look at you? Look down? On my phone?"

"Hmm," Daniel said, staring. "I think…you should glimpse at me. Keep your head forward but slightly towards me and your eyes should be on me."

"Okay."

Daniel was ready and began drawing. Every now and then I would get tired of the position and would look to the corner and Daniel would say, "Stop moving. If you move too much, I'll have to start over."

"Kay."

"Don't talk either." He smiled, his eyes looked up at me, then back to the page.

After 20 minutes, he finished. He sat next to me and showed me the drawing. It was nice, he drew me prettier than I was, but I wasn't complaining.

"You did a good job," I said.

"Thank you." He kissed my cheek. "Wanna draw me?"

I laughed. "I'm a terrible drawer. I can't."

"Come on, just for shits and giggles."

"Alright if you say so."

Daniel tore a sheet of paper out and placed it on the sketchpad. I took it and sat in the chair he was previously in. I wasn't good. I drew a circle for his head, straight lines for his hair, a lot for his bangs and some at the nap of the neck. I drew his body, his torso was about 3 inches tall, and I made his legs extremely long, and I drew a little stick figure that was supposed to show the size comparison. I showed Daniel when I was done.

He choked out, "It looks good." Then burst in laughter.

"See why I didn't want to do it?"

"It's cute, don't be upset. I'm laughing with you, not at you."

"I'm not laughing."

"I think it looks good. I'll even hang it on my wall."

"Please don't."

"Fine, I won't. But I still get to keep it."

"No, cause I don't get the one you drew of me."

"I'll draw another one that you can keep. How about that."

"Alright." I smiled sitting back on the couch.

The next morning, I left for work. I didn't want to wake Daniel, so I left without saying bye. Besides, he needed rest if he was gonna sit through Jessica's play. I was so lucky to work that day.

When I arrived, Jessica was clocking in. She looked tired and not in the mood. She looked at me and sighed, "You sure you don't want to go?"

"Yeah, I don't get off work until 4. I most likely would be late, plus I need to call my sister and eat."

"I get off earlier than you, I can grab food for you, and you can talk to your sister another time."

"Nah, it's okay. I haven't talked to her in a while, so I want to today. I'll go to opening night, how about that?"

"I'll hold you to it."

"Okay. Sorry, I'll make it up to you."

Jessica walked away without saying anything. She was moody in the morning, so I didn't take it personally. When I got to my register, I snuck my phone out and texted Anna.

"You wanna talk later tonight?" I asked.

I sat my phone on the counter next to me and waited for Anna to respond.

After a few minutes Anna replied, "Sure. You usually don't ask, what's up?"

"Nothing, I need to get out of something and I wanted to give you notice. That way you don't miss my call and I have to go."

"Ah I see. What's happening?"

"I'll tell you later, I gotta get back to work."

"Alright, ttyl."

I loved Anna. She was a life saver. We needed to catch up anyway. I had A LOT of things to tell her. About me and Daniel, and Jessica.

During the day, Jessica kept giving me looks. I don't know if she was angry at me for not going to her rehearsal or what, but it was so awkward.

I looked at the door and Daniel was standing there waving. I motioned for him to come in.

"Hey, why are you here?"

"I brought you some Panda Express," he said, handing me the bag.

"Aw, you didn't have to."

"I know, but I want to see you at least once today."

"You can't after the play?"

"I can, but are you going to be awake?"

"Probably. I'm not all that tired."

"Alright, well I'll just take that back."

"Nah, it's mine now."

Daniel laughed. "Let's share it on your break. When is it?"

"Uh… I can check if Loue can cover me."

"What's Jessica doing?"

"I don't know, but she's been giving me looks all day. I don't want to ask her. Plus, she's almost done."

"I'll ask. She can work register until her shift's over. Go punch out."

"Okay."

After a few minutes, Daniel walked into the break room. I asked, "Did you get Jessica to do it?"

"Yeah, she didn't complain either."

"Wow, you're the Jessica tamer."

"I don't know. I think she's not gonna argue if she wants me to go to her thing."

"That could be it too. But I think you have that charm."

"Yeaah, no." He laughed.

"I think so."

"Anyways," Daniel said, changing the subject. "I got vegetable lo mein and vegetable fried rice to be safe."

"You sure you didn't want something else?"

"I'm fine, it's for you."

"Well we can share, this is a lot."

Daniel and I were enjoying our lunch when Jessica came up. She looked at me then looked away.

"The lovely couple having lunch?" she mumbled.

"Yes ma'am," Daniel responded, taking a bite.

"That's nice," she said. I could hear her sarcasm. She was really pissed.

I ignored her and looked at Daniel.

"How long 'til you're done?" she asked. "We could hang out until my rehearsal."

"I can't hangout. I have something to do before I head over there. Just wanted to spend a little time with Maya before I go."

Jessica rolled her eyes. "Alright. Another 'important' thing.'"

"Yep." Daniel was pretty good at responding to her. He didn't seem phased at all.

"I guess I'll see you later night. See you whenever Maya." Jessica stomped out.

"Mm-hm." I was annoyed with her attitude. I wasn't required to go, and she shouldn't get mad because I had other things to do and after working 10 hours.

"What do you have planned after this?" I asked.

"Nothing, I don't want to hang out with her."

"Yeah, her attitude is ridiculous."

"Oh well, she'll have to deal with it. I don't even want to go now."

"You should, otherwise we'll have to hear even more of this."

Daniel rolled his eyes. "I'm only doing this for you."

"Thank you." I kissed his cheek.

After eating, Daniel went home. I sighed. I just had one more day until the weekend and a break from Jessica. She ruined my mood for the day. I kept thinking about her attitude as I worked. Even on the way home, I wondered if I should've told Daniel not to go. It was already too late, but she really didn't deserve to have him be there after the way she acted.

When I got home, I placed a frozen mac n cheese dinner tray in the microwave. I called Anna ready to rant.

"What's happening?" she answered.

I let out a huge sigh. "It's a long story. I have a lot to fill you in on."

I told Anna about everything with Jessica and how she was acting today.

"And now she's probably ranting to Daniel about me or something."

"Wait a second… You actually left her alone with Daniel?" Anna asked.

"Y-yeah…" I stuttered. "Is that bad?"

"Yes. You've been telling me about this girl Jessica eyeing Daniel for a long time."

"Yeah. I still think she kind of likes him."

"So why would you give her the opportunity to be alone with him?"

"…I don't know. I trust Daniel."

"Yeah, but I wouldn't trust *her*. Bitches will do anything to get a man."

"You're…kinda right." I nodded lowering my head.

"I would *not* leave my partner alone with another woman. Especially if they have a history or she's shown interest in them."

"Wait, you have a boyfriend?"

"No…kinda…I don't know what we are, but don't worry about it," Anna said, nervously. "We're not talking about me. We're talking about you and Daniel."

"Do you really think I should go there?"

"Yes, right now," Anna said. "Finish your food quickly and when I say run, *run* over there."

"What if there's nothing wrong?" I asked, scarfing down a spoonful of mac n' cheese.

"Just say you decided to support her anyways."

"Ok. That makes sense."

"Hurry and go before she jumps your man."

Anna and I laughed.

I got on the train to NYU. It was 5 PM. Jessica's rehearsal was until 7 PM so I was going to make it on time. When I reached the campus, I hurried to the location Jessica sent me. I walked to the door, my breathing was jagged, so I took a moment to catch my breath. I didn't want them to know I was running. I pulled the door open and could hear Jessica yelling. It sounded serious. I walked inside and walked quietly down the hall.

"I don't give a shit about your girlfriend," Jessica shouted.

"She can't find out," a voice said.

Wait… I thought. *I-is that Daniel?*

I ran to the corner and saw only Jessica and Daniel in the auditorium. My mouth dropped. I hid on the side of the stage and stayed quiet. I wanted to see what they were arguing about.

"Look," Jessica said. "You know how I feel about this. We can't hide what we've done any longer. And I don't want to."

"She means the world to me," Daniel said.

"Then what about me?!"

"I-I can't. I'm sorry." Daniel turned away.

Grabbing his arm quickly, Jessica said, "I know you want me like I want you. Stop fighting it."

He walked closer to Jessica.

"My girlfriend is important to me. I don't want to lose her." He closed his eyes remorsefully. "But you… you make me feel complete."

Jessica walked to Daniel and kissed him passionately. Daniel wrapped his arms around her waist.

CHAPTER SEVEN

I was shocked. Who could imagine seeing your boyfriend and your so-called friend kissing? Two people who claimed to be my "best friend." I wanted to flee but couldn't get my legs to move. How could he do this to me? If he really loved me, he wouldn't have allowed himself to be seduced by her.

Unable to bear it any longer, I managed to walk away. How could they do something like this and in such an open space. They were being reckless and didn't care about being caught. With each step, my pace hastened until I was running. The sky opened up and rain suddenly poured down as I ran into an alley and cried. I'm hideous, that's why he cheated not even two months into our relationship. Were they laughing at me? Was this a ploy to get me to sleep with him? She pressured me into sleeping with him and he was more than happy to accept. I opened my heart allowing myself to be intimate with him, in ways I had never experienced before. I stayed in a corner of the alley for 10 minutes. My phone rang, it was Daniel, I turned my phone off. I knew, most women would have cursed him out, but I didn't have it in me to go berserk.

I walked towards the street, the rain was a drizzle now. Maybe that would explain my red eyes, I could say allergies when someone asked or too much rain in my eyes. When I got on the bus, I was met with lovey dovey couples and it really stung. I walked to the back of the bus and looked out the window. I wondered what Daniel was doing, would he be waiting as usual outside my door, or would he wait until he heard me walk into my apartment. Either way, I hoped neither would come true.

As I exited the elevator, my eyes darted towards my door. He wasn't there. Uncomfortable and a bit disappointed, I walked to my apartment. I took my time slowly walking pass Daniel's apartment. I took so much time waiting for him but not once did I hear a peep from his apartment. Was he even home?

I sighed and entered mine. If he wasn't there, then I wasn't letting him in later. I flopped on the couch and screamed in a pillow. I was a wreck. How could one person make me feel so confused and weak? I loved him, that was for sure, but why was loving someone so hard? Only in those super sappy romances did things like this happen. I curled into a ball and turned to the back of the couch. I was exhausted from crying and needed some sleep.

I woke up 3 hours later. The rain was really coming down, there was a thunderstorm and lightning filled the room.

"What time is it?" I groaned.

I grabbed my phone, I forgot I turned it off earlier. When I turned it on, my phone buzzed. I had 25 missed calls and 40 text messages.

"Geez," I mumbled.

They were all from Daniel. He left texts like "Where are you?!", "Please answer me.", "I checked your home, why aren't you there?", "Are you safe?"

Was he looking for me the whole time? I was conflicted, I wanted to call him back and tell him where I was but at the same time, he kissed Jessica. I knew I shouldn't.

Someone banged on the door.

"Maya! Please tell me you're in there," Daniel shouted. "Please open the door! Why aren't you talking to me?"

I wanted to drown out his voice, so I ran into my room and covered my ears with my pillow. I could still hear his banging. I didn't want our neighbors woken up. It was 11 PM, he needed to be shut up.

I flung out of bed and rushed to the door. "Be quiet people are sleeping!"

"Where have you been?"

"That's none of your business. Now please go home."

I tried closing the door before Daniel pushed it open.

"Get out!" I shouted.

"Why are you so angry?"

"Why? Well maybe I wouldn't be so pissed if you hadn't made out with Jessica!"

Daniel flinched.

"What? Didn't think I'd know about it?"

"It wasn't what you think."

"Then what was it?"

"I was helping her rehearse for a play she's auditioning for."

"You know, I'm more offended not by the fact that you're lying, but that you would think that I would fall for such a dumbass excuse."

"It's the truth!"

"Yeah, because a person needs so much practice with a kiss scene."

"It wasn't like that." He rolled his eyes. "That was the end results of our rehearsing."

"So after pretending to have an affair, you actually developed an attraction for her and kissed her."

"No, that was what the script said."

"You didn't need to help her with the kiss. Once you were done with the actual lines that should have been it."

"That's not how it works."

"Did you forget in high school I was a part of the drama club and starred in numerous plays revolving this. Seriously, you really think I'm stupid?"

"There was no ulterior motive for that. I'm not attracted to her. Never will be."

"Yeah right."

"Maya, I've loved you for *years*, why would I risk losing you as soon as my dream came true?"

I shrugged. "Because I wasn't what you were expecting."

"Nah, our relationship is exactly how I imagined it would be."

"And how is that?"

"Don't worry about it. And don't worry about Jessica. What happened meant nothing, and we don't see each other that way."

"But you don't know if she doesn't."

"She's too rude to me. There's no way she'd like me."

"I'm rude to you too." I threw my hands up. "Whatever, it's going to take me some time to forgive. So please go home."

"You're not mad?"

I stayed silent as I motioned for him to leave.

"I'll call you later."

As he left, he leaned over to give me a peck on my forehead, I dodged it and closed the door.

I didn't know what to do anymore or what to think. I always criticized why women never left their boyfriends. But I could see why, it was a lot harder than I thought. I wondered why someone so strong as I am could be so weak in this moment. I called it, temporary insanity. I was moody because of this. And if what he said was true, there wasn't much to worry about.

The next morning, I woke to the same ringtone for Daniel. For some reason this time, I was fed up with it. I was annoyed by the tone of my favorite song, and I listened to it daily.

"Hello?" Daniel asked, his voice sounded rough and low.

"Yeah," I responded.

"How did you sleep?" he asked.

"Okay. If I hadn't been cheated on, I would've had a great night," I said, a little playfulness in my voice.

"Yeah," Daniel scoffed. "Like I said, she doesn't like me. She told me she liked some guy named Paul, so you don't have anything to worry about."

"Mm-hmm."

"I'm coming over, okay?"

I sighed and said, "Yeah it's fine."

As soon as I hung up, Daniel knocked on the door.

"That was fast," I mumbled, putting on my shirt as I walked to the door.

When I opened it, I was met with a bouquet of flowers. It was gigantic.

"Thanks," I said, grabbing the flowers.

I looked from the flowers to Daniel who had bedhead and still wore his pajamas.

"You didn't put any clothes on?"

"This is clothing." Daniel winked and walked pass me.

"Yeah, for bedtime," I retorted, as I followed him inside.

When I closed the door, Daniel pulled me close and kissed me.

"I'm so sorry," he said, his eyes were desperate. "She means nothing to me."

I laid my head on his chest and he held me tightly.

"Don't go near her again."

"But what about work?" he chuckled.

"That's the only exception."

"Okay."

Daniel picked me up and carried me to the room. He carefully placed me on the bed and climbed on top of me. I pushed him away.

"You think I'd do it with you after yesterday, you're out of your mind."

"How long?" he asked.

I didn't answer him. I turned around and went under the covers. Daniel wrapped his arms around me, and we lay in bed until the afternoon.

"Come on," I said, shaking Daniel. "We need to get ready for work."

Daniel groaned and pulled the blanket over his head.

"No," I said, pulling it off. "We're going to be late at this point."

Daniel rolled out of bed and headed for the door. "My clothes are at my apartment. I'll see you in 20 minutes."

"Okay," I shouted. "And don't fall back asleep."

We made it to Loue's a few minutes late.

"You're late," Loue said. "I expect that from Daniel but not you Maya."

"I know, but it was because of Daniel," I said, pointing to him. "He wouldn't wake up and then fell asleep again at his apartment."

"I couldn't sleep last night," Daniel pouted.

"Was it because of what we did?" Jessica asked, walking to the time clock. She looked at Daniel and licked her lips seductively as she punched out.

I looked at Daniel.

"I don't know what you're talking about. It was because of Maya," Daniel said, quickly.

"Sure," she said, sensually running her hand across Daniel's back as she walked by. Jessica looked at me with a vindictive smirk. "Bye Maya dear."

I didn't respond and walked to my register. I was fuming. There was no way Daniel didn't pick up on that.

She really just did that, I thought, my face was burning hot.

Daniel picked up on my anger and said, "She was just joking. She told me yesterday she liked teasing us. She said you were cute when you're angry and I'm funny when I'm nervous."

"That's not an excuse," I said, in a hushed tone. "Even just now, touching you the way she did. Not okay."

"I know," he said awkwardly. "It gave me chills."

I didn't say anything and grabbed some cleaning supplies and wiped the register and belt.

"I'll talk to her about it, let her know that's crossing the line. Please don't be angry."

I nodded and continued to clean as he walked away. I scrubbed the corners and the registers. It was the best way to let out my frustration.

"That's some mighty good cleaning you're doing right here."

I looked up. Jessica was standing there with a basket full of groceries.

"Well I prefer my work environment clean," I forced myself to say.

"Hmph, to each their own." She shrugged.

I began ringing up her groceries. I avoided eye contact. I really didn't want to talk to her. I wasn't confrontational, but I also wasn't the type to forgive and forget.

"I wasn't going to say anything," Jessica said. "But I need to confess as your friend."

Jessica paused and I looked at her.

"It's about Daniel and me," she continued. "We kissed yesterday. It was a little romantic and we ended up kissing. He's a nice kisser but that's beside the point. I'm sorry. He told me not to say anything about it when I talked to him just now. But I couldn't hide it from you, not anymore."

"Your total is $38.42," I said, as I rung up the last item and placed it in a bag.

"Please don't be angry. It was an accident," she said.

"I already knew about it. I saw you two last night. Daniel already explained everything to me," I said, placing her bags on the belt. "Just now, he was most likely referring to how touchy you are. Not about the kiss."

Jessica was shocked, her lips were moving but nothing came out. I looked at Jessica, a smug look on my face. Jessica grabbed her bags.

"Well, that's good he told you. We need to be honest about those things," she said, nodding her head. "I'll see you tomorrow at work."

"Yep, bye."

Neither me nor Daniel worked tomorrow. I laughed when she left the store.

The next day, I went to Mama, I wanted Makayla's opinion on Jessica. I wasn't sure what to do, I knew she was trying to get under my skin. We both knew Daniel only liked me, but I couldn't help but worry.

Jessica was prettier than me. Who knew when Daniel would realize it and dump me? At least I could get beauty tips from Makayla.

"Welcome," Makayla said. "Oh hey, it's rare to see you."

"Yeah, I actually came here because I needed your advice on something."

"Go for it," Makayla said.

I explained the situation to Makayla from when I first met Jessica all the way to them kissing and what Jessica did yesterday.

"Girl, you're more patient than I am," she said, shaking her head. "I would have confronted her head on and told her to back the hell up."

"This is the first time I've had to deal with this, so I don't know the correct way to approach her. She was so nice to me, and even gave me advice about dating. Said we were friends."

"And you said Daniel isn't catching on to what she's doing?"

"No, he thinks she's just being friendly. That's why I thought I was overthinking it. And lately, she's been saying and doing more rude things whenever possible. And it's mostly about our relationship."

"Wow," Makayla said. "She's rude and bold."

Makayla continued, "Women can be like that. They'll go after another woman's man rather than find a guy that's similar. It's shameful. But you can't let her do this, either confront her and tell her to knock it off or if you don't feel comfortable doing that, make it clear that Daniel only has eyes for you."

"How could I do that?"

"Hmm, maybe be super mushy and affectionate? Or flirt with him whenever she's around."

"Ok, I think I'll be really affectionate with him."

"Okay, you sure you can do that?" she asked.

"I'll be embarrassed, but I don't want her to win," I said. "I also wanted to ask if you could give me some fashion and makeup advice?"

"Hmm," Makayla said, tapping her chin. "You could give me your phone number and we can go shopping?"

I smiled. "Okay!"

Makayla thought this was a serious matter, and we decided to meet up Sunday morning to visit some top department stores. I was a little worried about the prices since I didn't make that much at Loue's and still needed to pay rent.

I made it to Time Square and walked to Line Store, our meeting spot. Makayla was already there. She looked so cool and stylish. She made a simple black and white crop top hoodie and jogging pants look amazing. She even wore matching heels. I looked at my outfit in the window as I got closer, I tried looking cute but decided to change because I looked stupid. I wore a hoodie, leggings, and regular gym shoes.

"Wow," I said, walking to her. "You really are fashionable."

"You think?" Makayla asked. "Thank you, you look cute."

"No way," I said, shaking my head.

"You do, most people try to rock styles that don't match them, but with you, any style looks cute. Only advice I would give about this one is you need earrings. Earrings always complete the outfit. It can change the dullest of outfits into something cute," she said. "As a matter of fact, let's go in that jewelry store and buy some for you to wear."

"Okay," I said, following her into the store.

When we walked inside, I walked to a counter and saw the price of the jewelry. I'm not kidding when I say that my heart stopped. I must have been showing how shocked I was, Makayla walked over to me.

"I know it's kind of pricey," she whispered. "There's a clearance section over there. Let's check that out."

We walked over. The earrings were so pretty. But the cheapest pair was $20. For *one* pair of earrings. I took out my phone and looked at my bank account. I had $700, but $500 was going to my rent stash. If I got the earrings, that would mean I could only get maybe 3 outfits. I didn't know how much makeup cost. I sighed. I wasn't going to buy any.

"Which one do you like?" Makayla asked.

I pointed to a pair of hoop earrings, they were gold and matched the design on my hoodie. "I like that one, but it's a little outside my budget, if I want to do more shopping."

Makayla called the clerk over. "Can I buy this pair?"

"You like them too?"

"No, it's not my style, it's yours."

"What," I said. "You don't have to."

"I know I don't, but you've never done this right? It should be fun and not you feeling bad about the pair you couldn't get."

"Thanks," I said, hugging Makayla.

"Of course hun."

I felt a little more confident with the earrings on. We walked into a department store not too far from the jewelry store. It was bigger than anything in my hometown. It was amazing.

"Let's go to the makeup department. I need to get some new lipstick," Makayla said.

We walked to the second floor, and a burst of perfume hit me, and threw me off guard.

"Wow," I said, coughing. "That's a lot of perfume."

Makayla laughed. "You'll get used to it."

I walked behind Makayla as she looked for makeup. I was nervous to ask if I should get some. I wanted to but I didn't want to look ugly even with makeup on.

"I was thinking about getting makeup," I blurted out.

"Really?" an employee asked. "You're so pretty, you don't need all of this."

"Yeah, you really don't," Makayla agreed.

"I guess…I just wanted to do a total makeover. I always wanted to try some."

"Well, we have a section over there where they do your makeup it's only $5."

"I think I'll try it," I said. "I'll go over there."

"Okay," Makayla said. "I'll be here."

I walked to the corner of the department. I saw the sign for makeovers. I walked into the section. A woman looked over. "I'll be with you in a sec hun."

"Okay," I said, sitting down in the waiting area.

After about 3 minutes she walked over.

"Sorry about the wait," she said, before pausing and looking at me. "You want makeup? Girl, you're gorgeous."

"Thank you," I said awkwardly. "I just want to try it. I wasn't allowed to wear it growing up."

"Okay, but you don't need much done. I'll just work on your eyes and eyebrows. Maybe lipstick…"

It was pretty awkward. She was too close, but it was worth it. When she handed me the mirror my mouth dropped. I looked a lot better than I did before.

"You looked pretty before, but now you're beautiful."

I didn't agree but I said thanks and went back to Makayla who was still looking at lipsticks.

"Daamn," she shouted. "Daniel's in danger if he doesn't put Jessica in place."

"I don't look that good." I laughed.

"Like hell you don't."

"Did you find what you were looking for?"

"Hmm, I like these two, so I might just buy them both. What do you think?"

"I would, that way you have variety."

"That's true."

"I wanted to get the lipstick and eyeliner she used."

"Ooh you gonna make Daniel's mouth drop every day huh?" Makayla laughed.

I smiled.

We spent so much time in just the makeup department alone we decided to just go to one store for an hour before Makayla had to work. We walked into a clothing store. It was very… pink. I turned around and Makayla grabbed my arm.

"You gotta wear more colors than just black," she said. "Let's go."

As we looked around, I spotted something hanging in the corner, it was a pink, short-sleeve dress with a lighter pink belt. It was cute. I walked to it and held it up to my body. I turned to the mirror. It went down to a little above my knees.

Makayla walked over and said, "That looks cute. You should try it on."

"Can I?" I asked.

"Obviously, if you're going to buy something, always try it on beforehand. It might be too big or might not work with your shape."

I nodded and headed for the fitting room. When I came out, Makayla cheered. I was embarrassed.

"Girl, you really are beautiful. You should wear this out, and we can do your hair. That way, when Daniel sees you, he'll be speechless."

"You think?" I said, looking down at the dress. "Can I just wear this out?"

"Yeah, just let the woman over there know. But we also need to get you better shoes. So let her know you're going to keep shopping."

"Okay," I said, walking to the lady.

She took the tag off and stapled it to a sheet of paper and told me to bring it to the cashier. I asked Makayla to pick out my shoes, I knew nothing about them. I just picked whatever fit. Makayla looked around and grabbed a pair of light pink and white sneakers. They were cute. We bought a few more outfits and checked out. Makayla laughed at my face when I saw the total, $160. That was most of my spending money until my next paycheck. But it was nice to treat myself sometimes. It's healthy for a person… is what I told myself.

I texted Daniel asking if he wanted to have lunch together at this diner I saw in Queens.

"Of course," he replied. "I can be there in an hour."

"Okay," I said, sending a smiley face and heart emoji.

As we walked back to the station, Makayla asked, "Be honest with me, how do you feel about yourself?"

"What do you mean?"

"Do you love yourself? Like when you look in the mirror do you see how pretty you are? After spending today with you, I feel like you don't see that."

"Well, to be honest," I paused. "I don't see it. I think I'm ugly."

"Seriously? You are beautiful. Even the women in the stores said it. Do you know many guys were checking you out when we left?"

"They were checking you out, not me." I shook my head. "And I know a lot of people tell me I'm pretty, and I appreciate everyone complimenting me, but it doesn't matter when I don't see it myself. I don't want people thinking I'm fishing for compliments, so I just say thank you."

"That makes sense," she said. "It doesn't matter what others think about you."

I nodded.

We arrived at the station. Makayla and I were going different directions. "I want you tonight, after your date to just look at yourself, and I mean really look at yourself. You're a pretty girl, and eventually your looks will fade. So I hope you see yourself as you are and enjoy it."

"I will," I said.

Makayla and I hugged, and I headed to the A line.

She was right, it was about time I fixed my insecurities. I had so many fun things around me. I wouldn't be able to fully enjoy them if I didn't get better.

As I walked inside the diner, I saw Daniel in a corner booth and walked to him. Before I could reach the table, Daniel looked up.

His mouth agape, he said, "You look amazing."

"Thanks," I said, smiling. I sat down, Daniel didn't say anything, he just stared at me. My face was a little flushed. "Have you been here before?"

He shook his head.

"Me neither. It looks good though."

Daniel opened his mouth but before he could speak, the waitress came over. We placed our orders, throughout it, Daniel's eyes didn't leave me.

"Do you really think I look 'amazing?'" I asked.

"You are, you're stunning." Daniel smiled softly. "I can look at you all day."

"Thank you."

After lunch, we rode the bus back to our apartments. We had a pretty great conversation. I remembered what me and Makayla planned about being more affectionate. I reached over and held his hand.

"This is nice," Daniel said.

"I know. I had a great morning and lunch."

"Come over to my place," he said. "I do have to run to Loue's though once we go back."

"Why?" I asked. I didn't want him to see Jessica.

"I just need to get some things. Do you want to go with me?"

"No, I gotta do laundry. I won't be able to see you for the rest of the day."

"Aww," Daniel groaned. "Okay, I'll just head over now. I'll see you later."

Daniel kissed my head and got off the bus. I waved to him as he walked away.

When I got to my apartment, I changed out of my dress and started cleaning. I walked into the bathroom and looked at myself. Was I really pretty? I stared for about 2 minutes, but I couldn't see it. I sighed and gathered my clothes. As I put them in the washer, I realized I forgot I ran out of detergent. I thought about asking Daniel to grab some on his way back, but I remembered I had to be more affectionate with him in front of Jessica. I put my outfit on and headed out the door.

I got to Loue's and grabbed the detergent first so I wouldn't forget…and I didn't want it to look like I was being clingy. After paying for it, I walked around the store so I could find Daniel. I looked around for a bit, before I spotted Daniel and Jessica by the floral department. In his hands was a beautiful bouquet. They were so close to each other practically hugging. Jessica looked Daniel in the eye, and he handed her the flowers. He had the biggest smile on his face as she smelled them. My heart sank.

Was he cheating on me with Jessica? They looked so happy together. The perfect couple. Jessica wasn't that much shorter than Daniel but just short enough to place her head in his neck. I held back my tears.

Daniel looked over and saw me. A look of dread washed over his face. I turned around and ran away.

"Maya wait," he yelled.

I kept running until I ran into a park. I was so sick of what he was doing. It was obvious Jessica was after him, but he chose to ignore me and did little things like that or kiss her. Handing her the flowers was my breaking point. He clearly liked her. Maybe he felt bad if he broke up with me after a few months dating or maybe he didn't notice his feelings for her until then.

"Maya please," he said, running into the park after me.

I didn't say anything to him. I didn't even look in his direction. I was fed up. He kept denying she was after him. At this point it was ridiculous. There was no way he didn't pick up on her feelings. He made a fool of me. I asked him to stay away from her. And he couldn't even do that. I tried so hard to look perfect for him. Changing my fashion did nothing to fix our relationship and my insecurities. I was desperately fighting to feel validated so that I could beat Jessica when *I* was his girlfriend. I was sick of it.

Then it hit me, Makayla was right. I really needed to find myself and love myself. I had gotten so hurt because of Daniel and Jessica and I blamed it on my looks.

Seeing that look on his face, he never looked at me like that before. My heart was hurting. I couldn't do it anymore. He needed to be with someone that made him look that way every day. Jessica was perfect for him. She was so dedicated to him. She would go to any length to get that out of him. Maybe he loved Jessica, but because he liked me for so long, he stubbornly thought I was the one he wanted. I needed to think logically. I shouldn't have to worry as much as I did.

I didn't notice I was crying until a tear slid down my lips. I bit my lip.

"I want to break up."

CHAPTER EIGHT

We stood in silence. Tears streamed down my face. I looked at Daniel who stared at the ground, his hands clenched. It was time. I didn't want to, but we needed to call it quits. He couldn't have been happy with someone as depressing as me, and I knew I couldn't make him happy. Daniel looked as if he was sucked into a void. As if he weren't there.

"I'm really sorry," I said. "It's just not working. I can't be the girl that's cheerful when you walk into the room, or the girl that wants to see New York every hour of the day. I can't be the girl you want me to be."

Daniel was silent.

"I know you've liked me for years but I'm not the person you expected me to be."

"I wasn't forcing you to be anyone." He finally glanced at me. "I just wanted to make you happy. I don't know how to date someone I longed to be with for years, but that's not a reason to break up with me."

"I'm not going to make you happy. It's not going to be the fantasy life you were expecting."

I couldn't forget the way he looked at Jessica, the scene flashed in my mind to no end. My heart ached like a thousand needles were being hammered into it. He was better with someone like Jessica. A girlfriend that loved him and showed it. I could barely kiss him without freaking out. I wasn't ready for a relationship. I didn't realize it earlier and, in the end, I hurt both of us.

"I'm being selfish, but I'm not ready for a relationship. I hurt you with my rash decision, but I just can't anymore."

"Did you even love me?" he asked, bitterly.

"I did, I still love you."

"Then why can't we stay together?" Daniel plead, as he stepped closer. "We can go through the process together. I don't mind waiting until you're ready, as long as you're with—"

I shook my head. "I can't, that's not fair to you. Just… go with Jessica and be happy."

"Jessica?" he asked, surprised. "What does she have to do with this?"

My face felt hot. "I have to go!"

I ran pass Daniel and out of the park. I couldn't tell if Daniel was chasing me, and I didn't want to. When I read those scenes where the characters broke up, I never imagined it would be this painful. I didn't want to experience that again. I ran off into the night, hoping to never see Daniel again.

A week went by and no word from Daniel. I knew he didn't care. He probably went right to Jessica. I imagined them at his apartment holding each other. I cried. I regretted breaking up with him, but he was probably already with her. I still worked at Loue's, but I planned on quitting when I came in for my next shift. I hadn't seen Daniel or Jessica at work and wondered if we were even on the same shifts. I just prayed Daniel wouldn't be there tomorrow. Every day was constant worrying about running into him, and to make it worse, him with Jessica. Even just grabbing my mail was nerve racking.

I wanted to move out. I planned to spend that week searching for cheap apartments in Brooklyn…. But I wouldn't be able to afford helping Anna if I moved. This apartment was the most affordable one I could find in New York. I wouldn't survive being jobless and at some place with high rent. I had to suck it up for a little bit longer.

I hadn't told Anna about my breakup yet. I didn't know how she would respond. Knowing her, she would call Daniel and curse him out, hop on a plane to curse him out, or nag me for being spineless and giving up on him so easily. I didn't want to worry her, especially because she was dealing with her own issues at home. But I needed to vent to someone. Anna and Makayla were my only friends. I bothered Makayla too much already, I didn't want to be annoying. I needed Anna's shoulder.

I reached for my phone and took a deep breath. I was nervous about her reaction but also if I could hold back my tears when I heard her voice.

"Hello?" she answered.

"Anna." I bit my lip. "Me and Daniel broke up."

I burst into tears. Maybe saying it out loud made it real, I don't know, I was so embarrassed I cried.

"Wait, what?" she shouted. "How and when?"

"Last week, I caught him with Jessica."

"Again?!" she interrupted.

"Yeah, he was giving her flowers. I got tired of him doing things like that and broke up with him."

"And this was last week?"

"Yeah."

"Why did you wait so long to tell me?"

"I'm sorry. I knew you would be mad. I didn't want to get nagged, or have you curse out Daniel."

"You know me so well," Anna grumbled.

"I'm sorry I didn't tell you."

"It's okay Maya. I'm not mad…at you. Daniel is so stupid."

"He really is. He was always playing dumb when I brought up Jessica liking him."

"I wouldn't be surprised if she told him already, but he was pretending so you wouldn't notice."

"I don't even know. I got all dressed up for nothing."

"You did?"

"Yeah, I was talking to Makayla about the kiss situation—"

"Wait, hold up. What 'kiss situation?'"

"Uh, well…" I started. "Right after you told me to go to Jessica's play, I caught Jessica and Daniel kissing."

"What?!" Anna shouted.

I moved the phone way from my ear and continued, "Yes they were arguing and ended up kissing. Daniel claimed it was nothing, and that they were rehearsing but…"

"But you believed him, didn't you?"

"I did," I cried louder and covered my mouth. After composing myself, I said, "He's full of shit, and I'm stupid for believing him."

"You're not stupid," Anna said, softly. "You trusted him. What happened next?"

"Makayla gave me advice and even went shopping with me. I had a makeover and everything. He apparently liked it and was staring a lot. But he fucked it up by going to Loue's."

"That all happened in one day?"

"3 days. I asked him to lunch, but instead of going home with me he went to Loue's 'cause he needed to grab something."

"Do you think he went just to give her flowers?"

"I didn't until you just said so. But he did invite me to go with," I groaned. "I don't know. What if he was planning on breaking up with me that day but I asked him to lunch, and he couldn't do it?"

"I mean, did he seem happy when you broke up?"

"No, he was angry and begged me not to."

"Then you know the answer. He wasn't going to break up with you. I'm just confused on why he kept doing all that shit if he still wanted to date you."

I shrugged as if she could see me. "…Beats me."

"Has he tried calling you?"

"No. I haven't seen him, nor has he called me. That's why I know he was glad we broke up."

"Why would he be?"

"'Cause he's probably with her."

"Then go bust him out. Go to his apartment right now and see if she's there."

"I'm not doing that. I don't want to see him. Plus, it'll just hurt more if I'm right."

"Do you want me to fly up there?"

"No, you only have a month and a half left. Focus on graduating."

"I could fail all my classes this semester and I'll still graduate."

"How?"

"I finished all my credits last semester. If I'd known I could've graduated, I wouldn't even be here."

"I wish you graduated too," I paused. "Also…how are things going? With you and Max?"

"I feel like it's gotten worse now."

"What's he doing?"

"Well, I had a friend over the other night and Max came into the den and made some…comments about us."

"Like what?"

"He commented on our pajamas, told me in front of her, that, 'I'm really filling out.' Or like when we were laying on the couch, said we looked sexy, and we were doing something 'extra' under the covers."

"Dude, that's so nasty."

"It really is. My friend was uncomfortable, I had to apologize so many times."

"At least you have a witness if anything happens. She experienced it as well so he can't deny it."

"Yeah, this whole thing is fucked up. And I know Jane isn't going to believe a word I say. Even if Max went out and said it himself, she would still blame me."

"Some women can't separate from their husbands. Even when they know he's wrong."

"Yeah."

"Just remember, if you can't handle it anymore and need to leave before you graduate, I can change your flight date."

"Okay. I might also stay at my friend's place too. Just until I graduate, I don't know though, Jane and Max might not like it."

"Give it a try anyways. If you have a way to get away from him, do that."

"Yeah... We'll see."

Anna grew silent. I could hear Jane in the background calling for her.

"I'll let you go. I can hear Jane." I laughed.

"She always has the worst timing."

I laughed.

"But Maya," her tone was serious.

"What's up?"

"Would you like me no matter what I tell you?"

"What kind of question is that?" I was confused on where she was going. "Nothing you do would ever make me hate you. Okay?"

"Okay," she mumbled. Jane called her again, I could hear her agitation.

"Tell me when you're ready. I will love you no matter what."

"I will. I better go to Jane."

"Yeah, bye Anna. Good luck with staying at your friend's place."

"Bye Maya."

I could hear Jane once more before the call ended. I wondered what she was pissed over. I didn't like her, and I especially didn't like Max. I wasn't all too sure about child molestation in foster care or after adoption, but I knew it happened. It was currently happening to Anna. He hadn't touched her thank goodness, but I just couldn't help but worry about her, or any future children they adopted if he wasn't caught and registered as a sex offender. Even thinking on it now, what Daniel's dad did was grooming. What if he had already touched my foster sister before she turned 18? He didn't get in trouble for dating her. I wished there were some way to fix this in the judicial system. Even if someone was legally an adult, that didn't mean they were mentally and emotionally mature enough. Foster kids always had a target on their backs. They didn't have anyone to protect them, and these kids were preyed on by older adults. There should be some law against these predators, whether the kid just turned 18 or not. I had to get my mind off it. The more I thought about how fucked up people were, the more upset I got. It was enough to help me forget about Daniel… a little bit.

I wanted to reenact the montage in romances where the heroine would binge other romance movies and eat ice cream. I could afford treating myself to some. I was too scared to go to Loue's, so I went the opposite direction to a convenience store. They had a lot of canned foods and frozen dinners I could buy cheaper than at Loue's. I had shopped there for a few months before returning to Loue's after dating Daniel. I grabbed 6 chocolate ice creams, 4 vanilla, and one mint ice cream. I also bought enough canned goods so I wouldn't have to leave my apartment for a bit. Anything to lessen the chances of seeing Daniel.

I hurried into my apartment and slammed the door. I didn't hear a peep from his apartment. I wondered if he was at work. I put away my groceries and plopped on the couch with the chocolate ice cream. I put on a romcom and ate away the pain. Which of course, wasn't a health way to deal with my emotions, but it was all in fun. I eventually had to move my little "scene" to my room. I couldn't focus on the movie. My eyes darted to the wall that separated me from Daniel, I looked at the cute line of plushies on the love seat, it was too distracting. The only disappointing part to my montage was that I couldn't go on a weight loss journey. If I had lost any more weight, the wind would've blown me away. I went into a food coma later that night.

I woke up to my phone ringing. I ignored it the first time, but whoever was calling didn't stop. I rolled over and grabbed my phone. It was Anna. "What's up Anna?"

"Maya," Anna said, distraught in her voice.

I quickly sat up. Fully awake I asked, "Anna what's wrong? Are you okay?"

"I can't stay here Maya," Anna cried. "Max…he…he tried to have sex with me."

"What?!"

"He came into my room tonight and tried to force himself on me. I made as much noise as I could, and Jane came in. But…she didn't get mad at Max, she yelled at me. She said I was 'teasing him since I became a senior,'" Anna didn't continue, she cried loudly.

"Oh my gosh." I was shocked. "A-are you still at their house?"

"No." She took a breath. "Jane kicked me out, I didn't want to stay either. Max just agreed with everything Jane said and lied that I called him in there."

"Where are you right now?"

"I'm just sitting outside. I called my friend. She's coming with her mom to pick me up. So I'm just waiting."

"I can try to get a flight for today. Do you want to do that?"

"Isn't it going to be expensive?"

"Probably, but I saved a lot of money. If you're not going to bring any more stuff, I can just use that."

"I wanna get out of here."

"Okay Anna," I said, softly. "I'll stay on the phone as long as you need me to."

"Just until they get here. I'm sorry I woke you up."

"Don't be. There's nothing you should be sorry for."

Anna stayed silent. I didn't say anything either. What could I say? Nothing I said could do anything to make her situation better.

"You know," Anna mumbled. "I knew this was going to happen, but it was still unexpected."

"Sometimes your gut feeling is right. He's been showing signs for months, right?"

"Yeah, ever since last summer."

"This might be too soon, but you need to file a report against him."

"There's nothing I can do. I'm already 18, I can't say he tried to molest me."

"He tried to do worse. Even if he didn't get that far, you can still press charges for attempted sexual assault. He most likely would have to register as a sex offender."

"I don't have proof, it won't matter." Anna paused. "I…think they're here. I'll text you when I settle in."

"Okay," I said. "But I'll stay on until you know it's them."

"Ok."

I heard someone calling out to Anna, "Are you alright? Sorry we couldn't get here faster."

"It's okay. Hold on," Anna said, and returned to the call. "They're here. I'll talk to you later."

"I'll look for morning flights. If not, it'll be later tonight or tomorrow. I'll send you the information right away."

"Alright, thanks Maya."

"Bye Anna, get some rest."

Anna hung up.

I wanted to cry. I couldn't bear to see Anna go through this, but I didn't have time to cry. I needed to get Anna to New York as fast as possible. I rushed out of bed to my laptop. I managed to get a flight for 1 PM. I texted Anna the details.

I wanted to prepare everything for her. I unpacked a box of her clothes and placed them in the drawers. I was thankful we had enough of her stuff there already. I looked through the boxes for anything else she needed right away and pulled them out. By the time I finished, it was 7 AM. I was tired, but I needed to get more food. I didn't want Anna eating the crap I ate. I got dressed and headed for Loue's. It didn't matter that I could run into Daniel. I was willing to put myself in that situation if it were for Anna. I needed to quit anyways.

After getting dressed, I arrived at Loue's just as he opened. No sign of Daniel and Jessica. I felt bad. Loue was such a good person. He didn't deserve the brunt of our breakup, but he still had Jessica and Daniel working there. I grabbed the foods Anna loved and a few drinks. As I headed to check out, Loue took over for someone. *Great,* I thought. *Here goes nothing.*

"Morning Maya," Loue said.

"Morning," I paused. "I'm really sorry Loue—"

"For what?" he interrupted.

"I have to quit."

He stopped ringing up my things. "How come?"

"Well, me and Daniel broke up and I just don't feel comfortable being here right now."

Loue continued to scan my items. He sighed immensely. "I understand. Breakups can be hard. I just wish it didn't have to affect work. If, and when you get over Daniel, you're always welcome to come back here."

"I will." I smiled. "It's just going to be too awkward."

I paid for my things and left. Loue was cool, even though I knew he wanted to say my decision was stupid, but that was the least of my worries. Now that I didn't have a job, I had to find another one quickly. I put away the groceries and deep cleaned my apartment.

I got to the airport just as Anna's flight arrived. I waited outside the uber. When I saw Anna, I hugged her instantly. "I'm so sorry about what happened. Are you okay?"

"I'll be alright. It just brought back some past trauma. But I'll recover."

I led Anna to the car. "I already unpacked your things."

"Thanks."

"Did you get any sleep?"

Anna shook her head. "I couldn't sleep. Me and my friend just talked about things."

"I didn't sleep either. Let's take a nap and maybe do something later?"

"Ok." She nodded. "Have you seen Daniel yet?"

"Thankfully no," I mumbled. "I haven't seen him since that night."

"You guys are gonna run into each other sooner or later."

"I know, but maybe we can move before then. I'm willing to break my lease."

"You won't get another apartment if you do," the uber driver interjected.

"Really? Crap." I leaned against the window. "Guess we're stuck."

"I would get it over with. Maybe stage a meeting or something."

"Never. I said I never wanted to see him again, I'm sticking to it."

"Whatever you say," Anna teased.

When we reached the apartment, both of us were knocked out the minute we lay in bed. When we woke up, we talked all night. I told her about quitting my job. We thought up plans to get out of the apartment without messing up my credit.

I called the landlord. I wanted to know if she was willing to let me out 5 months early. She questioned why I needed to move so early, and I explained that I had a personal problem and had to leave. She, as expected, denied my request. I was screwed. The more I did, the less it seemed possible to avoid Daniel. Was I bound to be heartbroken forever?

I wasn't giving up yet. I figured we could talk to Makayla about it. I knew I was too dependent, but Makayla was older than us and would probably have a solution or work around. I texted Makayla. She wasn't working that day and was cool with meeting up. I texted her my address, I would have been fine with meeting her somewhere public, but that would require me leaving my apartment and seeing Daniel. Makayla came at noon. I explained the situation to her.

"And after all that work we did. Damn fool," she grumbled.

"Exactly," Anna said. "But it's his loss."

"Mm-hm." Makayla shook her head.

"We were wondering if there was a way out of our lease?" I asked. "I already asked my landlord and she said no."

"Not really, but why not see if she can sublease your apartment while you're…" Makayla paused then did air quotes. "Out of town."

She continued, "If you say there's a family emergency and that you need to leave for a few months, then maybe she'll arrange something. Or just continue to pay for rent but go somewhere else for a few months."

"What do you mean?" I asked.

"Well, you could always get an Airbnb until you're comfortable running into Daniel. You can keep paying rent here but be on vacation."

"I could but I don't have enough to do both, and I just quit my job."

"I have a friend who runs an Airbnb. I could see if she's willing to let you crash there at a cheaper price."

"Please do."

Before Makayla could say anything, her phone went off. She looked at the number, she was hesitant but answered.

"Yes?"

There was a pause as whoever, was speaking.

"I can't right now. I'm in the middle of something." She rolled her eyes and stood up. "Please don't do that. I already did what you said. Ok, I got it. I'm on my way."

She hung up. She took a deep breath then faced us. "Sorry I have to deal with something. I'll call her today and if she says it's okay, I'll text you her number."

"Is everything okay?" I asked.

"Yeah, totally. I just have to go in for work. I switched shifts with someone and they're saying I agreed to today too. So I better go."

"Okay, thanks for all your help."

"No problem, good luck with your situation."

"Thanks."

Makayla left. Me and Anna made eye contact.

"I guess you also thought that was shady?" I broke the silence.

"Hella. The way she was begging whoever that was to not do whatever, was weird."

"I hope she's okay."

"Me too."

I called my landlord once more. This time I made an agreement. I said, I had to leave town because of a sick relative. I said I would stay another year if she agreed to sublease my apartment. She was still reluctant, but I guessed she didn't want me to keep calling her asking. With a fixup on the deal, she agreed. I had to come back to the apartment in August. She was willing to sign whatever paperwork I needed. I wasn't a good judge of character, so I asked her to choose someone. With my apartment problem out of the way, I just needed Makayla's friend to say yes.

We waited for word from Makayla. She texted later than she said. Her friend agreed to letting us stay in a room. We had to pay $150 a month. Which was reasonable. A room would be available next week which was hopefully enough time to find someone to take my apartment.

The time had come to leave. We packed the last box and put it in storage in the basement. I went back to the apartment to make sure nothing was left behind. The bright side was that we didn't have to take the furniture out. I looked around the apartment and walked into my room. On the bed were the plushies that Daniel got me. I stared as Anna came in.

"I took those out the box," she said. "I figured you'd want to take those with."

I shook my head. "They were gifts from Daniel. I didn't have the heart to throw them out, so I was putting them in storage."

"Oops," Anna said. She took the bears and left.

It was weird to see my apartment empty. Even though I had to come back in a few months, I felt like I would never return. I took a deep breath, held back my tears, and left the apartment.

The home we were staying in was in Flushing, Queens. It was two stories high and was brick, the lawn was clean, and a short gate surrounded the property. I looked at Anna and opened the gate. "Here goes nothing."

I knocked on the door and a woman my height answered. She was an older woman, in her mid to late thirties with caramel skin, she had brown hair, she was a little chubby, and she wore glasses. She wore a lavender dress and black flats.

"Yes?" she asked, her Spanish accent was strong.

"Hi, I'm Maya and this is Anna. We're Makayla's friends."

"Oh, come in, come in." She moved to the side and motioned for us to enter. Once inside, she hugged us. "Oh, it's nice to meet you girls. I'm Valery. I know you're going through somethings, and I hope staying here helps."

"Thanks, we really appreciate your hospitality."

"It's nothing, glad to help. Let me show you to your room." Valery walked up the stairs to the left of the front door and down the hall. There were 3 closed doors to the right and a 4th at the end of the hall.

She opened the door at the end. "We have a mini fridge over there, snacks and water bottles, and towels in the closet. It's a single bed but if you don't feel comfortable sharing, I can bring up an air mattress."

"No we're fine with sharing," I said, setting my luggage in the corner by the window.

"Okay, I'll let you girls settle in." Valery closed the door.

"This is a cute little room," Anna said. She jumped on the bed. "Feels weird, doesn't it?"

"What does?"

"You moving out your apartment and me moving to New York."

"Yeah, a little."

She rolled over and looked at me. "I'm glad we have each other though."

"Me too." I smiled.

Someone knocked on the door.

"Come in," me and Anna said in unison.

Valery opened the door. "I forgot to mention. We're having dinner tonight if you both would like to join us."

"Thanks, we will."

Anna nodded in agreement.

She smiled and left the room.

"Guess that takes care of dinner." I shrugged.

We unpacked most of what we could into the closet and dresser drawers. The rest we kept neatly in our luggage. I took a nap while Anna was on her phone. When it was time for dinner, we put on the nicest clothes we had and headed down. In the kitchen was Valery and a taller woman. She was skinny, her hair was blonde with black highlights, her skin was a few shades lighter than Valery's, she wore a business suit and high heels. She also looked like she was mid-thirties. They were preparing the table and talking.

"Welcome ladies. We're almost done," the woman said.

"Have a seat," Valery said.

"Do you want some help?" Anna offered.

"No, we have most of it done already," Valery said. Recognition hit her and she said, "Ah, I forgot to introduce you to my wife Carmen."

"It's nice to meet you," I said.

"Nice to meet you," Anna trailed after me.

"The pleasure's mine. Have a seat."

Valery and Carmen made a lot of food and apologized. They only ate for two. Another guest was supposed to join us but didn't. On the table was a bowl of rice and beans, Arroz con Pollo, which was chicken with tomatoes, garlic, and rice. There were fried eggs, Yuca—cassava root, they had Maduros—fried plantains, comida criolla with fish and a huge bowl of salad. I never had Cuban food before. It was heaven in my mouth.

Even though I had just met Carmen and Valery, sitting at the table eating together, really felt like a family. Something I never experienced at Margaret's home. She ate with her children, and the rest of us ate in our rooms. It was nice experiencing this. The laughter, the conversations, the stories, it was a real home. I felt silly thinking that way with strangers, but I couldn't help myself.

We learned a lot about Valery and Carmen. Carmen was 40 years old. She was a lawyer and worked for one of the biggest law firms in New York. Her hobbies were gardening, knitting, and playing guitar, though she didn't have time for any of these things, she always wanted to start her own garage band. Valery was 38 years old and owned a cleaning service. Her hobbies were baking, cooking, and volunteering at youth centers. She did most of the housework since Carmen worked more hours and her cleaning service wasn't as busy. After dinner, me and Anna went to our room. We talked for hours about dinner and laughed about starting a band with Carmen.

Over the week, me and Anna were settling in. We ate dinner regularly with Carmen and Valery. On occasion, the other guest would join us. We were getting used to the area and figuring out the best routes to the train station. I liked Queens more than Brooklyn. The walk to the train was significantly closer. I missed taking the bus, but the train seemed faster. Since Anna was new to New York, we spent a lot of time touring. I didn't want to spend money with no income, but I was willing to do anything for Anna to feel better. I still had a decent amount of money in my bank account but who knew when I would end up spending it on something important. I needed a job fast.

I mentioned that I needed to find a job to Valery and Carmen and asked if they knew any places that were hiring. Valery offered me a spot at her business. I, of course, took it. She was such a good person. She also gave Anna a job. It wasn't a guarantee that she would need our help, but whenever possible, she would tell us. It was temporary, so she didn't add us to the payroll. She said she would just pay us out of pocket for each job we did.

We started the next day. She told us in the morning, she wanted to show us the ropes. She said we were young and most likely wouldn't clean as well as they were expected to. Honestly, I agreed with her. I wasn't a bad cleaner, but I knew Anna had never cleaned before. Jane was a stay-at-home wife and did all the housework. When we were cleaning my apartment, she was so terrible I told her to just pack. It was going to be funny watching her clean.

When we arrived at the apartment we were supposed to clean, my mouth dropped. It was disgusting. Piles of trash scattered around the floor, a horrible rotten smell filled the air, caked on scum in the kitchen, on the floor and counters. I was scared to see how their bedroom and bathroom looked.

"I'm glad I brought you girls with me," Valery said, walking in completely. "I'm going to charge extra. This is just too much."

It took us 8 hours to clean the apartment. It was insane people lived in that kind of filth, that it could even get that dirty. I felt sick to my stomach having to clean it and I prayed future jobs wouldn't be as bad as that. Valery and her client argued about the additional money required but she was able to get it out of him. She handed me and Anna both $150 and told us to write how much we made working for her for tax purposes. She explained a lot about how we would need to file taxes. It wasn't her responsibility to teach us, but she believed since schools taught nothing on real life needs, adults should take the reins until they did.

Two weeks passed and we were used to living there. Carmen and Valery were nice, the other guests were cool depending on who it was, of course. Lately Anna was disappearing more than usual. Through sheer luck, Anna was able to explain her situation to her teachers and they were willing to let her take her final exams online. She had to go to the public library to take it. While she studied and took her finals, it still felt like she wasn't there as much as she used to be. Instead of coming to our room right after she finished, she was hanging out with Carmen a lot and spent a lot of time on her phone. I wondered who she talked to, but it also wasn't my business…. Something was off but again, I hoped, she would tell me when she was ready.

There wasn't enough work for us, Valery already had a lot of employees that needed the jobs more than we did. When we did work, we were grateful and hardworking, but eventually I needed a more stable job. Where and how I got it was another story.

When I woke up, Anna was long gone. It was 7:30 AM. I took a shower and went to the kitchen to look for Anna. Valery was clearing the table.

"Morning Maya," she said. "You missed breakfast."

"Sorry. I'm still not used to waking up this early."

"That's alright. I can fix you something."

"No, it's okay. I can eat some ramen later." I was hoping she didn't force me to eat like Daniel did.

"If you say so," she said. "But if you get tired of garbage food, let me know and I will make real food for you."

"Yes ma'am." I nodded. "Is there any work today?"

"No." She shook her head. "I'll get you if there is."

"Okay."

"You moved to New York, right?" she asked, as I was leaving the kitchen.

"Yeah, I came to New York for a better life, but I only became more depressed."

"People come to New York to live," Valery said. "When you're down you don't come here to be depressed, you come here to feel alive again. You need to spend some time finding what makes you happy."

What Valery said moved me. I shouldn't have been feeling the way I did. I came to New York City for a better life, not to let my past haunt me. I came expecting happiness and fun to be handed to me, and I did nothing to help achieve it. It was time I moved on and enjoyed what was in front of me. I had Anna, I made new friends, I wasn't alone anymore. And rather than stay focused on the things that hurt me, I needed to focus on the people that cared about me. Happiness would soon follow.

I said bye to Valery and went to my room. I feared what the outcome would be, but it was a risk I needed to take. I yawned and relaxed in bed. There wasn't much of a reason to stay awake.

Anna burst into the room. "Maya! Maya!"

"What is it?" I asked.

"Look at this newspaper," she shouted.

"Shh, it's 8 in the morning. Don't wake up the other guests."

"I don't care, this is way more important." Anna shoved the newspaper in my face.

"Since when did you start reading newspapers?" I laughed.

I looked at the page and in bold letters it said: **Looking for Maya Reed**.

"What does this have to do with me?" I asked.

"Just read it," she said.

I rolled my eyes and read the article. Not even halfway through, my heart stopped. It was an article about a woman that needed to find her daughter.

"W-wait," I stammered. I continued to read. "No way."

My arms trembled as I held the newspaper. The beginning of her story seemed just like what happened with me.

"That's definitely about you," Anna said. "Turn to the next page."

I turned the page as fast as I could. On the back, was a picture of me when I was 4. There was no mistaking it. This was written by my mother.

> "...She's 19 now, and I was given little information on where she went. If anyone knows where Maya Anderson is, please contact me at 551-XXX-XXXX.

Anna stayed silent as I finished reading. When I was done, I sat the newspaper on the bed.

"What are you going to do?" she asked. "Are you gonna contact her?"

"Should I?" I asked.

"I mean, I would." Anna shrugged. "You can finally have answers."

"…You're right," I agreed. "…I just don't know. I'm scared."

"Why are you afraid?"

"I—I don't want to be hurt, you know? I spent 14 years without her. Always wondering what I did to deserve being given up. I can't stomach hearing she didn't want m—"

I cupped my face with my hands and cried. I was trying hard to hold back my tears. I went through so much by myself. I spent so many years constantly thinking about the fact that my mother didn't love me, that I was unwanted. When I watched my classmates go home with their moms while I walked "home" alone, the lonely birthdays, and the mistreatment from Margaret. Years of hurt I bottled up inside, at that moment, poured out.

"But if that were true," Anna said, hugging me. "She wouldn't be going to such lengths to find you now. And if she did give you up on purpose, sometimes people make tough decisions on emotions and do something they regret. You won't know the truth until you ask her."

I didn't say anything but hugged Anna. After about 5 minutes, I was calm enough to speak again.

"I really want to know why she gave me away."

"Then text this number," Anna said, handing me the newspaper and my phone. "It's better you figure things out. No matter what the outcome is, good or bad, I'll be here for you."

"Thanks Ann."

I dialed the number and took a deep breath.

"Is this Angela Reed? I have information on your daughter."

My heart was racing. My trembling hands gripped my cell tightly.

"And now we wait," Anna said.

As soon as she finished speaking, my notification went off. We flinched so bad Anna burst into laughter.

"That scared the shit out of me!" She laughed holding her chest.

"She responded," I said.

"That was fast." Anna leaned over. "See, if she wasn't serious, you would have gotten a reply like two days from now. What's it say?"

"Thank you for reaching out! Please tell me all you can!"

"I'm—" I stopped typing. "I don't know."

"Maya." Anna leaned back onto the bed. "I need you to take a deep breath and write it's you."

"I'm just scared. Logically I know I should just say it. But I just…I'm just really nervous."

"I know, but it's a simple text. You can tell her and not talk to her until you're ready. But I know you, and I know you want to. You just need a push."

I looked back to the phone.

"I'm Maya Anderson… Or Maya Reed, I guess."

"It's sent," I said. My heartbeat hadn't calmed, it sped up.

"I'm proud of you Maya." Anna hugged me.

My hand started to vibrate, I looked down as my ringtone grew louder. She was calling me. I panicked and threw my phone across the bed.

"Nope." I shook my head. "I already texted her, I'm not ready to talk to her."

"Just let it ring," Anna said. "Then tell her you aren't ready to talk on the phone."

I nodded and reached for my phone. We watched it ring. When it ended, I wrote, "I'm sorry. I'm not ready to talk over the phone."

"That's okay. We can text," she responded. "I just can't believe you found my article so quickly!"

"I didn't. I don't read newspapers. My friend saw it and told me."

"I'm thankful to your friend." Another text came through, "I know you said you weren't ready to speak to me, but would you like to meet for coffee and talk?"

"She wants to meet for coffee," I relayed to Anna.

"Are you ready for that?" she asked. "If so, say yeah, and plan for like next week or something."

I nodded.

"Does next week Friday work for you?"

"Yes! It does! Why don't we meet up for lunch?"

“Okay.”

“I don’t know if you’re still in New York, but I’m in New Jersey.”

“Yes, I’m currently in Queens.”

“Hmmm...I don’t think I’ll have time to make it to Queens and back before I go back to work.”

“Say you’ll go to her,” Anna said, over my shoulder.

“I can go to New Jersey.”

“Great! I’ll look for a quiet café, and text you the details.”

“Okay.”

“I need to get back to work. Thank you for reaching out to me Maya.”

“Bye.”

“You okay?” Anna asked, softly.

“Yeah, I’m fine. This is just crazy. Life changing crazy.”

Anna laid her head in my lap. “If you and your mom make up, are you gonna leave me?”

“Of course not,” I said, flicking her forehead. “I’ve been with you for practically all my life. You’re my sister for life. If my mom wants me to go wherever with her, and you can’t come, I’m not going.”

“Okay,” Anna said, relieved. “It would be weird without you.”

“Now you know how I felt after you got adopted.”

We both laughed and I hugged Anna. She was my one and only family.

CHAPTER NINE

A week went by and tomorrow was the day I had lunch with my mother. I was freaking out. I knew nothing about her. What was she like? All I had was a twisted memory of her neglecting me. I don't remember her being violent, just not feeding me. As an adult, I had to think of it rationally, hear her out and discern whether it was a lie or not. I had time over the past week to get my thoughts together. I deserved to know the truth, no matter how hurtful it may be.

Anna watched as I threw all my clothing out of my suitcases and drawers. Each article of clothing I threw, she said, "That's cute… Why not that?"

"Anna," I whined. "I'm serious. This is very important. What if she's a nice person but sees me looking ugly and decides she doesn't want to talk to me?"

"Then she wouldn't be a nice person," Anna said.

"…But I still can't help but think something's gonna go wrong."

"If it does, which I highly doubt, I'll be here for you."

"Thanks. What about this?" I asked, grabbing the outfit I wore when me and Daniel broke up.

"Girl, that's cute." Anna sat up. "You should wear that."

"Only thing is, I wore this the day I broke up with Daniel."

"Different occasion," Anna quickly said. "Don't let that stop you from wearing that."

"I'll wear this then."

"Go to sleep now so you don't look tired."

"Yeah."

I laid my outfit on the table and lay down. It was finally happening. I said goodnight to Anna and fell asleep.

I took a deep breath. 10 minutes before I had to leave, I stared in the mirror, I looked decent. I couldn't recreate how I looked that day. But it didn't matter, I was seeing my mom. I wasn't trying to wow anyone.

I arrived at the diner, or at least the sidewalk in front of it. I was scared to step on the property. Even walking through the parking lot sent chills up my spine.

I entered the diner. I glanced around before sitting in the waiting area for her. My heart was pounding. I wanted to leave and never come back. But I knew I would regret not hearing the truth when it was within my grasp.

I took out my phone to text my mother when a woman walked up to me.

"Maya?" she asked.

I looked up. She was beautiful. Her skin was a little darker than mine, her hair was long, black, and straight. She wore pearl earrings and a pearl necklace that complimented the yellow dress she wore.

"Y-yes," I stuttered, standing up.

She smiled warmly and said, "I could tell. You have your father's eyes."

She reached over and hugged me. I kept my hands to my side until she let go.

"Shall we sit down?" she suggested.

I nodded.

My mother asked the waitress to sit us further in the back. I guessed for more privacy. She had a lot to explain, maybe she didn't want people to know she gave away her daughter. I stayed quiet as we sat down. She thanked the waitress as she handed us the menus.

"What would you like Maya? Order anything, it's my treat."

"It's fine," I sternly declined. "I can pay for myself."

"I'm sure you can, but I invited you out to lunch, the least I can do is pay for it."

"Why? So you can feel better about not feeding me years ago?" I bit my lip. I didn't mean to say it aloud.

She kept a straight face, but I could tell by her eyes that she was hurt.

"Maya," she said, softly. "There's a lot of things you don't understand from back then. You were very young. I'll explain everything after we order. But for now, it's my treat."

I looked at the menu and just went with an omelet and a muffin.

After placing our orders, my mom looked at me and said, "We have a lot to cover. I don't know if you want me to explain everything from the beginning, or if you want to ask me questions—"

"I want you to explain everything."

She sighed and nodded. "I don't know if you remember your father dying when you were younger…."

I nodded.

"Okay…. Me and your father weren't very responsible with money. We spent the first 7 years of marriage travelling. I got pregnant with you, and we decided it was time to settle down. Caleb found a job and I stayed home to take care of you. Everything was perfect. We had the perfect little family for 3 years. Then," she paused. "Caleb died in a car accident."

"How?"

"Drunk driver," she said, quickly, then paused to take a deep breath. Continuing she said, "We didn't prepare for any of that. No one expects to die at 34, your father didn't have life insurance. We won enough money from the lawsuit I filed against the driver. *He* managed to survive…. It was enough to cover Caleb's funeral costs and rent for a few months until I found a job."

She continued, "I applied for government assistance, but I had too much money at the time and was denied. We managed for a year but as the money dwindled, I knew I needed to find a job. I spent every day searching. While I did, I paid our neighbor to watch you. I came home late but still managed to make you something to eat."

"I remember that a little differently," I interrupted.

"And how is that?"

"You came home from work and would go in your room… all you did was cry. I had to find my own food."

"No Maya," she said. "I made you dinner. Do you really think you at 3 years old knew how to prepare food for yourself? I was exhausted and still grieving yes, but I didn't have a job and I left your breakfast and dinner on the coffee table for you. Lunch was something I left to your babysitter. I can see why you thought you were fending for yourself, but you weren't."

I didn't say anything else. Was it possible I messed up my memories? Before she could continue, the waitress came over with our plates. My mother kept quiet and thanked the waitress as she left.

"We were falling on hard times, Maya. I was incredibly stupid back then, I was only rejected from benefits once, and I thought I would be rejected again, so I didn't try. We were soon to be evicted. I couldn't stand to lose you or see you homeless. I called my mother and asked her to take care of you. She couldn't house both of us. Not long after, I lost contact with your grandma. I knew you were going to be safe, so I didn't worry and focused on finding a job and a home. I spent almost two years living in my car."

"Why didn't you just stay in a shelter?" I interrupted again.

"A shelter is one of the last places a woman would stay. In general, many homeless women are escaping sexual abuse or domestic violence. I didn't have to go through that of course, but I still harbored the same fears of what it would be like in a shelter."

She continued, "Finding a job while living in a car was difficult. I didn't have anything to put on the address line and no phone number. I eventually found a minimum wage job and a cheap apartment. Once I was on my feet, I went back for you… only to find out my mother passed away and you were put into foster care. I was heartbroken. I searched everywhere for you. It took me 4 years to locate you. They changed your name to 'Maya Anderson,' my mother's surname."

"So you already found me? Why didn't you just take me back?" I asked. I wouldn't have changed anything in my past because I would have been separated from Anna and everyone else, but I wanted to know why she didn't even try to get me if she was better.

"I tried," she said. "I contacted Child Protective Services about getting my parental rights back. How it works is, when your child is placed in foster care, if they're in foster care for 15 out of 22 months, the court can decide to terminate your parental rights. Which of course, I was way out of that time frame. I did everything within my power to prove I was your mother and that I was fit to take care of you."

She took a sip of her water and continued, "The judge, as well as your caseworker, did everything in their power to prove I was unqualified to take you back. I was a recently homeless, widowed, Black woman. They questioned why my mother had custody of you before you were placed in foster care. I explained numerous times I was struggling to make ends meet after your father died. It was the only way to assure your wellbeing. I was persistent, but I was still new to it, I didn't know my rights. The right to visitation. I did send you letters, daily in fact, but none of them were responded to…."

"I never got any letters," I said.

"Really? Your address was…. right?"

"Yeah." I nodded. "I bet my foster mom threw them away. Wouldn't surprise me."

"Well, truth is, the judge issued a 'no contact' order, meaning I couldn't see you or speak to you. I still sent them. She was following the judge's orders."

"Why did the judge do that?" I asked.

"I'm not sure." She shrugged. "I was very determined to get you back. He most likely did it out of spite."

"Man, that's stupid." I shook my head. "Margaret could have looked the other way or something so I could know you still wanted me."

"I can see why she wouldn't. She could get in trouble I believe if she did let me speak with you."

"There's more to it than that, trust me," I said. "What made you look for me now?"

"The order expired when you turned 18. Legally I could speak to you. However, when I finally got ahold of 'Margaret' she told me she didn't know where you were and to stop contacting her."

I rolled my eyes. A typical Margaret response.

"I was furious. She just lost all traces of you after you aged out?"

"She didn't care, she threw me out."

"What?" my mom shouted, before lowering her voice. "She threw you out?"

I nodded. "She wasn't a nice person. She was abusive. She didn't feed us, she shaved my hair, the only thing she didn't do was put her hands on us. or at least me. I don't know what she's done to other kids behind our back."

"They left you with an abusive person but acted as if I were the abuser?"

"I don't think they knew. She was smart in how she did it."

"I'm going to report her, someone has to."

"She deserves it."

"We're off topic now," she said. "Maya, there's nothing I can do to change the past. But would you forgive me for not being in your life? I would like to from now on."

I didn't know how to respond. Was what she said the truth or was she making it up to feel better about herself? I felt relieved to finally talk to her and clear up what I had been harboring since I was a kid. But I was scared. What if I said yes and she decided she didn't want to stay with me if I screwed something up? At that moment, I understood where a lot of my lack of confidence came from. Feeling like I was rejected by my mom made me distrust everyone. If my own mother didn't care about me, who would? I was afraid of rejection and distanced myself so I wouldn't be hurt again. It was about time I took more risks and opened my heart. Even if it was just a little bit at a time.

I took a deep breath and nodded. "I forgive you."

My mother's face lit up, she reached over and hugged me. I hugged her back that time.

"This might be moving too fast for you," she said, as we sat back down. "Would you like to come live with me? Make up a little of the time we missed together?"

"Thank you, but I want to live on my own, besides, I'm with my foster sister right now. I don't want to separate from her."

"I understand." She smiled. "Let's make sure to keep in contact."

"Okay." I smiled.

I waited outside while my mom paid for lunch.

"Alright," she said, hurrying out of the diner. She smiled and sighed. "This is goodbye, I guess. At least for now."

"Yeah, we'll stay in touch."

"Of course we will. I'll hunt you down if you stop talking to me."

I laughed awkwardly.

"Do you have a job? Where are you working."

"I'm part time at a friend's cleaning service. It's temporary… until I can find a better job."

"Okay. And where are you staying right now?"

"I'm at an Airbnb in Queen—"

Before I could finish, my mom interrupted, "An Airbnb?! Are you homeless right now? You and your foster sister can stay at my place until you find an apartment."

"Thank you, but I'm not homeless," I chuckled. "Um, I have an apartment, it's just…I just got out of a bad breakup with someone that also lived there. I—"

"Is he harassing you?"

"No, nothing like that. Just, I didn't want to have to talk to him," I said. "So I subleased my apartment until I go back."

"Well Maya," my mom said, reaching into her purse. She took her wallet out and a stack of money.

"No." I defensively threw my hands in front of me. "I don't need anything."

"I don't care." She grabbed my hands and placed the money on my palm. Holding my hand gently, she said, "This is for you. Spend it on rent or whatever you want."

"Mom, I don't need it."

She smiled widely. "That's the first time you called me 'mom' since we got here. Take it, it's the least I can do. Go shopping and get something cute, I don't know. Just take care of yourself."

"I will." I put the money in my wallet. "I'm glad I finally know what really happened."

"Good, I'm happy you forgave me."

We hugged one last time before parting ways. As I walked to the station, I felt a rush of relief. I felt a lot lighter, like someone took 50 lbs. weights off my chest. The world seemed brighter. And I'm sorry what I said may seem overdramatic, but that's what it felt like. I finally figured out what was holding me down.

When I got back to the Airbnb, I was excited to tell Anna everything, from the moment I arrived to how I felt on the way home.

"I'm happy for you," Anna said, hugging me. "I told you there was probably some kind of misunderstanding."

"Yeah. I feel like a new person kind of…. Sorry, I'm being corny."

"How?" she laughed.

"'Cause I'm overreacting."

"Not at all, I would actually be worried if you weren't acting this way."

"I suppose it's normal…."

"I just can't get over Margaret, that dumb bitch."

"My mom said it was because she could get in trouble."

Anna scoffed, "As if she cared about that."

"I guess," I mumbled. "I mean, she had to get in as many jabs as she could. She's so evil. I'm going to report her to foster care. She doesn't deserve to take care of those kids. I don't think she spent a penny of that money she got on us."

"See, I'm all for getting her in trouble," Anna said, as sassy as she could. "But that would separate the kids. I'm pretty sure they're as close as we were to each other."

"I know, but they deserve to be in a safe and loving environment. They'll still stay in contact if they wanted to."

"I guess…" Anna reluctantly gave up.

She knew I was right. I was going to call on Monday. Margaret was nothing but added stress to kids in foster care. It was about time one of us stood up and said something.

"Well, since your mom gave you a shit ton of money…" Anna rolled onto her back. "We should go shopping."

"She said to use this on something I need."

"No. You said, your mom said, 'spend it on whatever you want, even clothing.'"

"She said go shopping not buy clothing."

"Same shit." She rolled her eyes. "You feel like a 'new person' right? Let's change your wardrobe to fit the new you."

"I don't know Anna. That's so cliché."

"Come on," she whined. "We said we would do something if you met her today. I wanna go shopping!"

"Anna…"

"Pleaassee. I barely got to do anything since I got here. Just move into this place and walk around."

"We didn't just walk around." I rolled my eyes. "Touring the city isn't just 'walking around.'"

"That's what it feels like. Let's go to some designer stores."

I sighed. There was no winning against Anna when she wanted something. "Fine, let's go tomorrow morning. Is that fine with you?"

"Totally." Anna got up. "Well go to sleep then. We're getting up early."

Anna got dressed and opened the door.

"Where are you going?"

"Nowhere." She looked awkwardly. "I'm just going to the store. I want some snacks."

"Want me to come with?"

"No it's fine. I won't be that long." Anna scurried out the room slamming the door shut.

I wonder what she's really doing, I thought.

That was like the 10th time Anna did something shady since coming to New York. I knew she had some huge secret she wasn't sure she could tell me, but I wasn't going to push it. She would tell me in time, I was certain of it. I wondered if she had a boyfriend, but she wouldn't hide that. She was open about her relationships. I felt kind of guilty. Yeah, I said she would tell me in time, but I was really curious. I didn't have much going on in my life. I needed some kind of action.

I changed into my pajamas and snuggled into bed. It was way too early to go to sleep, why did Anna urge me to? I didn't have anything else to do, I decided to watch videos on my phone until Anna came back, then we could watch a movie.

As I played a mobile game, I got a text from my mom, "Did you get home safely?"

"Yes," I replied right away.

"Great! Do you have any plans for today?"

"Not really, probably watch movies with my sister when she gets back."

"That sounds fun! I was just checking on you. I'll leave you alone now."

"You're not bothering me but have a good evening."

"Thank you, sweetie. Bye."

"Bye."

I couldn't wrap my head around speaking to her. It felt weird. Especially because I held so much resentment for her over a decade. Over time, I hoped I would feel comfortable.

After about two hours of watching whatever videos popped up, Anna returned. "What took you so long?"

"Huh?" she said, confused.

I laughed. "What do you mean 'huh'? You went to the store for snacks two hours ago. You don't even have anything."

"I put them in the kitchen…."

"You know we aren't supposed to do that. We have a fridge and dresser in here."

"Well I ate them then. I was hungry."

"I know you're hiding something and I'm fine with that. But you gotta make sure you don't leave any holes in what you say."

"Sorry Maya," Anna said, sitting on the end of the bed. "I'm just not ready yet."

"You don't have to tell me what it is, let me know when you're ready. No rush."

"Ok."

"Well, if you don't have anything else planned, let's watch some movies. It's way too early to sleep."

"Yeah, I don't mind. What are we going to watch?"

"I didn't plan that much."

Anna pursed her lips and said, "Let's…just see what's on…"

We spent 10 minutes scrolling through movies and finally decided on two. A romance and a rom-com. It was dreadful to watch. They reminded me of the mess my love life was. I still couldn't believe I wasn't over him. Yeah, a few weeks had passed but surely that was enough time… right? Anna also looked uneasy. I didn't ask why, but it confirmed she had problems with a relationship. Maybe she was being considerate of my feelings and didn't want to talk about her issues. One thing was for sure, hell froze over because Anna had fallen in love.

The next morning, we sluggishly got up. This seemed more like a chore than a day out. I wanted to sleep for another 2 hours, but I knew Anna would throw a fit. We got dressed and headed to Manhattan. My mom gave me $700. Which was a lot of money, but it wasn't enough to have a whole day of shopping. Unless we shopped at cheaper, nation-wide stores, not the designer stores Anna wanted.

"Let's go in there." Anna pointed.

It was a very…bright and colorful store… "I didn't know you liked stores like these."

"Not for me, you. This is your makeover day." Anna pulled me into the store.

"Come on Anna," I groaned. "I prefer darker colors. Except the few pieces I have from when Makayla and I went shopping."

"Yeah, and you looked super cute. You don't fit the goth emo look you're going for. You don't even wear all black. It's like you're part wannabe goth but afraid of goth kids."

"I'm not afraid of them, I just like wearing darker clothing…. I'm not even goth."

"Eh, I disagree." Anna dragged me through the aisles. "It's your insecurities, desperation and fear of change that's causing you to think you want to wear them."

"We got therapist Anna over here." I rolled my eyes.

"You know I'm right." Anna let go of me and started looking through a rack. I did the same next to her. "You're afraid of change, and until someone gives you that push, you'll stay in that little comfort bubble."

"Wow, that's kinda deep…"

"Yeah, I know. I've lowkey been thinking of applying to college here and going into Psychology. Ya know, help people like us."

"What college?"

"I don't know, like CUNY or something."

"I mean you have amazing grades, so I'm sure you could get into any of them. What made you want to do this?"

"Just to help people. I was talking to my friend, and she helped me realize that's what I want to do." Anna pulled out a frilly dress. "This is sooo you."

"You're funny," I said, sarcastically. "I'm glad you found what you want to do with your future."

"Yeah."

We looked around some more. It was a medium sized store, so it wasn't that difficult to go through. I kept Anna's advice on keeping an open mind, got a few cheap skirts that looked cute. The tops were too much, I wasn't that ready to leave my "comfort bubble." I needed long sleeves or at the bare minimum, short sleeves *without frills*. Anna found a dress for her friend, but I reminded her to pick out things for herself.

We moved from store to store buying outfits I never would have worn two months ago. We even bought business suits. Just an array of styles I would try over the summer. I bought makeup and jewelry, different kinds of shoes from my favorite, sneakers, to business shoes and heels. It wasn't healthy to force myself to do things I wasn't ready for, but I just needed to go for it. I was too scared otherwise. There was a first for everything and everyone must step out their comfort zone at some point.

We finished shopping. I decided to save the last $200 for emergencies. When we got home, we searched makeup tutorials and I studied which ways worked for me. I kept it simple, just eyeliner, mascara, and lip stick. Other styles were overpowering, and I didn't look like myself.

We spent the night trying on different styles of clothing. We laughed when we wore the business suits. I don't know why it was funny, but we were just being silly, plus it was weird wearing them. It didn't suit either of us. Anna's grunge style to my "wannabe goth" style.

Overall I was glad I went out with Anna. Something that felt like a chore became a fun experience. No matter how cliché it might have felt.

A week went by, and I had an idea. While Anna was working on my "transformation," we also needed to celebrate her graduation from high school. That last week of school with finals was chaotic for her. We still didn't know if they were going send her diploma to her adoptive parents or if the request to send it to Valery and Carmen's house was accepted. Regardless, she worked hard to get to where she was, and it was sad she didn't get the chance to walk the stage with her friends and classmates. It wasn't fair she missed an important part of finishing school.

That's where my idea hit. Since she couldn't enjoy the fun of graduation, I was going to see if Carmen, Valery, and Makayla were up for doing our own graduation ceremony. It would take a lot of planning, and it would be difficult to do in our home.

They were all for it. So Valery set up a cleaning job for Anna to do by herself and we met up for a plan. We talked for hours on what to do. We would do the graduation walk at Makayla's theatre club. They were able to book the stage even during the summer with professor approval. She could get us 30 minutes of their practicing time to do the ceremony part on Thursday, 2 days away. Then we would go to Bowne Park for a picnic and celebration.

Makayla and I bought the balloons, cake, a fake diploma prop, drinks, and a present for her. We were buying separate gifts. I also bought a cap and gown. It wasn't an official one from her school, but I saw Anna looking at photos of her friends at graduation and I remembered the color. If it wasn't so last minute, I would have invited her friends, but there was no way they could afford a last-minute flight to New York. Not to mention, the cost of a hotel and whatever else they would need all for one day, not even, a few hours. Makayla was going to keep all the party accessories and bring them to her club.

Carmen and Valery were going to cook a picnic for Anna. How they were going to do it without her noticing was another thing, but the idea was fun.

Thursday came around…finally, and I woke Anna up at 8 AM to get ready.

"Why?" she complained.

"I'll tell you when we get there." I pulled Anna out of bed. "Dress nicely, comfy but kinda formal."

She got dressed mumbling under her breath. She put on a white crop tank top and a long maroon skirt that went to her ankles and sandals.

"Nothing nicer?" I asked.

Anna gave me look and I dropped the subject. I wasn't gonna force her to wear anything she didn't want to. She was grumpier than I was in the morning. I put on a floral dress with mid-sleeves and went down to my knees.

The train ride to NYU, Anna kept her eyes close. I felt bad making her wake up, but she would, hopefully, like the reason later. We met up with Valery. She carried the bag with Anna's cap and gown, and we led her to the bathroom. We told her to put on what was in the bag and meet us by the front doors of the auditorium.

While she put it on, I ran to check on everything else. It looked amazing. They put the balloons on the first few seats, Makayla's club members were sitting in the audience, there was a podium and Carmen waited behind it. She was the one who would hand Anna the diploma.

"This looks great! Thanks for all your help," I said.

"It's no problem at all," Makayla said. "Unfortunately, a few of our members are gonna be late so it's not as big a crowd as I hoped."

"It's okay. They're more than enough. I appreciate you guys giving us part of your rehearsal time."

"It's all good. We just gotta hurry before the director comes. She'll be here at 10 to check on us."

"Okay. We'll hurry up. Are you still able to come to the park with us?"

"Yeah, I can. I won't be able to stay long though."

"That's alright."

Anna tapped the door. "Can I come in?"

"Not yet," I said, running to the door. I went out making sure she didn't see anything inside. I smiled when I saw her in her gown.

"What are you guys doing?" she asked.

"Exactly what it looks like."

"Where did you get this from?"

"Bought it. Now no more questions." I tapped on the door and peeked inside. "Ready?"

Carmen nodded and everyone went into their seats.

"Okay. Close your eyes."

"Maya…"

"Just close them," I demanded.

Anna closed her eyes and put out her hands. I took them and carefully guided her into the auditorium. I stopped just in front of the steps and told Anna to open her eyes. Her eyes widened as she looked from me to the students in the audience and to Carmen waiting for her on stage.

"I don't know what to say…" she stuttered.

"It's alright. We know how hard you worked to graduate. Graduation is an important part of life. You deserve the right to walk just as much as everyone else."

Anna cried. "I wanted to walk on stage."

I hugged Anna. I whispered, "I know."

Anna gained composure after a while. She laughed. "I wish you would've told me. I could've worn something prettier."

"Shoulda listened," I teased. "When you're ready, head-on stage. I'll be sitting up front."

"Can you record?" Anna asked, handing me her phone.

"Sure. I was gonna record on mine, but you can just send me the video."

"Yeah."

Anna waited until I was sitting and recording, she nodded to Carmen she was ready.

"Anna Davis," Carmen shouted.

The crowd erupted into cheers. Anna smiled and walked up the steps. She took her time walking to Carmen, waving at the audience and at the camera, she shook Carmen's hand with her right hand and took the diploma with her left. Carmen said something to Anna, and Anna walked off stage.

"Is it always this fast?" she asked, sitting next to me.

"No, it's annoyingly long, so you were saved from the hours of waiting to call your name," I said.

"I don't mind either way."

"So anything you wanna say to the camera?" I pointed her phone at her.

"I did it. Hi everyone. Fuck you Max, fuck you, Jane." Anna laughed and took her phone. "Thank you, Maya."

"No problem. But we aren't done yet."

"What do you mean?"

"Your graduation party. Well, not really a party but we have something else planned."

"Nothing embarrassing right?"

"…Maybe."

Anna rolled her eyes.

We took pictures in the auditorium. We thanked the theatre club and headed to Bowne Park. There was an area a few feet from the pond. We sat our picnic blanket down and our belongings. We took a few more pictures because Bowne Park was beautiful and sat down to eat. A smile never left Anna's face.

Feeling accomplished with Anna's graduation, it was time to move to the next step in my "changed" life. Finding a job. But I was terrible at searching for one. I wish schools taught us basic life skills instead of useless classes we wouldn't use in everyday life. I thought about asking for help, but I felt it was time I stopped relying so heavily on those around me. Otherwise, I would've never learned.

I got online and looked for openings in the Queens area. If I could find something close, that would've been a blessing. It was weird that there weren't many places hiring. There were a few restaurant openings, but I didn't want a minimum waged job. It wasn't cheap living in New York, and I had to provide for Anna until she found a job too. It was hard, I wasn't in college, I had barely any experience outside of waiting tables and a few months cashiering. Loue's paid a decent salary but that was definitely out of the question. Out of curiosity, I searched Loue's to see if they were hiring. Of course, they were. It wasn't much of a surprise. He barely had employees that lasted longer than 2 months. Why they all left was beyond me. He was a good boss, pay was good for a grocery store, I doubt they would find a place more accommodating. I wasn't one to talk though.

I spent about an hour searching. I didn't want to just sit at my laptop all day looking. I was impatient. I would just need to spend maybe an hour a day looking. There wasn't much of a rush anyways. I had enough money, and I was working for Carmen. Even if it wasn't much, paychecks were paychecks.

I texted my mom. *Some* help wasn't bad. "Hey mom, if you know of any places hiring with good pay can you let me know?"

She replied right away, "Of course. I'll help you look for some job openings. Do you need money? I can send you some."

"No, I don't need it. I just need to find a better paying job. I go back to my apartment in like 2 months. So I want to be able to comfortably afford rent and still have spending money."

"Okay, that's a good way to focus on your finances. I'm still at work, so I must go. But I will look."

I texted bye. I hated asking for help, especially asking her. Not because I still held resentment for her. I was ecstatic that I could have a good relationship with her. I just felt like it was too soon for me to ask her for certain things. Regardless of her being my mom, we just rekindled after 14 years. I didn't think it was appropriate. What if she wasn't fine with it? But at that point I was desperate for a job. If she didn't want to help, she would just say she couldn't find one and move on, I wouldn't ask her to continue searching. I was an adult now. I didn't have the luxury to ask my parent for help. If I were still a kid when we met again, I would be more comfortable, but not at 19.

I put my laptop away as Anna came into the room. She was texting, not actually looking where she was going, and taking bites out of a granola bar. She sat on the bed, still not looking at me.

"Texting your friend?" I asked. I wanted to tease her, but I didn't want her to shy away from whatever relationship she was getting in.

"No."

I pursed my lips. It was a little awkward watching her text so intensely. "Who are you texting then?"

"Jane." She stopped texting and looked at me. "She's refusing to send me my diploma. She's yelling at me for 'seducing' Max. Apparently, my teachers contacted CPS and they're investigating what happened. Now Max is divorcing her, and she thinks I had some kind of hand in it. I'm just so tired of this. She's saying after all she did to provide me with a good life, I could do her like that. But I didn't choose to be adopted by them. I didn't *choose* to have a fucking creepy ass father and a mother that's ignorant and in denial." She went back to texting again.

"Block her. You don't owe her anything. She can't hold that over your head. She chose to adopt a child. Just because she did, doesn't mean you have to take any verbal or physical abuse from them. You can request another diploma."

"*Two* people have complaints about the same thing. *Two*," Anna continued. She was so upset I didn't think she heard what I said. "At some point you would think she would admit he's a fucking problem. Who knows how many children they've adopted that he's harassed?"

"Exactly. In a way, because Jane hasn't done anything to stop him, she's getting her karma. And his will follow soon. Just tell her to fuck off and block her number. You don't deserve how she's treating you, and she isn't entitled to a response."

"You're right. I'm wiping my hands clean of them. I'll block them both until I can change my number."

Anna sighed. She cupped her face and cried.

"Anna," I said. I hugged her. I didn't know what to say to her. My heart hurt seeing her upset. "Everything's going to be alright. You're here with me and surrounded by amazing people. You have your friend, there's so much going on here, you have a lot ahead of you. Don't let these losers stop you from living your best life."

Anna nodded, still resting her head on my chest. We sat there for 10 minutes. Just me calming her down.

Anna rested her head in my lap and said, "Uh, since we're here..."

"What is it?"

She paused. She didn't say anything. She looked at the bed and fiddled with her phone, tapping the screen. "Since I'm already sad, I guess this is a good time to say this..."

I didn't respond. I just waited for her to tell me what she wanted to say. It was weird for her to say, "Since I'm already sad." What did she think she would tell me that would upset her?

"I…I'm dating a girl…"

"Oh…" I said. I wasn't expecting that.

She continued still not looking at me, tears streamed down her face again. "My friend, the one I've been telling you about is actually my girlfriend. We've been dating for two months. I really love her. She's so beautiful and smart, I…. You aren't saying anything, are you mad?"

I mean, I wasn't mad. I just didn't know how to respond. I didn't care if she dated a man, woman, or a non-binary person. I just didn't know what to say. After a bit of time I said, "I'm not mad. You love who you love. Doesn't matter what gender they are. I told you I would never hate you, no matter what you told me, and there's nothing wrong with being lesbian. I think I'm more shocked by you dating someone for two months and loving them, than you coming out."

Anna laughed. "I know, it's crazy. Even I don't understand it. But there's just something about her that makes me happy. you know?"

I nodded. "It's understandable. I was like that with Daniel. It's an inexplicable feeling… the way they make you feel. I'm just glad you told me. I've been trying my best not to be nosy."

Anna wiped her tears and sat up. "I'm sorry for keeping it from you. I just didn't know how to tell you."

"Don't be. That's something that can't be said easily. I know you didn't wanna hide it, but you were worried. At the end of the day, I'm glad you felt comfortable enough to tell me. What's her name?"

"Tiana."

"That's a pretty name."

"Yeah, it is. I was thinking of inviting her here once one of the rooms was available."

"Do it. If you wanna see her, this is a good time to."

"Okay. You'll love her."

"If you love her, I know I will too." I smiled. "Just don't be too lovey-dovey. I still have a shitty love life right now."

"I'll try my best."

I was happy Anna finally told me her secret. She'd been wanting to tell me this I think since she last visited. It was probably a huge weight off her chest. I still couldn't fathom her loving anyone though. She protested it since she was a kid, but there she was, head over heels. I never thought the day would come or at least not until she was in her mid-twenties. I kind of suspected she was dealing with romance by how she'd been acting. But I didn't think I would be right.

We spent the rest of the night talking about Anna's girlfriend. Anna's face was bright, and her eyes sparkled with each mention of Tiana's name.

CHAPTER TEN

I was stressed. I still couldn't find a job. It was the last week of June, and my search was going nowhere. I got on my laptop and searched for jobs. I knew I shouldn't have been picky, but I just didn't want some of these jobs. They looked like too much work and didn't pay well enough. I felt incompetent, the decent jobs I did manage to find, I had some ok interviews but never got a call back. It was pointless.

For a while, I was honestly contemplating going back to Loue's. I knew I would get hired easily, and with some negotiating I could even up my pay. But I just couldn't face Daniel. I couldn't stand seeing him and Jessica flirt in my face. I definitely was *not* going to let that happen, I was humiliated enough.

Everywhere else in my life was swell. Anna was comfortable telling me more and more about Tiana, Makayla was hanging out with us more, she was on summer break, she hung out with Carmen and Valery almost every day after theatre, then before leaving, she would come and talk with us.

It felt great having so many people to hang out with. It was crazy that a year ago, I was alone in my apartment binge watching movies. It felt surreal.

As I wallowed in self-pity over not getting a job, my mom called me. "Are you still looking for a job?"

"Yeah. I can't really find anything that pays enough."

"Well, I was speaking with a good friend of mine. He owns a cosmetics company and is looking for new hires in the sales department. I told him about you. If you're interested, he's offering a paid internship. Depending on how well you perform, you could be hired full time."

"That sounds amazing." I was shocked. Who knew my luck was getting better? I was frustrated that I couldn't find the job myself, but

I took where help was offered, and this was a great opportunity. "Is it okay that I don't have a degree?"

"I told him you were 19. He prefers employees with a degree or some experience. But sales doesn't require a degree. He's willing to look past you not having one if you work hard."

"Oh my gosh. Thank you!"

"Of course. It's the least I can do," she said, softly. "I'll text you his business number. His name is Oscar Robinson. *Call* him. Don't text. Alright?"

"Alright."

"Let's go out to dinner sometime. You and your sister. It'll be my treat."

"Yeah, let's do that. I have to check with Anna what time she's available."

"I have to get back to work. Let me know when you two can, and I can set up a reservation. Bye hun."

"Okay. Bye."

I sat my phone down. Who knew my luck would turn like that? My mother was a saint. I knew she was going above and beyond to make up for the years we were apart. She explained everything to me, I understood, and I forgave her. She didn't have to keep trying to prove she was a dedicated mother. I was opening my heart to her each day regardless of how much she did for me. My mom texted me his number. I was a little nervous. I didn't know how I should speak to him. I didn't want to sound inept.

I dialed the number and a woman picked up. "Vlosam Cosmetics, Deena speaking."

"Hi, I would like to speak with Oscar Robinson."

"May I ask who's speaking?"

"I'm Maya Anderson."

"Do you have an appointment with him? I'm not seeing you on his schedule."

"Uh. My mother and Oscar Robinson spoke about me. He's expecting my call."

"…One second, let me see what I can do."

I waited on the phone for 3 minutes listening to that one song I have no idea what the name is, but it's played on almost every companies' hold line. Deena came back to the phone.

"Hi, Ms. Anderson?"

"Yes."

"Generally, you need to schedule an appointment. Even over the phone. Mr. Robinson is going to overlook it this time. But in the future, please call ahead and schedule with me. Okay?"

"Ok. Thanks."

The line clicked and I was back to the waiting music. I was about to start humming it before the line clicked again.

"Oscar Robinson, how can I help you?" His voice was deep.

"Hello. I'm Maya Anderson. My mom… Angela told me about the sales internship."

"Ah yes. Hi Maya. Angela told me a lot of wonderful things about you. Are you interested in the position?"

"Yes."

"Great. What would you like to know?"

"Um, how much does it pay?"

"What do you think you should be paid?"

"Maybe $16 an hour?"

"A full-time employee in our sales department makes on average $19 an hour. How about we start you at $17.50?"

"Y-yeah, that definitely works with me. So what kind of work would I do?"

"There's a lot. To name a few, our employees sell products to businesses and customers, look for potential buyers and answer questions. I'm not quite sure what they'll want you to do, but as an intern, I'm sure they won't give you anything too difficult."

"Okay. When can I start?"

"Let's see…" he trailed off. I could hear him flipping through pages. "I would say 2 weeks from now. As a formality you will still need to go through an interview process with the head of sales. What time are you available?"

"Any time."

He mumbled to himself, "Next Monday is the 4th of July, so she'll be out of town…. Then I will put you down for next Friday at 11 AM. Sound good?"

"Yes. Thank you for the opportunity."

"Of course. Anything to help."

It was crazy he was willing to give me a chance. I knew my mom had a role in it of course, but I wondered how good of friends they were for him to take a risk with someone so inexperienced. I wasn't complaining though. This was a good job. And being paid $17.50 an hour. I was part time but still, that much money? I was so grateful to them for giving me a shot. I just needed to do well to impress whoever my boss was going to be. They weren't going to be as biased as Mr. Robinson was. I had one business suit and a few somewhat formal dresses.

I was nervous, but I mean, I wasn't going to be denied when the CEO himself, hired me. I was still going to do my best.

It was our last month in Queens. Tiana, Anna's girlfriend… I loved saying that, was visiting the last week of July. Makayla was on break and Carmen took a 2-week vacation. There was a lot planned for that month. The last month before reality was forced on me.

The week prior to the first day of July, Makayla proposed we take a trip to a beach and enjoy the fireworks. I was excited to go. It was my first time at the beach. We would all pitch in for a 3-bedroom Airbnb in Rockaway Beach, where, I had no idea, I was leaving that to Makayla, Carmen, and Valery, as long as it was affordable, no more than $200 a night.

We planned on spending 4 days there. It was last minute, so Valery couldn't take a long vacation from her business. She had already scheduled services for the 6th-15th and I had my interview on the 8th. They managed to find one for $150 in Rockaway Beach, about a mile from the shore. Not even a 20-minute walk. Why it was so cheap was beyond me, but I wasn't complaining. It was better than travelling back 'n forth, and better to feel like a vacation than a day out.

The next issue was a swimsuit. It was the only thing I didn't buy last month. I didn't think I would be swimming any time soon. I needed to find something cute but comfortable.

I asked Anna if she wanted to go swimsuit shopping. Of course Anna said yes. We planned to go the day before our trip.

We went to a cheap store, I wanted us to save up for our half of the Airbnb. Anna protested wanting to go to a major department store, but I couldn't afford it. Anna bought a pastel pink 2 piece. The top had ruffles that went around the body, and the bottom was plain and tied on both sides of the hip. I bought a 2 piece and a cover up. The top and bottom were navy blue, the cover up was lace black, it hung like a poncho that covered down to mid-thigh. Anna was trying to convince me to show my body off, but I wasn't comfortable. I was sure it was going to be cold. We quickly packed and went to bed.

When we reached the home, it was smaller than the picture. It still looked nice though. We didn't have to meet the homeowner. He left the key in the mailbox with a note. Valery read as we walked into the house.

"'Thanks for choosing my home. I'm also on vacation so perfect timing for both of us. Unfortunately, a few days before your arrival, the kitchen sink stopped working. So I suggest getting bottled water.' You'd think he would tell us about this before we arrived," Valery complained. "'Everything else is working fine, hot water runs out quickly. That's about it. Enjoy your vacation. – Frank.' Welp, Carmen, want to go with me to get water?"

"Sure," Carmen said, setting their bags down. "There's a room with a double bed, that's for me and Val. You girls can choose from the other two rooms, they both have 2 beds."

"Okay," we said in unison.

After they left, we checked out the home. It was a ranch home. When you first entered the house, there was a short hallway and 2 steps at the end, once you went past the steps, the living room was small, there was one large navy-blue couch, and two armchairs on both sides, a flatscreen in the middle, there was a black circle metal coffee table. If you looked to the right, the kitchen was in the corner and a hallway just before it.

We were indifferent to who got what room. Me and Anna chose the room at the end of the hall. Makayla and Carmen and Valery's rooms were opposite each other in the hall.

In our room, there were two twin beds, a dresser, and a closet to the left of the door. The walls were turquoise, and the bedding was navy blue covers and pillowcases. The room was plain, but the bed was comfortable.

After Carmen and Valery came back, we spent the first night unpacking food, clothes, and ended the night with a movie.

The next day, Anna and I were woken up at 8 AM, why it was necessary for us to wake up that early was beyond me.

"What do you need?" Anna asked, dazed.

"Nothing, let's get up now, eat and head to the beach," Carmen said.

"It's only 8, it'll be too cold," I chimed in.

"We won't leave until like 9:30 or so. Valery and Makayla are making breakfast right now. You two are the only ones still sleeping."

"Okay." I yawned. "We'll get ready and help with breakfast."

"Alright," Carmen said, closing the door.

Anna groaned, "Who has a schedule on vacation?"

"Them." I laughed.

We got ready and went into the kitchen to help. Most of it was already cooked. They only needed us to put plates on the table. They made scrambled eggs, pancakes topped with whip cream and blueberries, sausages, and bacon.

After breakfast we changed into our swimsuits, grabbed everything we needed and walked to the beach. We got there at 10 AM just as the beach opened. It was almost empty. Only a few others were there and far away from where we were. I stabbed my umbrella into the sand, set up my towel underneath it and lay down. I didn't want to get in the water yet. I was going to let them test the water temperature first. It was still cold, I could hear them screaming as they went in. I laughed and closed my eyes. It was peaceful. The sound of the waves was relaxing. I took a deep breath, taking in the smell of the water and the cool breeze gently caressing my skin.

Anna shook me awake. "Maya! Geez, you've been sleep for like 10 minutes."

"Really?" I sat up and rubbed my eyes. The beach had more people on it. Almost 5x the number of groups before.

"Let's go in the water."

"Is it still cold?"

"Not really. It's warmer."

I looked around the beach, I didn't see the others. "Where'd they go?"

"Huh? Oh they went to get some food. They'll be back."

"Okay." I stood up and went to the shore. The waves hit my legs and I trembled. It was *not* warmer. Anna had gotten used to the temperature. "Nope."

As I turned to run away, Anna grabbed my arm and pulled. "Come on, it's gonna be cold when you first go in. Let's have fun before it gets even more crowded."

"Fine." I sighed. I walked deeper into the water. I was waist deep and shivering. I squatted to cover my entire body in the water and came back up.

"See it's not that bad," Anna teased.

I splashed her and swam away.

We played in the water for another 20 minutes then spent the rest of the time looking around the boardwalk. We headed back to the Airbnb later that afternoon. We watched some movies, then went out for ice cream. Valery and Carmen went on a date while me, Anna, and Makayla hung out in our room.

"I never asked," Anna said, changing the subject. We were originally talking about scenes in movies we hated while playing a card game called Jackass. "Makayla, do you have a boyfriend?"

I looked at Makayla. I never thought about it. I barely knew anything about her except that she went to NYU and was majoring in theatre.

Makayla looked awkward then said, "Well, we aren't really dating but I am talking with a guy."

"Oh?" Anna moved closer. "What does he look like?"

"Tall…" Makayla replied.

"And?" I said.

"And he has short hair."

"And?" Anna and I said in unison. I could tell Makayla didn't really want to say much about him. But I just wanted to tease her a bit and then leave her alone.

"And he has green eyes, muscular, he's also in theatre. Um, there really isn't much else I know. We talk randomly, sometimes he'll ask me to come over, and I don't know. We aren't dating, I'm honestly not all that interested in him."

"Why don't you break it off?" I asked.

"I can't tell you," she said.

"Okay," I said. I saw Anna about to keep pushing and I softly kicked her, while Makayla wasn't looking. "I hope your situation gets better."

"Me too," Makayla said, dully. "Me too…."

After a while, I broke the silence and said, "Anna did you talk with Tiana about coming to New York?"

"Yeah, so far she doesn't need much. We're still waiting for other guests to leave, then Carmen and Valery are going to let us know if she can take a room."

"That's good. And I'll have a whole room to myself again for a week."

Anna scoffed, "Don't get used to it."

It was quiet again. Makayla was still brooding over whatever her situation was. I wished she would tell us and rant about it. But it was her life and if she wasn't comfortable saying anything, then there was nothing I could do. Anna, however, didn't catch on to not talking about it again.

"Are you sure you're alright?" she asked.

"Yeah really." She didn't look up at us.

"I mean, we're friends, right? No matter what the situation is, we're not going to judge you or laugh at whatever's going on."

"She's right," I chimed in. "You don't have to tell us if you don't want to but just know we aren't gonna look at you any different. I mean I told y'all every step of my mess with Daniel. I doubt it could be worse than that."

"It's way worse," Makayla said. She took a deep breath and said, "Okay, I'll tell you. But please don't tell Valery and especially not Carmen."

"I promise," I said.

"I won't." Anna shook her head.

"Well this has been going on for a few months now. The guy I'm talking about caught me changing my grade in one of my classes. Everyone was gone and my professor left herself logged in," Makayla said. She noticed the shocked look on our faces and said defensively, "I normally don't do things like this! But that teacher has been harassing me for the last 3 semesters. She's the only teacher that teaches these classes so I couldn't avoid her. This was a gender studies class and I needed it to graduate in the fall. She was constantly giving me bad grades even though my answers were right. She'd already failed me once."

"Why didn't you report it to the school?" I asked.

"I did the first semester she gave me a C, but they defended her and not me, so I had to do this."

She continued, "And I was the last one to leave so I just changed a few assignments and boosted myself from a D to an AB. He came in from the other door and caught me. Since, he's been threatening to tell if I don't date him. I have one semester left. If I get caught, I'm going to get kicked out, as well as whatever charges they'll sue me for."

"That's why you don't want to tell Carmen," Anna said.

Makayla nodded. "I just have to put up with it a bit longer until I graduate then I can block him and move on with my life."

"Damn," I said. I had no idea how to help her without getting her caught for changing her grade.

"So yeah… we aren't dating. I don't like him, but I'm stuck with him until December. Hopefully, he'll lose interest in me before then."

"Sorry for making you tell us," I said.

"No, don't be. It feels good to tell someone else. At least now I have you guys to rant to whenever something happens."

"Of course you do," Anna said.

We heard the front door open and quickly started playing Jackass again. Carmen and Valery came into our room, and we all played card games until it was late. Carmen and Valery left first. Makayla thanked us once more then went to bed herself.

It rained the third day of the trip, so we all just hung out in our rooms, Makalya hopped from room to room until settling in ours and talking more.

It was our last day at Rockaway Beach. It was the 4th of July and there was an event on the beach. It was crowded like usual. The sidewalks leading to the boardwalk were filled with parents and their children playing with sparklers and other fireworks. The designated barbeque area was packed. We swam for a bit and walked around the boardwalk. It seemed more crowded than usual. So we decided to come back in the night when the fireworks were happening.

We had fun even at the Airbnb. We bought a bunch of fireworks like sparklers on the way home and played in the yard for hours, going in and out for popsicles. When night came, we walked back to the beach. The fireworks had already started but we didn't miss much. I put my towel on the sand and lay down to watch the fireworks. It had been a long time since I saw them.

I didn't know why, but whenever I had to leave somewhere, I felt sad. We were only there 4 days but thinking about going back made me sad. I liked staying with Valery and Carmen, but soon, I would be going back to my apartment. Back to seeing him…. Those 4 days would be something I treasured forever, simple, or not.

I sighed as I grabbed my luggage and left the room. It was time to head back to Flushing, Queens. 4 days just wasn't enough, but me and Valery still had work related things to do.

When we arrived at home, I plopped on the bed and sighed. I hated travelling. Anything longer than 20 minutes was too much. We still had a lot of fun things to do in July, but I felt like I needed to get my priorities straight. Which sadly meant studying a bit about sales and what was required of the job.

After I reenergized, I got on my laptop and searched "what do sales employees do"? It seemed like a lot of work. The part that stood out to me the most was the fact that I had to speak to clients. Well, something that job would do was improve my communication skills…. I wasn't going to back down because of that one flaw. My mom and Mr. Robinson gave me this chance, I wasn't gonna let them down. This was also a good way to prove to my mom I could do anything.

Besides, it was part time. I wouldn't have to deal with them all day and the first few weeks would most likely be training. They wouldn't risk putting someone inexperienced with potential clients.

I looked into what sales did then retired for the night. I had 1 and a half days left until the interview. Sleep was more important.

It was Friday and I made sure to arrive at 10:45 AM, just to be safe, and possibly leave the impression I arrive early to work. The building was only 4 stories high. When I arrived at Vlosam, the atmosphere was intimidating. I was overwhelmed with how busy it was. I cautiously walked to the receptionist.

"Excuse me," I said. "I have an interview with the sales department."

He stopped typing, looked up at me and went back to typing. "Name?"

"Maya Anderson."

"Thank you," he said, still typing. "Okay, take the elevator to your right to the 2nd floor. Sales will be the third door down."

"Okay, thank you."

"You're welcome, good luck."

I reached the 2nd floor and went to the sales door. I knocked and opened it. It was dead silent, I could hear faint typing, maybe someone whispering, I didn't mind the silence. I wouldn't have to talk.

"Excuse me," I whispered. Most of the office looked at me. "I have an interview at 11."

"You're early," a woman at a desk separate from the others said loudly. It could have also been in her regular voice, but the silence amplified everything. She was focused on her computer. She looked like she was in her mid to late 40s. Her hair was blonde, gray hairs sprinkled randomly. She wore red, thin, rectangular glasses and a blue business suit.

"Sorry. I prefer being early. I can wait."

"No need." She stopped whatever she was doing and looked at me. Her glasses halfway down her nose as she examined me. "Have a seat."

I walked over to her desk, no way she was having the interview there. Everyone would hear my answers. I looked at the name tag on her desk, "Deborah Williams."

"So I see you were already hired by Oscar."

"Yes."

"Hm. Wonder how…." She furtively rolled her eyes, but I was able to see over her monitor. "If he's already hired you, what's the point of this interview?"

"He said for formalities."

"That was a rhetorical question…. Do you have any experience in sales?"

"No. I studied some of the tasks and how sales work in general, but I have never worked in sales."

"Hm. So you need training…" Deborah exhaled furiously. "Just doesn't make sense. When did he say you start?"

"Next week. He didn't give a specific date."

"Of course he didn't. There really isn't a point to this interview… more like a waste of time. You start Monday at 8 AM. I'll create a training video for you. You'll spend all day training. I expect you to understand it without any questions. We aren't going to hold your hand through this."

"I understand."

"Good. That's all. Nothing more to speak about. I have a lot of work."

"Thank you for the opportunity, have a nice day."

"Shouldn't thank me. I wouldn't have given you one," she mumbled, clicking away at her computer again.

I didn't respond. When I left the office, I rolled my eyes. She was a huge bitch for no reason. Prejudging me without even watching me work. And even if was I bad at the job, that didn't mean it was acceptable to be rude.

"Deborah's" disrespectful attitude gave me enough motivation to excel at that job. I wasn't going to let her write me off that easily.

I arrived at the Sales Department at 7:50 AM on Monday. Deborah of course, "scolded" me for arriving "so early." But I wasn't going to arrive exactly at 8 or later, then she would complain about that and use it to get me fired. I had my own cubicle in the corner farthest from the door, facing away from the window. I loved it. There weren't that many people on that side of the office, and I was away from Deborah. I spent all day like she said, watching botched training videos she made. They were all over the place, but I still managed to get the gist of it. The concept was easy. I knew where my problem was. Associating with clients. I needed to come out of my shell, get over my social anxiety.

When my shift was over, Deborah called me to her desk. "Understand it?"

"Yes."

"Huh, okay. Any questions?"

I knew she was setting me up for something. She literally said the other day to not have questions. "Not related to the videos no."

"Then what's your question?"

"When will I have clients?"

"Not for a long time. You aren't even close to ready. Understanding the concepts of sales isn't the same as being good at it."

"When do you think I'll be ready?"

"Who knows, certainly not this month."

"So…what am I supposed to do?"

"Hmm." She tapped a pen on her lips. "I'm going to have you work with Joanne. You'll shadow her for now."

"Okay."

"You're done for the day."

"Do you have a work schedule for me?"

"Nope. I'll have one next week. You're part time, right?"

"Yes."

Deborah took out a notepad and wrote something. "This is your schedule for the week. I'll have someone create a schedule for you soon."

I took the note and said, "Thank you."

When I arrived at home, I flopped on my bed. Anna was relaxing next to me.

"Exhausting day?" she asked.

"Yeah, and my boss is a huge bitch."

"Why?"

"She just is. Like making snide comments every 5 seconds," I said, my face buried in my pillow. "She's salty over Mr. Robinson hiring me with no experience."

"Tough shit," Anna said. "Her boss hired you. Nothing she can do about it."

"Except make my life a living hell until I quit. Or she'll try and get me fired."

"Yeah, but isn't your mom friends with him? She'll just ask him to rehire you."

"I don't want to cause trouble for them. I'll just do my work and be good at it. Leave no room for complaint."

"Is it at least fun?"

"Not in the slightest," I quickly responded, almost cutting her off. "I spent all day watching videos, I have to shadow someone, and worst of all, at some point I'm going to have to talk to people."

"What's wrong with that?"

"Everything. You know I hate talking to strangers. And you know they're gonna expect me to smile and be overly friendly."

"Sucks."

"Yep. But a job's a job. My mom worked hard to get me it. So I'm not gonna complain too much about it."

I read for a few hours then went to sleep at 10 PM. A "grownup's bedtime." I didn't work tomorrow, but it made sense to get used to that sleep schedule. I preferred staying up late into the night though.

On Wednesday, I still came at 7:50 AM. Regardless of how many times Deborah blew a fuse. I punched in and sat at my desk. I waited patiently until whoever Joanne was, showed up.

"Maya," Deborah said, waving me over. A short woman with caramel skin and curly hair down her back was waiting at Deborah's desk. "This is Joanne. Joanne, she'll be shadowing you for the next few weeks."

"Alright." Joanne walked away and motioned for me to follow her. "What's your name?"

"Oh, Maya."

"Like she said, I'm Joanne. I work from the office. Sometimes I meet face to face with clients, but I mostly do online work."

"Okay."

Joanne explained what she was doing, but I spent most of the time just looking over her shoulder. Sometimes she would tell me to do the next client, but Deborah would yell at us. She *really* didn't want me doing anything. It was so annoying. It was boring just looking at Joanne's screen and trying to hear her phone calls. How was this helping anything? And of course, it wasn't Joanne's fault. She was really trying to help me. Deborah was clearly trying to sabotage me. There was no explanation for refusing to let Joanne give me hands-on training. If the task was easy, there was no way I would mess it up.

And all that week, it was a repeat of Joanne trying to train me and Deborah blocking her, *and* Deborah ordered me to get them coffee. Yes, I was technically an intern, but that didn't make me their gopher. I should have been learning the ropes properly. Did I learn anything? A little, but only thanks to Joanne taking lunch breaks with me, away from Deborah and explaining her tasks.

Deborah handed me my schedule for the next few weeks. I only worked Monday, Wednesday and Friday, 8 AM to 4 PM. I didn't mind those hours. But it just felt like Deborah was trying to give me as little hours as possible.

Over time, I was understanding my job more. Deborah still wouldn't let me have my own clients, but she eventually let Joanne train me properly. I had 2 or 3 sales, but Joanne had to convince most of the clients I spoke to, to reconsider their decision and she was able to fix those mistakes. But overall I was a natural.

It was the last week of July and Tiana was coming to visit Anna. They managed to book Carmen and Valery's other room. It was kind of weird sleeping alone. I had gotten so used to sharing a bed with Anna that I stuck to one side of the bed. Tiana wouldn't be arriving until the next day, but Anna wanted to setup a surprise for her. She was so cute. She was excited, Anna had wrapped up all the gifts she'd gotten her over the past 2 months. She bought desserts, and special sodas you could only get in New York, she bought other things but didn't tell me what they were.

I was excited to meet Tiana. I was curious about the type of woman who could make Anna fall so head over heels. This same girl told me day in and day out she didn't believe in love, it was a waste of time, and she would never love anyone. Yet there she was, setting up a romantic surprise for someone.

The next day at noon, Anna went to La Guardia Airport to pick up Tiana. I made sure to wear a nice outfit. I wore a kind of loose-fitting baby blue short sleeved shirt tucked into black flare leggings, I wore blue hoop earrings, I made sure to wear matching socks. First impressions mattered and I didn't want to look sloppy when I saw her.

When they arrived at the Airbnb, I greeted them at the door. Tiana was beautiful. She had long dreads about midback, she wore black glasses and had hazel eyes, her ebony skin was glowing, and she wore the brightest smile. She was absolutely gorgeous. No wonder Anna fell for her.

"Hi Tiana," I said, extending my hand. "I'm Maya."

"It's nice to meet you, Anna told me a lot about you," she said.

"All good things hopefully." I laughed awkwardly.

"Obviously," Anna joined in.

"Do you guys have anything planned for today?" I asked.

"I don't think so," Tiana said, looking at Anna. "I do wanna go sightseeing at some point."

"We can," Anna said bashfully. "I was thinking for today we just chill in the room and catch up. Then for the rest of week we can shop."

Uh-oh there she goes with shopping, I thought. Out loud I said, "There are a lot of great things to see."

"Yeah, we're gonna visit a bunch of places, but I think for now we go up." Anna grabbed one of Tiana's bags and gave her a slight nudge.

"It was nice meeting you. Better follow Anna before she gets too impatient." Tiana grabbed her other suitcase and went upstairs with Anna.

Seeing Anna so lovestruck was funny. All she wanted was for them to be alone, I wasn't offended or anything by her rushing our conversation. Besides, she was Anna's guest, it would be awkward if she hung out with everyone but her.

Neither Carmen nor Valery were home, and they wanted privacy, so I left. I didn't know where to go. I just walked. It was a nice day. The sun was shining, the sky was a beautiful deep sky blue, clouds strolled past ever so often, it was warm. That was the first time in a long time that I was by myself. It felt weird. I was so used to having Anna or the others with me, or surrounded by people at work, that I was uncomfortable being alone. I liked the peaceful atmosphere but at the same time, I felt like something was wrong.

I went to Mama's, but Makayla wasn't there. I figured she was focusing more on her theatre club. I kept walking past. I fell in love with the hectic part of the city, the horrible traffic, impatient drivers, the overcrowded sidewalks, tall buildings, the random gusts of wind and the unfortunate woman who forgot to wear something under her dress, and the lights of time square. Growing up in a small town, when I first came to New York it was overbearing, but now I don't think I could live without it.

I saw a new business being constructed. It didn't say what company was being built, but depending on what it was, I would check it out. It was 2 PM. I thought about going somewhere nice to eat for lunch.

There was a West African restaurant not far from where I was. I decided to go there. It was different from what I normal ate, but I was in the mood to try new things.

It was a small restaurant, there were about 15 tables inside. 5 on both sides of the restaurant and 5 in the middle. There was a map of Africa on the wall, circled in red were the countries the foods were from. I looked at the menu. There was so much to choose from. After a while, I went with Poisson Yassa from Senegal which was fish and onions, from the description on the menu, it was marinated with lemon and other seasoning. I ordered Eddoe Soup from Liberia, which was eddoe, a vegetable that kind of tasted like potatoes, I'd never heard of it until then so that was the best way to describe it. The eddoe was cooked with hot peppers, onions, garlic, and fish, it was spicy. And then Moin-Moin from Nigeria. Moin-Moin was a pudding made with black-eyed beans (or honey beans), seasonings, red peppers, and onions. I wasn't expecting the large portions. It was too much to eat, but I made sure to try each dish.

Satisfied, I was going to ask for the check when I heard my name. I looked behind me and Deborah and Mr. Robinson were being seated. They hadn't noticed me. I hunched over and continued eating, taking small bites of the Yassa.

"Why would you hire her?" Deborah whined.

"Because I think she has potential," he said, confidently.

"Not even close. She doesn't understand anything, she doesn't pay attention when I train her, she's too young and inexperienced to work with me."

My mouth dropped, to think she would stoop so low.

"I think you need to give her a shot. You're too cynical. You can't expect her to learn when her teacher isn't trying to teach her."

"I do my best at my job! But she just doesn't get it. You're more ruthless than I am when it comes to firing incompetent workers. So why are you defending her?"

"If you must know," Mr. Robinson paused, and sighed. "I'm friends with her mother. I'm doing this favor for her."

"You can't bring your personal life into your company!"

"Like you said, it's my company, I can do whatever I want."

"But it's affecting my department!"

"Then do a better job training her."

A server came over to take their order. They waited until he was out of earshot before continuing.

"I can't if she's not smart enough," she whispered.

"I believe Maya's an intelligent young woman. Now, I'll ask you politely not to insult her. Whether she's with you or not."

"I'm sorry…but give it some thought. Your company is more important than whatever relationship you have with her mother. Maya just isn't ready for this kind of job. She should be at a job for a teenager."

"I disagree. It's better she starts working jobs like ours early in life. Even if she grows tired of this company, she'll be able to take her experience and get better jobs."

"She doesn't deserve it," she mumbled.

"That's not your decision to make."

"I just think people need to work hard to get to where we are. It shouldn't be handed to them."

"How do you think I became CEO? Through hard work? No, it was handed down to me. So by your standards, I shouldn't work here either right?"

"It's different for you," she mumbled again. Her tone was quieter every time she spoke.

"Not at all," he said. There was a moment of silence before he spoke again, "How about this, I'll move Maya to marketing. If she can't handle it as you say, then I'll speak to her mother and have her fired. If she's able to handle the tasks I give her, what do you think should happen to you?"

"I don't know. Give me time to think about it. However, I work damn hard at my job. The best you've ever had. Don't think I'll just offer to quit over a child."

"Grown woman," he interrupted. "I won't fire you, but this is a bet, right? You need to give me a stipulation. You have the rest of the week to think about it. Do you agree?"

"Yes..."

"When Maya arrives at work, tell her to come to my office. I'll inform you on what work I'll give her."

"Okay. She won't make it."

Mr. Robinson didn't respond. Soon they were speaking about work. Most likely what they came on lunch for, but Deborah tried crying to the big boss because her harassment wasn't working.

The server came over with my check, I asked for doggie bags, paid for my meal and secretly left the restaurant, hoping they hadn't noticed me. I wondered what exactly my mom and Mr. Robinson's relationship was. Friends wouldn't fight that hard, "risking" as Deborah put it, his company all to make my mom happy? It wasn't my business, but it was questionable.

When I got home, I put my leftovers in the fridge and relaxed the rest of the night in my room. I could hear Anna and Tiana laughing away.

I was dreading having to look at Deborah when I went into the building. I was going to do my best pretending I didn't hear her lies, but just thinking about it annoyed me. I was happy to be transferred, I wouldn't have to see her anymore, but I would miss working with everyone else.

Just as Mr. Robinson directed, Deborah, with a smug look on her face, sent me to his office.

"Good morning," he said. He sat on the corner of his desk tossing something in the air. "Have a seat."

That was the first time I saw his office. It was spacious, the back wall of the office was all windows, in the front part of the room, were armchairs, one small couch, and a thick, dark wood coffee table. The side walls were covered with bookshelves, and in the back of the office, was his desk, neatly decorated, a large, padded swivel chair for himself and a hard office chair on the other side. If he wasn't such a nice man, I would've thought his office was part of an evil lair.

I sat down in the chair opposite his side.

"How's everything going in the Sales department?" he asked.

"Good, I understand most of it. I just have a little difficulty selling."

"Yeah, your sale's chart is low, but it's only been a few weeks, I expected you to have low numbers. Are you understanding Debbie's training?"

"Debbie?" I asked.

"Deborah. You don't call her that? She prefers to be called that."

"Oh I didn't know."

"That's alright. How's training with her?"

"I haven't trained with her. I trained with Joanne. She was very thorough teaching me, but 'Debbie' wouldn't let her teach me everything. So I started late on a lot of tasks. I didn't start talking to Joanne's clients until last week and I still don't have my own clients."

"Huh," Mr. Robinson said. He wrote something down and said, "Well, it's good you didn't learn anything else. I'm transferring you to our marketing department. How does that sound?"

"Good. It's better to learn multiple departments."

"Uh-huh. Well Shay knows you're coming. Do you know where marketing is?"

"No."

"Take the elevator to the 3rd floor. They have the whole floor. Look for Shaylia."

"Okay. Thank you for the opportunity."

"It's my pleasure."

I left his office and went to the 3rd floor. It was louder than Sales, not by much but there wasn't awkward silence. I looked around and went to the only person not working. He was an older man with a short gray afro. He twirled a pen in his hand and was learning back in his chair. I looked at the name on his desk, "Howard A."

"Excuse me," I said. He flinched and sat up in his chair. I held back my laugh and continued, "I'm looking for Shaylia."

"She's over there. You see the woman in the black dress?" he said, pointing with his pen. "That's her."

I thanked him and walked over. She was speaking with someone, so I waited quietly until she looked over.

"Can I help you?"

"I'm Maya. I was transferred here."

"Oh yeah, I'm sorry. Slipped my mind. Oscar told me you needed training. Do you at least understand how marketing works?"

"Sort of. It's like sales but you guys do the promotions and stuff."

"Close. We do a lot more than that. We track trends and monitor our competition. We're all about innovation, I expect creative and unique ideas. We communicate with the rest of the company, we help improve sales processes, monitoring and managing social media, and we haven't even scratched the surface."

She continued, "Some might disagree with me, but we're honestly the most important part of this company. If it weren't for us, I can guarantee this company would have collapsed years ago."

I nodded. I sort of regretted changing. It seemed like a lot of work, but maybe I wouldn't have to do everything. So far, the vibes in the office were significantly brighter than Sales. Obviously because of Deborah.

Shaylia, once she was done helping someone else, did a quick training session. She didn't think it would be too hard for me to understand. She gave me a few test products and told me to come up with good ideas for each one. I didn't think I was creative, but I had to help Mr. Robinson win that bet.

I didn't do well my first time, but Shaylia told me what I did wrong and how to determine if it was good. By the end of the day I had a better grasp of Marketing than I did 2 weeks in sales.

I worked every day that week. Shaylia was the *complete* opposite of Deborah. She didn't think I should work less hours, she wanted me working more because I was inexperienced. Deborah thought it was so horrible that I worked there, she would rather ruin her team than just train me properly.

I spent some time with Anna and Tiana. I didn't want to intrude on their time, but sometimes they would come down to the living room and play board games with us. It was fun hanging out with her.

By the end of the week, Shaylia was praising me. I felt confident, and I was giving better ideas. She wasn't going to give me my own project just yet. However she said soon I would team up with Howard and have real products.

Saturday came and Anna and Tiana said their goodbyes. Anna was quiet the rest of the day. I didn't bother her. She was sad over her leaving and there really wasn't much I could say to make her feel better.

"Wanna go shopping tomorrow?" I asked. "It'll be our last time for a while shopping here."

"Yeah," she said. She turned over and smiled. "You're paying though."

I rolled my eyes. "Fine. But next time you have to pay if you suggest shopping."

"Deal."

With how my job situation was going, everything was falling into place. The next step was to hold my head high and go back to my apartment… no matter how scary it was. Just thinking about seeing Jessica and Daniel walk out of his apartment, made me tremble.

Sunday night, we were finishing our packing. We procrastinated until we had to stay up late.

"I don't want to leave," Anna said, glumly. "It's fun here."

"I know, but we have to go back. I already made a deal with her. She'll mess up my credit if I don't go."

"Damn." Anna leaned on the bed. "Are you gonna be alright?"

"Yeah, why?"

"I mean, living next to Daniel."

"I'm over him. It'll probably be awkward if he does or says something weird, otherwise, I'll be a-okay."

"I don't know Maya. You tend to bottle things up. I'm pretty sure you aren't telling me something."

"Like what?" I laughed, nervously.

"Like the fact that you aren't over him."

I smiled. "I'm over him."

"I doubt it."

"I am, really. Don't worry about me, okay?"

"Ok Maya. But don't do anything rash."

"I won't. Let's pack our things so we don't have to in the morning."

Anna didn't respond. She knew I was full of shit. However, she wasn't going to pressure me into telling her how I really felt. Either because she knew I would never tell her, or she knew I was lying even to myself.

After we finished packing, we headed to bed. I lay there awake. It was really happening. Tomorrow was the day life resumed.

CHAPTER ELEVEN

It was time for me and Anna to go. Carmen and Valery were very kind, but we couldn't stay longer. We would become a bigger burden than we already were. In the kitchen we spoke with Valery.

"Are you sure?" she asked. "You're always welcome to stay longer."

"Thank you," I said. "But we've stayed too long. Besides, we have to go back."

"Are you sure?" she asked.

I nodded. I never met friends as kind as her and Carmen. They were nice enough to let us use one of their rooms at a ridiculously low price and made us feel at home.

After talking with Valery, Anna and I left. We loaded our bags in the cab and waved goodbye. I sighed and went into the car. I looked out the window as we left Queens. My thoughts went back to Daniel. Where was he? Was he okay? The regrets I held for ending it filled my head and my heart hurt. I took a deep breath.

"I'm gonna miss them," Anna said, breaking the silence. "They were so nice. Way nicer than my parents and the wicked witch of the Midwest."

"Yeah," I said. "We'll probably hang out with them again."

Anna could probably tell I didn't want to talk. She glanced at her phone then out the window. I slowly looked out the window. I closed my eyes, traffic was bad, it would be a while until we reached Brooklyn.

I opened my eyes to the driver yelling for me to get out. I sluggishly rolled out of the car and Anna pulled me up.

"Jeez, you were out the whole ride. He was gonna throw you out any minute."

"I could tell," I sneered, flipping him off as the tires screeched and he sped off.

"Are you really up for this?" Anna asked, concerned.

"Yeah, we made a deal with the landlord. We have to honor it," I said. "Besides…I'm over him…."

Anna didn't say anything. She just stared before turning to go inside. I couldn't convince Anna any more than I could myself. I took a deep breath and walked inside. Three months had passed since I was last there. If my luck really did get better, maybe he moved out?

My heart pounded as we reached the 6th floor. My thoughts were running wild. *What if Daniel still lives here? What if he comes out as we enter my apartment?*

The elevator doors opened, and my eyes shot to his door. I felt instant relief he wasn't there. I darted to my apartment, Anna could barely keep up.

"Maya, slow down," she complained. "The likelihood of him still being here and coming out right now is next to none."

"Yeah, but I don't want to risk it," I whispered, scrambling to take the key out the door as I entered the apartment.

Anna rolled her eyes and followed me.

I felt a little nostalgic seeing my apartment. I took a deep breath to hold back my tears. I was pathetic. Hung up over one guy. Yeah, he was my first for everything, but there was no reason to be the way I was. I should've moved on, yet there was I about to cry over a cheater. *I guess it really isn't that easy to get over someone.*

Anna groaned as she brought the last bag in. "Thanks for the help."

"Huh, no problem," I said, snapping out of it.

"I was being sarcastic. Why didn't you just hold on to your bag when you opened the door? I did everything."

"I'm sorry. I got lost in thought. Just thinking about you know, past events here."

"Well stop, you were doing well. Every time you think about him, slap yourself."

"Why would I do that?" I laughed.

"I don't know. Better than thinking about him and getting all emotional."

"Nah. I'll just try not to. And if I do, I'll start a conversation with you."

"Eh, if you say so."

"Yeah, and to make sure I don't run into him, I'll stay in the apartment. You'll do all the grocery shopping and anything else we need."

"Hell no, I'm not a servant. We'll *both* do it. You can wear a disguise or something, I don't know."

I sighed. "I really hope he moved out."

"I hope so too. But I also wish he still lived here so I could smack him once."

"Anna, no."

"I said once, geez."

"Not even once. We'll play the high ground and pretend he doesn't exist."

"We can do that too…."

The next couple of days I didn't hear a peep out of Daniel's apartment. I wondered if he really did move out. To be honest, I was disappointed. Deep down, I really wished I could bump into him. I imagined him seeing the changed me just like in the rom-coms. The protagonist came back months later smoking hot and independent and their ex was like, "Damn you look great." And she rejected all attempts of getting together again.

…Except, I wasn't smoking hot, and I was kinda dependent on Anna's support. But I was independent from needing him. Nonetheless, I was a changed person after we broke up. Yeah, he was the reason I grew so much as a person, but I was bound to change anyways. He needed to know I was good without him…. Regardless of him being my every thought.

After removing everything from storage and unpacking, I made us food and we spent the rest of the night hanging out in our room.

Working was a good distraction from Daniel. Not only was I excited to do my own projects, but I was also happy to be out of my apartment for 9-10 hours. And after work, I took my time going home. I met Anna at Mama, hung out with Carmen and Valery, and went grocery shopping at whatever store I was close to. I wasn't coming home until 10 PM and I went to bed right after. Was it healthy to use work and friends to keep my mind off Daniel? Absolutely. There wasn't any advice I heard that said otherwise.

Due to my enthusiasm at work, Shaylia was giving Mr. Robinson positive feedback. I was so proud of myself. Hopefully, that was enough for Deborah to shove her foot in her mouth. By the second week of August, Shaylia was giving me more chances to pitch ideas. And every idea was a success.

Mr. Robinson called me into his office. "Maya you've excelled greatly since transferring. I'm offering you the chance to lead the marketing on a major collaboration we're having with Luna Cosmetics."

"Really?" I said, astounded.

"Yes, and if you pull this off, I might promote you to Marketing Coordinator. Hellen is planning to move to another branch in a few months. I want to offer this position to you first, but only if you can pull off this event. Think you can do it?"

"Y-yes," I stuttered. "Thank you for the opportunity!"

"Of course. Keep up the good work," he said. As I left the room, Mr. Robinson said, "You can start planning after your week off."

"Okay."

I was oozing confidence. Only a month working there, and I was offered a great position. It really made me feel like I could do anything. I certainly fell in love with marketing. Never would have imagined working here years ago. I thought it was a boring job, but it was actually fun.

I rested in bed reading about Luna Cosmetics. They specialized in lip gloss and eyeshadow, but the new products were introducing lipstick, eyeliner, blush, and other makeup products. They were a fairly new company founded 2 years before. I took notes on their logo and how they designed their packaging. I set my phone down beside me and stared at the ceiling.

"Maya, we gotta go to a grocery store," Anna said, coming into the room holding an empty carton of orange juice.

"For what? We still have food," I said, sitting up. I did NOT want to go to Loue's. That was ground zero for running into Daniel and Jessica.

"I need juice though."

"Go to a convenience store or something."

"I don't know the area, but I'm pretty sure Loue's is closer. I know you're saying no because you don't wanna risk seeing them."

"I don't Anna," I whined. "He's bound to be there. Or at least Jessica. No one else is going to hire her except Loue."

"And?" Anna gave me an "I don't give a fuck" look. "You need to go. Show her how much more attractive you are than her."

"I doubt it. She's really pretty and regardless of my looks, she already got Daniel. She 'won.'"

"She didn't '*win*' anything. You gave him up. You're still the winner. Besides, he'll cheat on her too."

Anna pulled me off the bed. "Let's go. I'm thirsty."

"Fine."

I found my "nicest outfit" and Anna did my makeup. I looked fine. We walked to Loue's, and I couldn't go inside. My heart was racing, I would finally see Daniel.

"Come on," Anna said, softly.

I followed her inside. It felt weird. Like I hadn't been there in years. It was nostalgic. Everything was exactly how it was when I left.

"Maya," Loue shouted, from across the aisle. "Good to see you. How have you been?"

"Great. How have you and the store been?"

Loue rolled his eyes. "Stressed. You quit, and Daniel quit not long after. I'm stuck with Jessica in the mornings. My assistant manager is back though."

"I'm sorry. Why did Daniel quit?"

"Same reason as you I assume. Breakups are hard."

"Yeah, Jessica just couldn't stay away from him," Anna scoffed.

Loue looked at her confused.

"I'm sorry. This is my sister Anna. Anna, this is my old boss Loue."

"It's a pleasure," he said, shaking her hand. Whispering he said, "Now what was this about Jessica?"

I laughed. Loue was as nosy as ever. "Jessica basically stole Daniel from me. The entire time I worked here, she kept making advances towards him."

"What? And she got him?"

"No, I broke up with him, I figured they should just stop sneaking behind my back."

"Oh man, I never thought Daniel as the cheating type."

"Neither did I." Anna sighed.

"Yeah, I'm not mad though. It was better to find out sooner than later."

"Yep. Look, I know you probably don't want to work here with Jessica. But is there any way you're able to work again?"

"I don't know. I already have a part time job. Anna could though."

"I mean I could…" Anna said. "But why not work both jobs?"

"I'm willing to be flexible with your other job. I just need competent employees," Loue begged.

"I guess I can. That way we can afford a bigger apartment when my lease is up."

"Yes," Loue said, desperately. "Please consider it. Hell, I'll even shorten Jessica's hours and work hers around yours."

"I'm fine with that."

"Great. If you can come back tomorrow or the day after, we can get your paperwork done."

"I can come in tomorrow. Anna can too."

"Alright, I really appreciate it. I'll let you two get your groceries."

"Ok. See you tomorrow."

"Nice meeting you." Anna waved as he walked off. "I hope he fires her."

"Nah, he wouldn't. He doesn't like her, but he's her uncle, and his brother always hounds him to rehire her."

"Damn that sucks."

We continued to shop, I figured we could stock up on food. As we walked to check out, reaching the end of the aisle, I almost hit Jessica with my cart. She was running through the aisles.

"Geez," she shouted, stepping back. She looked at me and after recognizing me, gave me the nastiest look possible.

I didn't say anything to her and walked to the register. I could hear Anna scoffing. She was holding back everything until we were away from there.

"I'm sorry," the cashier said. "I'll speak to her after this."

"It's okay. I used to work here. I'm not bothered by her."

"Oh you did?" the woman said. She was short, her hair was black and down to her shoulder. She wore black glasses and a white uniform. She must have been the assistant manager.

"Yeah, I quit two months ago."

"Ah, during my leave. I'm Maria."

"Maya, and this is Anna. She'll be starting here soon."

"Oh yeah. Loue already told me you two were coming back. Thanks we really need the help."

"Yeah, it's good to be back."

We finished checking out and left the store. Anna couldn't hold it in anymore. "Was that bitch Jessica?"

"The one I almost hit with the cart? Yeah."

"You think she's pretty? Not even."

"She is pretty."

"I don't think so at all. Just because she puts makeup on, doesn't mean she's pretty. No amount of makeup could hide that face. How could Daniel choose her over you? You're waay prettier."

"Thanks. But I think she seduced him. She basically threw herself at him. Plus, I think he just likes overly feminine women."

"Nah, it was probably the sex, no other way. You're a way better option. Nicer, prettier, smarter…"

"You're only saying that because you're biased."

"I'm saying it because it's true."

"I don't think so. But it's whatever, really, I don't care anymore. I'm glad he quit so I don't have to worry about bumping into him."

"Daniel? Yeah, that's better. But if they're dating, he's gonna come to pick her up."

"Please don't say that."

"Sorry, I take it back." She laughed.

It was fun walking home. Anna spent the whole-time roasting Jessica. I was grateful Anna was with me, she made every situation better.

The following week was okay. After agreeing to work at Loue's again with an increased wage, I wasn't going to ask for too much, but we agreed on $16/hr. I started that week. Since I was on break from Vlosam, it was a good time to relearn everything at Loue's. Afterwards, I would work mornings on Tuesday, Thursday, and Sunday. Jessica had the ugliest attitude towards me, and it took everything to hold Anna back. Yeah, I was Daniel's ex, but if she was with him, there was no reason to have an issue with me. *She* was the one who took him from *me*, not the other way around. Thankfully starting the next week, she would have a later shift.

My job at Vlosam Cosmetics was going perfectly. I was finally returning to work. I was nervous I would mess up, but I wouldn't let that stop me. I worked diligently, day in and day out, planning and designing what I wanted to do to promote the product. I wanted to throw a launch party to get it into stores and maybe potential customers. I had a few kinks I would work out once it was approved.

Mr. Robinson approved it. I wasn't expecting him to agree to the party, but he was as supportive as always. I didn't even have all the details down, but I guess he trusted me. "Trial and error." He probably expected me to fail somewhere, but that was part of growth. I was a quick learner and whatever mistakes happened I'd learn from.

I was nervous planning such an important event by myself. So I asked for a team to help with planning. I requested Joanne from sales and Howard was my mentor, so he was all for it and Shay preferred supervising. We spent day in and day out working. Planning the venue, decorations, how the product would be placed, etc. It was more work than I thought it would be and the days until October 15th grew shorter. I trusted my partners for the project, but I couldn't help but feel like my ideas were stupid and I was messing up.

I realized there were parts of my life I hadn't changed and felt worse. What did I change in the months since I had broken up with Daniel? My wardrobe? How did that help in the slightest? I made more friends, had fun, I had an amazing job, met my biological mother, but I didn't actually *fix* myself. I lacked confidence. It wasn't something that could be fixed in 2 months.

Yes, my life had gotten significantly better, and I was grateful for that, but I still couldn't get over my insecurities and depressing thoughts. Was I in depression? I didn't know. I wasn't going to self-diagnosis myself, but I also didn't have the time and willpower to speak to a therapist. I barely told my thoughts to Anna let alone a stranger. I was scared of therapy. If I could change one thing at that time, it would have been that I went to therapy. It would have saved me a lot of pain and confusion.

Regardless, I sucked it up for completing this project. I had a lot riding on this. I needed to force myself through it.

As the weeks went by, I was feeling more confident in our work. It was coming along better than I imagined. Seeing it in person was better than trying to visualize it. Unfortunately work at Vlosam was the only thing going smoothly. At Loue's I only saw Jessica a few times when Loue forgot to separate our shifts… or did it intentionally when important loads came in. Sadly, I was moved to the grocery department because of my inflexible schedule, and I only worked part of my shifts with Anna. Since I worked mornings, Loue had her in the evenings. I didn't know if it was because we were friends or not, but it sucked.

It seemed like more tension was rising between Anna and Jessica. I didn't know if it was because Anna was defending me or if Jessica was targeting her for something else. I wanted Loue to switch our schedules, so she didn't have to spend 8 hours with Jessica. I could handle 5 hours every other day, she didn't even want to talk to me. We would be more civil than those two were. I was worried my marketing team would disagree with the time switch. But they preferred working on projects in the morning. It was more relaxing and gave them more time to wake up. They preferred client meetings in the afternoon. They just assumed I couldn't with my second job.

I spoke with Loue on my next shift and requested to change with Anna. I didn't tell Anna about it because I knew she would protest it. She loved chaos and drama. Loue agreed and starting the following week I would be working with Jessica again.

Of course, Jessica couldn't be civil. She took every opportunity to belittle me or "accidentally" do things to me, like knock over my cart or U-boat or sometimes bump into me. She usually did it after Anna left. Anna started her shift at 9 AM and it overlapped with Jessica's at 1 PM and mine at 4 PM. Jessica was clearly afraid of Anna. She had met her match. I was fine with being Jessica's target if Anna wouldn't have any more problems.

Jessica's petty behavior was slowly getting the best of me. I did everything in my power to not snap on her. Kill her with kindness, but sometimes that just wasn't enough, no matter how respectful and mature I was towards her, she wouldn't return it. Eventually I was going to tell Loue why I thought she should be fired. She was crossing too many lines and my patience was growing thinner.

I took the frustration I had towards Jessica and poured it into my party. It was the best way to vent my anger. I cared enough about this project that it made me forget whatever problems she caused me the day before. But how much would that fix?

Only 3 weeks remained until the cosmetics party. I was nervous, everything had to be perfect. I didn't want to embarrass Mr. Robinson and prove Deborah right. I would have a successful event and enjoy my promotion. Did I think I could be marketing coordinator? Not in the slightest, but I knew marketing was a better fit for me, and Mr. Robinson believed in me. I wasn't going to let him down.

The venues we were hoping for were all booked. So we settled on one of Vlosam's rooms. They were rarely used, why, I didn't know but it was more convenient to hold it there. We chose a more isolated location from the main part of the building. They called it the "Rose room." It was 2,600 sq ft. The walls were white, the floor was light wood, and there was a partition in the middle of the room, we booked both sides, so we had it retracted. There were tall windows about 3 on both sides of the room and 2 on both sides of the front doors, there were 6 hanging lights on both sides of the room, there were diming settings, so I hoped the others would agree to maybe keep the lights down or at least for half the event.

While Joanne and Howard kept planning and buying items we needed, me and Shay spent time at the Rose room decorating. We had a strict budget and couldn't hire people to do it for us. We split our tasks in half. Shay worked in the front of the room, and I worked in the back.

As I was setting up tables for refreshments, I noticed two large doors in the back. I was curious about what was on the other side. When I opened the doors, there was a huge garden. The gate blocking the garden from the street was tall, a gray painted lattice design and was lined with trees inside and outside the gate. It was beautiful. I knew Vlosam let others book their rooms, but I wondered if the garden was for weddings. The garden was separated by 4 small stone walls. Closest to the building were flowers, different varieties perfectly organized. I couldn't tell what species they were. On the left side facing the building, were yellow, purple, and blue flowers, and on the right side, were pink, red, and orange flowers. There were red roses. They looked pretty, but I hated the stench of flowers. I couldn't explain how they smelled, but I just couldn't handle it.

On the other side of the first two walls, and in between all four walls, were metal benches, nothing special, and towards the back of the garden, were vegetable pots. I saw tomatoes, bell peppers, cucumbers, cauliflower, on the left and jalapenos, eggplants, squash, broccoli, and a few more on the right. It looked like a community garden. But I wasn't sure. There weren't any signs any where inside.

"What are you doing?" she asked, and I headed back.

"I was looking at the garden. I was thinking we could maybe leave the doors open and guests can view the garden. If it's not too cold or the flowers don't die right away."

"Huh," Shay said, walking to the garden. I followed behind her. She looked at the flowers and said, "I doubt these will be alive in 3 weeks, but we could check with Joanne and Howard and see what they think. It could be a huge attraction if we decorate it beautifully."

"Uh huh, but I saw vegetables in the back, so we should check to make sure this isn't a private garden. If it's not, we should still block off the vegetables."

"I agree. But for now, let's focus on what's already on our plate and add on if we have time."

"Okay," I said. I grabbed the tablecloths and continued putting up tables.

At 3 PM, we wrapped up. I had to go to Loue's and Shay still had her own work. They couldn't take off from work like I did. It was unfair but complaining wouldn't change anything.

I went home to change into my uniform and headed to Loue's. I wouldn't be lying if I said I didn't look at Daniel's door…it was only a passing glance. I wondered why I hadn't seen or heard a peep from him once. Was he okay? Was I… lucky… enough to not see him again? It was looking more and more like he moved out. So rather than risk seeing me again, he moved out? He probably did it because Jessica asked him to. I didn't think he was the type of guy to be that hurt over our breakup that he uprooted his life to escape me, only Jessica was capable of being that petty.

When I arrived at work, Anna was ready to leave. I was bad at remembering her schedule, but we only worked an hour of our shifts together. Unfortunately, Jessica was working a full shift. I figured Loue probably forgot about separating our shifts, or he couldn't. I wasn't sure how I would deal with her when Anna left. She gave no fucks about being mean to Jessica, and Jessica, weirdly never bothered me when Anna was there. Maybe she was afraid of her, or maybe afraid it was 2 vs 1 if she started an argument. Whatever the reason was, I knew the moment Anna was gone, Jessica would go bitch mode again.

Me and Anna worked in the same aisle. We talked about my project, gossiped about Jessica, Anna gushing over Tiana, just random things.

It hit 5 PM and Anna wasted no time punching out.

"Can't even go overtime a little?" I asked.

"Nope, I spent my entire day here, I'm going home."

"Fine, I'll see you later."

"Yep," Anna said, running out of the break room.

As Anna left, Jessica came into the break room for her lunch. She rolled her eyes at me and went to her locker. I didn't want to deal with her and started towards the door. She mumbled something but I didn't care about what she said.

Most of the evening went okay. I passed Jessica throughout the store and in the backroom. There was a new load at 7 PM and we had to get most of it done before the third shift came. It was only me, Jessica, and a new hire, Matthew. It was a little stressful, but we were making progress. 10 minutes before our shifts ended, Jessica approached me. I knew it wasn't going to be good, but I humored her and stayed.

"I heard you and Anna talking about me," she said, her hand on her hip.

"Okay and?" I asked. I was cleaning up the back. We didn't finish the load, but I was neatening up what was left.

"And it's starting to piss me off. I let it go earlier, but the more I saw you, the more I started thinking." She walked away from me and sat on a stack of pallets. Continuing she said, "Are you really that obsessed with me after whatever happened between you and Daniel? Like, how is that my fault you didn't listen to my advice and lost him."

I rolled my eyes. She just couldn't let that situation go. "Well, first off, *I* dumped Daniel."

"Because you guys were having problems."

"Secondly," I said, ignoring her. "You're the one that can't let things go. You got Daniel, right? So why bother me and be a bitch? What? Are you that threatened by his ex?"

Jessica looked confused. I assumed hopefully she saw how childish and immature she was being and was thinking, "Why was I rude to her?"

Jessica finally responded. She smirked and said, "You're right. Me and Daniel are dating. I won in the end. You should get over yourself. There's no reason to sic your ugly, gay little doggie on me just because you lost your man. That's *your* fault, not mine. I'm willing to overlook your shitty behavior, but don't expect me to be friends with you and that bitch of yours. I don't trust you not to try and steal him back."

"I don't want him back. That's why *I* broke up with *him*." My throat hurt, it grew tighter by the second. Hearing her confirm their relationship hurt me. I wanted to cry but I wasn't going to let her see me upset. "Enjoy your time with him, really. I wish nothing but happiness for Daniel. I don't want to be your friend. You're a conniving bitch that does things behind other's backs. Like I said, I had no issues with you. You mean *nothing* to me. But I won't ignore your bitchy behavior and I especially won't let you talk about Anna like she's a dog. She's a good person and a real friend, something you wouldn't know. You live your entire life bitter to the point you would attack an 18-year-old girl. How sad. You're threatened by her and the fact that she's way prettier than you, more successful and can get anyone she wants. You can't handle someone as kind as her, so you bother her. And you lose *every time* you try. You can't even get a man without spreading your legs."

Jessica stood up, her face was red. I wasn't scared of her. And I wasn't holding any punches anymore. Say all she wanted about me, but Anna, that was crossing the line.

I continued, "You knew Daniel how long? And only recently he showed some inkling of interest in you. Not because he had feelings for you. 'Cause you used sex to get him. Daniel was in love with me for years. I didn't have to lift a finger to get him. If you have nothing to worry about, then you wouldn't be this defensive towards me. But don't think you can keep him. He'll grow bored of you, and whatever sex positions you throw at him and go for someone he *actually* loves. Lose him how you got him, don't forget that."

Before Jessica could respond, I walked away. I wasn't letting her have the last word.

"Fuck you, you bitch," she yelled.

I flipped her off and left the back area. I punched out, grabbed my belongings, and ran out of the store. I ran until I was two blocks away. I stopped for breath and burst into tears. My heart was racing, and my body shook as if it were below $0°$ and my throat hurt, like it was closing. I couldn't breathe. I was proud of myself for finally standing up to her. I felt bad for talking about her methods for getting men, but it was the only thing I could think of that would hurt her like she hurt me. I hoped me cussing her out would make her leave us alone. I walked the rest of the way home. I was still crying and looked like a mess. There was no way I would let strangers see me cry. The night air was refreshing, the cool air was helping me calm down. I was able to breathe again, and my thoughts cleared. I wondered if I should tell Anna about what happened, but I thought if she did, the next day she would try to fight Jessica or something. I laughed thinking about it. Anna definitely would.

When I got home, I told her a watered-down version. Just Jessica telling me her and Daniel were dating, her insulting me and me cursing her out. Anna was ecstatic that I cussed her out but was livid about her confronting me. I told her I handled the situation and that she didn't need to do anything. I wouldn't be at work to stop anything from happening the next few days and needed her to promise not to go after Jessica. She reluctantly agreed after a while, and we spent the rest of the night talking shit about her. It was fun to rant. I got everything out of my system when I stood up to her, but I still wanted to talk shit, one last time before I washed my hands clean of her and Daniel for good.

CHAPTER TWELVE

Only two weeks remained until the party. I requested time off at Loue's so I could focus on the event. I didn't feel comfortable leaving Anna alone with Jessica, but she insisted everything was fine. She would be on her "best behavior." I hadn't seen Jessica since the night we had that argument. Anna told me Jessica was quieter than before. She still picked petty fights with Anna but kept to herself most of the shifts they had together. I—Even though Jessica instigated the argument that night, I still felt bad for shaming her, I didn't know if it was considered "slut shaming" but I thought I crossed a line myself that I shouldn't have. No matter how much of an asshole she was, the way I treated her was uncalled for. What she was doing wasn't even bad. That was just her method for ensuring a relationship. Everything else she did was horrific. But I was in the heat of the moment and said the wrong things. Did she deserve to have her feelings hurt? Honestly, yeah, but that wasn't the way to do it. But it was whatever. I wasn't going to apologize, and I wasn't going to think about her or Daniel again. Only when Anna brought her up, or when I went back to work, would I acknowledge her.

As for Daniel, I was the only one still thinking about our relationship. He had already moved on... of course before I even broke up with him, but he was in another relationship and never thought about me. So why was I constantly thinking about him? I still had feelings for him, there was no way I could deny that any longer. But was I even trying to get over him? I moved away for a few months and barely thought about him. The moment I came back to my apartment, it was like all our memories together flooded into my mind and I was trapped in never ending pain. I was going to do my best to get over him. Hearing Jessica confirm their relationship was the push I needed. I had my resolve. It was stupid how I was acting, embarrassing. From that day forward, I would stop thinking about him. When I left my apartment, I would look the other way, when I went to Loue's, I would only think about work. I was going to dedicate myself to moving on. From that moment on, the success of the party was the only thing on my mind.

I spent all day and night working in the Rose room. I waited for the arrival of the furniture. We ordered a small divider to put at the front door to separate the room from the check in. On the other side of the divider was a podium for the Luna Cosmetics employees to speak. We had dining tables as well as booths. The booths were in the back half of the room, a row against the wall on the right side, in the middle past the partition line, and the left side against the wall. The dining tables would be in the front half of the room and some in between the booths and there was a counter installed for alcohol. I put most of it together by myself after the others went back to work.

I hoped they liked how I did it. I was starting to doubt myself again but snapped myself out of it. I had 3 amazing coworkers helping, it wouldn't go wrong. Everything was going as planned. We had a good turn out on RSVPs. If they showed or not was another thing.

On the way home a week before the event, I spotted a small graphic design company called Lightning Corp. It was in the building that was constructed back in July. I wrote down their information. I hadn't heard of them, I thought everyone deserved an opportunity. There would be major companies at Luna's product launch.

We would put up the rest of the decorations 2 days before the event. I checked on the garden to see if the flowers were still alive. Most of them wilted. So I put in my notes to mention cancelling the garden. The room itself looked flawless without it. We could order more flowers if it didn't look right. The flowers were arriving the day of.

I was biased and ordered our desserts from Mamas. We did the actual dinner at some catering company. Honestly, I didn't care who they chose for catering, I left it up to Joanne. I didn't even know who she booked, but I trusted her tastes.

After working for hours, I got back to my apartment at 11 PM. I didn't even look at Da—at the other apartments. I walked with my head high and into my own. Anna was on the phone with her girlfriend. So I was quiet as I got ready for bed.

As I lay there, I thought about everything up to that point. How I started in New York all the way to my attempting suicide and where I was then. Me and Anna living together, meeting new people, an amazing job, and so much more, none of the amazing things I experienced would have happened if I jumped. That was something I did owe, the name I wouldn't utter until I was over the person that owned it. I would never forget what that person did.

Only 4 days remained until the party. I hadn't even thought about what to wear. It was a black-tie event. I didn't have anything appropriate to wear. I could easily blame my lack of attire on planning the event, not procrastination. But I needed to go someplace cheap but with nice "sophisticated" dresses. At that point, anything would do. If it fit me, I would buy it. Anna couldn't come with me, but I could find something by myself.

I found a small shop in Brooklyn. It was a small business. They had a variety of dresses. I looked through the dresses and came upon a navy blue, turtleneck halter neck dress. It was simple but pretty. It was floor-length, and the front, just above the chest was lace. I didn't know what material it was, it was soft and stretchy. As sad as it was, the price was $120, and this was one of the cheaper options in the store. I wanted to call my mom to figure out what kind of jewelry worked with it. I felt bad because I hadn't talked to her since she got me the job at Vlosam. But I could also blame that on the Luna product launch.

Once I left the store, I called my mom. I asked about what jewelry was appropriate to wear. She said to keep it simple. Hoop earrings and a bracelet were fine. I had both at home, so I was thankful for only having to spend $125. When I got home, I put the dress away, and found my nicest pair of silver earrings and a silver bracelet. I was going to leave my hair down, but I wasn't entirely keen on it.

Two days until the party. We started decorating the Rose room. We had too many decorations. We went with a pastel blue colored theme. It matched the design on the makeup packaging. We spent the two days putting everything up, Luna Cosmetics sent us pastel blue balloons last minute. They wanted those somewhere in the room. It had their logo on one side and their name on the other. It was a pretty balloon. I wanted to take one home… but I was an adult, I could withstand the urge.

The day of the party arrived. I arrived early in the morning. The event was from 7 PM to 10 PM. I spent the day making sure catering was alright as well as making sure there were no last-minute problems. I planned to leave at 4 to get ready and come back at 6 in my dress.

Before leaving I took one last look at the room. The moment had come, and my heart was racing. The party could've been a bust and I got fired for embarrassing Vlosam or I did so well, I was promoted to vice president… not that that would ever happen. but maybe enough to make everyone think about it for a millisecond.

I glanced across the room. We had pastel blue and white stars and clouds hanging from the ceiling. A cardboard crescent moon hung from the corner above the product table in the front. Luna Cosmetics wanted the moon. We were iffy about it, but it turned out nice. The tablecloths were off-white, on every other table and booth were a small vase of blue roses. The catered tables were to the right of room facing the front doors, Mama desserts to the right of the food. Neither companies would arrive until 6:30 just so the food wasn't sitting out for long. We had wine, soda, and water at the bar.

While the Rose room looked nice, deep down I was unsatisfied with how it looked. It was how Luna envisioned it so at least they were happy. And at the end of the day, it was the product selling that was most important and would determine the success of the event.

When I got home, I quickly showered, moisturized, and put my dress on. I put on my earrings and the bracelet. I still had no idea what to do with my hair. Anna suggested a bun, so I went with that. She helped me put it in a bun, leaving a coil of hair out on the right side of my head and one in the back. She helped me put on my makeup, mascara, black eyeliner, and red lipstick. I looked… different. I wasn't used to seeing myself so elegant. I liked it. I would probably dress like that again for the hell of it.

I grabbed a small black wallet purse, a long jacket that went down to just under my butt, and I headed out. I didn't sit on the bus or train. I didn't want to wrinkle my dress. I wanted to look as perfect as possible.

I got to Vlosam at 6 PM. There was a coat check in, not a part of our event, but they stayed open for it. Shay and Howard also arrived early. Joanne was on her way. We looked over things, helped catering set up, sadly Makayla wasn't the one to deliver the desserts. I hoped she was doing well. This was her last semester, so she was busy. I didn't want to bother her, so I didn't text her. When she graduated, I wanted to throw her a party better than the one for Luna Cosmetics.

Guests were arriving by 6:45, earlier than I thought they would. I thought they would come late. Thankfully, most of the set up was done. Just a few last-minute fix ups with the catering.

I sat at check in. I checked off guests until 7. Howard took over because Deborah and Mr. Robinson wanted to speak with me.

"You did a splendid job," Mr. Robinson said. "And you did this by yourself?"

Before I could respond, Deborah said, "No, one of my employees helped her."

"Yeah, Joanne, Shay and Howard helped me plan it. I couldn't have done it without them."

Deborah smirked at Mr. Robinson, who looked slightly annoyed.

"She can't put all the credit on us," Joanne said, walking up. "We helped with certain things she was never trained on. The ideas, the decorations, everything was designed by her. We just oversaw the more difficult aspects. So Maya *did* put all of this together. Due to a low budget… we couldn't hire anyone to help set up. Maya did most of that herself. So she should take credit where it's due."

Joanne smiled at me and excused herself. Mr. Robinson's facial expression had lightened. He was greeted by some big shot CEO and left to speak with him.

"Well there's more to come Maya," Deborah spat out. "You're still an employee of mine. Therefore I expect you to sell products, I want at least…15 packages of Luna makeup sold by the end of the night. That should be enough for you right?"

"I was transferred to marketing. Why do I have to sell the product?"

"Because you haven't been officially transferred. You're still listed as a Sales employee." Deborah smirked. "You should be able to do this, miss star employee."

"I can," I said. "I've learned a lot about the makeup items they're selling. So it shouldn't be hard to do."

"You say that now." Deborah looked unamused. "You struggled months ago and haven't had any training since your little party planning. I'd *love* it if you did learn something, but don't get cocky Maya. Only 3 hours to sell, sell, sell."

I nodded and walked away. Selling 15. I laughed. I could sell myself 15 products. I'd take multiple colors of lipstick, blush, and eyeshadow, maybe see if Shay wanted some lip gloss. Deborah didn't think about that loophole. But I wasn't going to do it. I wanted Mr. Robinson to be proud that he hired me.

Sadly, I wasn't allowed to sit in the corner while they talked business. I looked around the room as it grew more crowded. There were 30 people so far, and that wasn't even half the amount of people invited. I took a deep breath. Since Deborah had me doing sales that meant, Joanne was there for the same thing. I looked for her. Joanne was already speaking with some businesswomen. I walked up and listened as she explained the Luna Lip Balm. She was giving detailed descriptions, more than I thought was necessary, like the way it felt on her lips, that the smell reminded her of her childhood, and so forth. Surprisingly, they ordered a line of their lip balms.

When she was done, I asked, "Is it okay if I shadow you for a bit? Deborah wants me to sell 15 products by the end of the night."

"You're not even in our department anymore." Joanne rolled her eyes.

"She said I haven't transferred yet, so she can make me do this."

Joanne shook her head. "Yeah, you can. It's very simple. Here."

She handed me a sheet of paper for putting in their orders. This was the worst part about doing orders. It made zero sense to me. Another failure of school, not teaching us how to use spreadsheets properly and data input, things needed in the real world.

I walked with Joanne as she spoke with potential clients. Sometimes, she had me speak. I failed a few times, but Joanne still managed to get them to buy something. Over time, I was more comfortable and was able to explain well enough for people to show interest.

After an hour I had 5 sales, which was good. In no time I would reach 15. Deborah really low-balled thinking I wouldn't accomplish such a small amount. I couldn't wait to see her face when I reached the quota, I was even going to get more than required. She was the kind of person to use giving me a low number as an excuse to discredit me.

The schedule was set for Luna Cosmetics to give a speech. I sat down at a table near the back with a plate of chicken, rice, and cheesecake. I listened as someone from Luna Cosmetics spoke. He was short, just barely tall enough to be seen over the podium, his hair was slicked back, and his accent was strong. He spoke for 15 minutes explaining each product they were selling. I didn't mind, it saved me time, I could just ask people if they wanted to buy it.

When he was done speaking, I put my plate away, grabbed a glass of ginger ale and scanned the room for potential buyers. I asked around, most had already put orders in. With how pro Joanne and Deborah were, they probably already sold to everyone in the room. Which screwed me over, but surely, Joanne left some for me.

I saw a man standing on his own drinking a cocktail. He looked standoffish like me, so maybe that scared the others off. I walked up to him.

"Excuse me sir," I said. He looked at me. He didn't say anything, so I continued, "Did you hear the spokesman for Luna Cosmetics earlier?"

He nodded.

"Are you interested in buying some? Do you have any questions?"

"Who would I be buying it for?" he said, his words slurred, and he took another sip.

"Uh, maybe a special person in your life. For your company. You could give this as gifts to your employees."

"Hm," he said, still not all there. He was spaced out and not really thinking.

I smiled. "I'll come back later once you figure out who or what you want to buy this for."

"No need," he said. "I'm not interested in buying."

He walked away, or rather stumbled away. It had only been an hour and 15 minutes since the party started and he was hammered. I wasn't judging.

I paced around the room looking at the sheet. Only 5 sales. Then I remembered Loue. He wasn't invited but he was still a business owner. I ran to a corner, behind a group of men that blocked me from being seen and I called him.

"Loue's Grocery, Loue speaking?" he answered.

"Hey, Loue. So remember that event I was planning for?"

"Uh-huh."

"I have to sell some makeup for a company called Luna Cosmetics. Would you be interested in ordering some for the store? It'll be cheaper now if you order from the release party, and you could have it in your store before everyone else."

"We don't really sell makeup though."

"You do. I see it all the time. Why not have a nice brand of makeup. You could charge a pretty penny for this."

"How many sells do you need?"

"At least 15 and so far, I have 5. My coworkers are snatching up sales."

"…Alright," he said. "What kind of products do they have."

"They have lipstick, lip gloss, lip balm, blush, eyeliner, eyeshadow, and a bunch more."

"'A bunch more,'" Loue repeated. "Just put me down for the ones you listed. Maybe 3 cases of each one."

"Okay. Thank you, Loue, I owe you."

"We're even for you coming back to help. This better sell."

"It will, they're a super popular company."

He gave me his information and I thanked him again before hanging up. Deborah wouldn't know who was there or not, and a sale's a sale.

6 down, 4 more to go. I smiled. I texted Anna an update on how everything was going. I figured, I could text while no one could see me. The men behind me weren't paying attention to me. They were taller too, so they probably couldn't even see me.

When I was done sending the message, I put my phone back in my bag and squeezed my way through the group of men. I looked around for any other buyers. I saw Deborah a few times. Still mean looking and bitter even when she was eating or alone.

I found Howard and talked with him for a bit. He was manning the check in for late stragglers. He was bored, he had the worst job, just standing there checking off names. He could go into the party for a few seconds, longer if someone else took his spot. I did for 5 minutes while he went to the bathroom and got a plate of food.

I looked at the guest list. There were a lot of major corporations attending. I was glad I knew about that after the party planning otherwise I would have been too nervous and shut down. I skimmed the list to see if the graphic design company showed up. They did, they had 3 employees show up. Only two of their names were written down because of lack of space. I was glad they were taking the chance.

Howard came back and I was sadly sent back to scouting buyers. I refilled the drink I had, and I looked around the room again. My eyes glanced slowly at every face, especially if they were alone.

I made it to the back of the room and looked across to the other side. My eyes opened wide, and I froze. It was like time had stopped.

Daniel was across the room. He wore an off-black tuxedo and had a drink in his hand. He was talking to the drunk guy I spoke with earlier. I wondered if that was his boss.

He looked so good in that tuxedo, his hair was slicked back, and his smile was as charming as ever. I could tell he was uncomfortable talking to the drunk guy, his nice smile, was accompanied with a weird wrinkle on his face that only showed when he was awkward, and his dimples were barely showing, so it was definitely a fake smile.

My heart raced as if it had picked up boxing and practiced on my chest. His nice, soft eyes looked at the drunken man with care. I could stare into his eyes all day.

I snapped out of my trance. *What is Daniel doing here?!* I thought.

I ran and hid in a booth, practically spilling my drink on the way. What was I going to do? He was the last person I wanted to see. My face was hot. Why was I feeling that way? I hadn't thought about him in so long, I was sure I was over him. As I wallowed in my pitifulness, Mr. Robinson sat with me.

"You did an excellent job Maya. I made the right decision hiring you."

"Uh thank you," I said, sitting up. I had to snap out of it. I couldn't let him ruin this night and my chances of getting promoted. "I couldn't have done this without your guidance."

"I can't take any credit." He shook his head. "You took the minimal directions I gave and made this. Let's see how many sales we can get. Keep up the good work."

"Thank you, sir." I shook Mr. Robinson's hand, and he left the booth.

I sighed. I needed to get my head in the game. I didn't work so hard the past few months for him to screw everything up. I had to avoid him for the rest of the night. If he was there for work, I would speak to him only as a formality, nothing more. I chugged down my drink and stood up.

Game time, I thought.

Forty minutes passed and no sign of Daniel. *Maybe he went home?* I was ecstatic. I made 14 sales total, which was good enough for someone on my level. Only an hour and a half remained until the party was over, and I was lucky enough to not see Daniel. The night was going great.

Mr. Robinson waved me over to a group of people. I smiled and walked over. "Maya, I would like you to meet Chris Whelming, COO of Luna Cosmetics."

"It's a pleasure," he interrupted, and shook my hand. "Our product is selling off the wall."

"Gina Thomas, CEO of East Coast Cosmetics," Mr. Robinson continued.

"Nice to meet you," she said, shaking my hand."

"And Porsha Kim, CEO of Daringly free cosmetics."

"It's a pleasure to meet you." Ms. Kim shook my hand.

Why is he introducing me to important people? I thought.

"Maya," he said, gesturing to me eagerly. "Is the orchestrator for this event."

"You did an amazing job." Ms. Thomas shook my hand again.

"Thank you."

"Maya, I want you to pitch an idea for an up-and-coming product."

My mouth dropped. No way he was putting me on the spot. I thought, *This must be part of that test.*

"Well," I paused. I looked around the room for inspiration. He didn't tell me anything about the product. I glanced from object to object until I saw him. Standing in the corner across the room was Daniel. We made eye contact and he gave a slight nod. I looked away. *How long was he staring at me*? My mind went completely blank.

Shit, I thought. I didn't want to ruin this opportunity.

"Maybe one that involves…love." I was bullshitting as much as I could. "I would need the full details on what it is you're making, but how about the product for now is lipstick. There's a person waiting for their lover. They spend every day sitting by the window, but their partner never returns and each letter they send, they seal it with a kiss. We can base the line off common things we feel when we're in love or even heartbroken."

The CEOS and COO nodded their heads.

"I like it. It needs work, but for coming up with it on the spot, I think it's a good idea," Mr. Whelming said.

"I agree," Ms. Kim said.

Mr. Robinson gave me a low thumbs up, just out of view of the others. I was surprised they liked it. But I guessed I would have to remember what I said just in case they really wanted to continue with it.

"We have more people to speak with, but it was great meeting with you Maya. I hope to work with you in the future," Ms. Thomas said.

I shook their hands and they walked away. I glanced over to where Daniel was.

He smiled and walked over. "It's been a while, how are you?"

Avoiding eye contact I said, "Good. A lot happened and I'm feeling great. How about you?"

"I'm okay. I take it you work for one of the companies?"

"Yeah, Vlosam. I… set up the event."

"Really? You did an amazing job."

"Thanks… w-what are you doing here?"

"I'm a graphic designer for Lightning Corp. A few of my colleagues and I are here to look for business.…"

I mentally rolled my eyes and kicked myself. Me wanting to help a small company put me in that situation.

"I want to apologize," Daniel continued.

"For what?"

"You were right," he said, ashamed. "About Jessica. She… was trying to take me away from you."

I didn't say anything, just thinking about their relationship made my heart ache.

"After you broke up with me, I was really fucked up. I stopped showing up to Loue's, and… it just got bad. Since I hadn't answered Loue's calls, he sent Jessica to check on me. I told her what happened," he paused. "She was so happy we broke up. She confessed she had feelings for me and that she wanted to go out with me. And…"

"And?"

"I agreed. It was more for the rebound. But I…. When you dumped me, you mentioned Jessica and I being together…. It took me a while to figure out what you meant. Did you, when we were together, think I was cheating with Jessica?"

I nodded and said, "Yes. The kiss incident, the way you looked at her versus how you looked at me, I could tell you were in love with her."

"In a way, you were right. Deep down, I couldn't admit that I did have some feelings for her. I was interested in her since I started working at Loue's. But when I saw you again, I couldn't let go of my feelings for you. I was being stubborn, but Maya, I *never* cheated on you."

I looked down. I really wanted to cry. I bit my lip and held back my tears. He really admitted it. Hearing him say he loved her when we were together was worse than just having a suspicion. Did he really love me?

He continued, "I was hurting you and I was too stupid to realize it. I'm sorry. If there's anything I can do to make you forgive me, I—"

"I'm not mad," I interrupted. "I was heartbroken yes, but I'm not going to hold it against you. I—I have to go now, but I hope you and Jessica have a happy life together."

I turned around quickly. I couldn't hold my tears in any longer. I didn't want him to know I wasn't over him. I walked away, almost running, and out into the garden. Maybe it was the cold breeze, but once I was outside, my tears flowed relentlessly. I had to keep going, out of the sight of the party guests. Quietly, I cried, my vision blurred, I walked fast to the dimly lit vegetable garden. Most of the plants were dead. Only a few of the plants were still alive, barely hanging on. As I walked past the wall, I heard leaves rustle behind me.

"Wait," Daniel said, grabbing my arm. "Me and Jessica aren't together. We didn't last 2 weeks."

I didn't face him, I couldn't. I wanted to end it there. Seeing him only brought back pain. But… I didn't want to be apart from him, not anymore.

"At first, I really did believe that I liked Jessica. But as time flew by, I realized it was nothing more than a physical attraction. You and I weren't very intimate, which, I was fine with. I wanted to make sure you were comfortable. But I think mixed with the feelings I would have had for her if I hadn't met you again and the lack of intimacy between us, made me think I liked her. I had this woman throwing herself at me, it made me confuse lust with love."

"Where are you going with this?" I asked, wiping my tears.

"I didn't like Jessica. The few days I was with her, I couldn't get you out of my mind. I realized that I am madly in love with you and seeing you tonight confirmed it."

"I don't want to sound crazy or forceful," he continued. "But this is the third time we've met again. I think we're meant to be together. I don't know if you still love me, but if you do, don't you think this is a sign?"

"I—" I stuttered, "I don't know. I don't want to be hurt again."

"I promise I will never make that mistake again and hurt you."

I didn't respond. I really needed to think about it. How he made me feel when we were dating, if he was compatible with the new me, and if he would really value me for me. I loved Daniel, I wasn't going to deny it, but I didn't want to repeat the same thing. Was I ready for a relationship?

"I want to say yes, but I don't know if I'm ready," I finally said. "I'm not sure if I'm ready for a relationship and I don't want to waste your time."

"You're not wasting my time." He laughed. "I told you before, I don't care how long I have to wait, just as long as you're by my side. If you need time, I can wait."

"It could be years."

"That's fine," he said, walking closer. "I'll wait for you, till death us do part."

I laughed. "What are we married now?"

"I hope to marry you one day."

"But not now."

Daniel reached over and hugged me. "I'm happy I got to see you again and I hope we never fall out again."

"Me too," I said, turning around.

Daniel lifted my chin, he gazed lovingly into my eyes, his warm hand cupping my face. He kissed me passionately. I was swept away by his warm lips and his strong embrace. Our lips parted, but we still held each other, our eyes closed and our foreheads touching. I missed his kisses.

"Can we talk for a bit?" Daniel asked, whispering.

I nodded. "For a little bit."

I led Daniel to the benches on the other side of the wall. The bench was so cold, it felt wet, which of course worried us both. We didn't want to walk in like we peed ourselves. We laughed. We went from a cheesy moment to an embarrassing one.

Daniel sighed. "It's crazy that I can't escape you."

"Me neither. I was doing my best to get over you."

We were silent, before I continued, remembering what Jessica said, "You said you dated Jessica for 2 weeks after we broke up?"

"Mm-hm." He nodded.

"You don't have to lie. Jessica told me a few weeks ago you two were still dating."

"What?" Daniel said. He was so shocked he yelled, "No, I promise, we dated 2 weeks in June. Nothing more."

"I wonder why she lied… but I guess that's just something she does for you."

"Yeah… which would explain why she texted me last week."

"What did she say?"

"When I broke up with her, I told her even though you and I had broken up, I still wasn't over you… and for a while, I was contemplating trying to get you back."

"Good thing you didn't since I wasn't even home."

"Yeah," he exhaled. "That would've been discouraging. But anyways, she texted me saying you guys got into an argument, which I didn't believe, you aren't that outspoken, and she was saying you said you didn't care about me anymore. That you hated me and her for what we did to you. That you didn't want anything to do with me, and Jessica could have me. Then she proceeded to say she couldn't take it any longer and defended me against you."

I rolled my eyes and laughed. "That woman. We did get into an argument. She started it and she said something mean about me and Anna. I did say that I didn't care about you and that you two belonged together but only because she told me you two were dating, I didn't want her to think I still cared about you."

"That hurts a little." He laughed. "But I get why you said it. And doesn't matter since you admitted to liking me."

"I've changed," I said. "I'm not really the same Maya you knew."

"That's alright. Can't wait to meet this Maya." He smiled. "I do want to know what you were thinking back in spring."

"What do you mean?"

"Like what was happening between me and Jessica."

"Just that you guys were sneaking behind my back. You defended Jessica no matter what, even though she instigated most of the situations, you said I was partially at fault…. Then the kiss… but at this point, I know it was planned by Jessica. I don't think she calculated me showing up though."

"What about the day in the park?"

"Well, I needed to buy detergent, so I went to Loue's and…. And the way you looked at Jessica when you were handing her that bouquet. You looked so in love and happy." The image of them flashed in my head, I held back my tears. It still hurt. "You two were so close, you guys looked like the perfect couple. That was the last straw. It confirmed my suspicions, and I just couldn't do it anymore. Even if I misunderstood that, I knew you would come up with some weird excuse and make me feel like I was the one overreacting. Like that was normal. I really thought she was the person that could make you happy."

"And she's not, you are," Daniel said. He held my hand and lifted my head to look at him. "You really did misunderstand. And I'm not lying to you or anything. I went there to get those flowers for you. Jessica saw me and asked why I was looking so happy. Then she suggested 'practicing' handing you the flowers but with her. I was stupid to listen to her advice. I was so oblivious to what she was doing…. I feel so stupid."

"Don't be, she was a friend with ulterior motives. You wouldn't have known. But that's one of the reasons why I'm afraid to get back with you," I said, moving my head from his hand. I looked him in the eyes and said, "I want someone who listens to me and my concerns and not brush them off, and you ignored me throughout our relationship."

"I'm sorry," he said. "I should have listened. Pretty sure if I did, we wouldn't have broken up."

"I feel like it would have happened anyways. I wasn't ready for a relationship and rushed into one because I had a warped understanding of relationships and thought it would work out like the movies," I said. "I had a lot of insecurities that weren't going to be fixed if I stayed with you."

Daniel nodded.

"I still wanted to date you, but as I am now, I see that there was a lot I wasn't going to learn staying with you. It wasn't your fault or the relationship, but my own personal problems."

"I know what you mean. Our breakup also helped me. One, and I'm being very serious, it made me realize I do love you and it's hard to get over you. Two, I had a twisted fantasy of dating you. You weren't and aren't the same person I thought you were. You weren't the same teen who liked and disliked certain things. I didn't know much about 19-year-old you, and I couldn't adjust to the you that was in front of me. Instead of figuring out who you were, I tried to conform you to the you in my mind and that was wrong of me. If you give me another chance, I want to get to know the new you as well as the you before."

I smiled. "Okay."

Daniel looked at his watch. "We've been out here for a while. Do you need to go back in?"

"Yeah," I said, standing up. "We should talk about more misunderstandings. I'm pretty sure, half the time we dated, I was jumping to conclusions."

"That's fine with me."

I hugged Daniel. He still felt warm. I hugged him a little longer so I could warm myself up. I needed to go to the restroom and fix my makeup before Mr. Robinson found me. Daniel opened the door for me, and I went in. "I'll see you soon."

"Yeah." Daniel smiled.

After cleaning myself up in the restroom, I felt rejuvenated... motivated. I did my best to finish Deborah's quota. Daniel bought makeup boosting me to 15 sales. I finished the rest of the party perfectly.

As I said bye to the guests, Daniel waited on the side of the building for me.

"You didn't have to wait," I said, walking to him.

"Yeah, well I don't know if I have your current number."

"Oh, here. I'll text you." I sent Daniel a smiley face. "Well, I'll talk to you later."

Before I could walk away, Daniel grabbed my hand. "Wait. I don't want to leave you just yet. Can I walk you home?"

"You sure it's not going out of your way?"

"You still live in the same apartment, right?"

I nodded. "Yeah. Is your place close to there?"

Daniel smiled. "I still live in the same building. Just on the 3rd floor."

"Why did you move?"

"Hmm, kind of an obvious reason, I didn't want to see you. I needed to get over you and no way to do that with you next door."

"Yeah, I understand. I recently came back to mine."

"Did you go on a trip?"

"Something like that. Don't worry about it. I guess that explains why I never saw you."

"Same to you."

We walked home just catching up with each other. I told him about meeting my mother and reporting Margaret. He told me about how he was hired at Lightning Corporation.

EPILOGUE

After the party, me and Daniel started off as friends. We spent a month talking about everything that had changed for us prior to the event. Mr. Robinson thought I needed some more training and experience before becoming marketing coordinator. He used it to motivate me and prove Deborah wrong. Even though he didn't say it, it was also so he wouldn't lose whatever bet they placed. I wasn't disappointed, I didn't think I was ready that position either.

Turned out, Deborah lied about me not officially transferring to marketing. She knew she was going to lose the bet with Mr. Robinson and desperately needed something to use against me. I never found out what Deborah betted on. Alas, she still worked there, so it wasn't her job.

My mother and I are on better terms. I made sure to visit her every two weeks. Surprisingly… but not really, Mr. Robinson and my mother were dating. I mean, how much Mr. Robinson backed me up, kinda gave it away. I don't feel right working a job handed to me, but it was a nice gesture, and I'm grateful to both of them.

A few months had passed, and Daniel and I moved in together. We started dating again 4 months after the party. Moving in wasn't planned. After Tiana visited New York, she wanted to move there as well. My apartment wasn't big enough for three people and there weren't any available apartments in our building. I wasn't comfortable with Anna being on her own. She was an adult of course, but I was still protective over her. Our apartment complex was one of the most affordable in the city and in a safer neighborhood. Anna, Daniel, and I discussed it and Daniel offered for us to move in together. I added Anna to the lease when we went back to my apartment in August. When it was time to renew it, I didn't renew mine, Anna applied to take over the lease, and it was approved. Daniel added me to his. It was a difficult process honestly.

I moved in with Daniel. Anna and Tiana in my old apartment.

As for Jessica, after seeing Daniel pick me up from work, she figured out after a bit of PDA that we were dating. Surprisingly, she didn't cause a scene. She stayed silent as she left. She quit Loue's the next day. And I, regardless of how a lot of problems that happened in my relationship with Daniel was caused by her, and her petty behavior when I started working at Loue's again, I still felt bad for her. To put that much love and devotion into someone only for it to blossom into nothing was heartbreaking. One of the most important things I learned throughout my journey was, you can't help who you love.

But I think where Jessica went wrong was not knowing when to give up and stooping to such lows. If by some luck she had succeeded in snagging Daniel, her karma wouldn't have been good, the same would've happened to their relationship. Regardless, she—I hoped, learned from this. She was also young, around the same age as Daniel, and would find someone that cherished her for her.

I can't help but laugh at myself. I still had a lot to learn, but I talk as if I know the answer.

BONUS STORY
A Life Worth Waiting

"**T**his is Daniel. He'll be starting in grocery for a while before learning front-end," Loue said. He was an older man. He looked very tired and miserable when I first met him. But I couldn't blame him. There were only 6 employees including myself.

I moved to New York a month before applying to Loue's Grocery. There wasn't a real reason why I moved to New York. I was just bored of Missouri. My father and I moved from state to state because of his work. After he divorced Margaret, he married my foster sister Rebecca. Homelife… was just uncomfortable. Having a "mom" 2 years older attending the same college, it was disturbing. And as expected, their marriage didn't last long. Rebecca had matured and realized she didn't want to stay with an old geezer. They argued constantly and I couldn't handle it anymore. My dad helped me get an apartment in Brooklyn, paid for my plane ticket and I left Missouri. Two weeks later, they filed for divorce.

I felt bad for my dad. Even though what he did as wrong, he was still my dad, and it was sad seeing him alone and heartbroken, but that was better than staying married to Margaret. Every now and then I thought about my foster siblings. How they were holding up against her and if they had gotten adopted. Anna was my main source of information, but she hadn't contacted me in 4 years. I tried my best not to think about Maya. Sometimes, well most of the time, she would pop in my head, but since moving to New York, I hadn't thought about her. I was pretty sure I had finally gotten over her. I had enough of my unrequited love. I wanted to live my life.

I had other relationships, but the women I dated could tell I was in love with someone else and dumped me. They were in the right, anyone would break up with someone that didn't love them. I just wished one of them would've stayed and helped me lose those feelings.

Loue continued, "Jessica."

"Yes sir," a woman, I presume Jessica, interrupted, raising her hand. Damn she was actually…kind of hot.

"I need you on register while Jorge shows Daniel the ropes."

"Right away sir." She saluted.

I thought she was cute and playful. If I worked with her, that low staffed store would be worthwhile.

I worked hard over the months. I stayed as many employees came and went. I worked a lot of shifts with Jessica. Man, she really was beautiful. I genuinely believed she could be the one to end my one-sided love.

"Daniel, the load's here," Jessica said, walking to the register.

"Okay and?" I said.

"And that means you and I switch."

"Hmm… nah, I don't think so." I smiled.

"I don't want to work on it by myself."

"You aren't. Tyshawn is back there."

"He gets off soon."

"And when he does, we can switch." I smirked at Jessica and returned to work.

I liked giving her a hard time. It was my way of flirting. I hoped she picked up on it though. I mean, there was no way she wasn't interested right? Not to toot my own horn, but I was handsome. Women especially loved my gray eyes and dimples. And the way she spoke and looked at me, I could tell she wanted me. I just… I wanted to make sure she was the one. I didn't want to invest so much time on her, and she dumps me like all the others. She had some unattractive flaws like how she treated Loue and the job, and her endless complaints, but when you care about someone, you overlook those qualities and remember the good ones.

As I stood there, I thought about whether I should ask Jessica out or at least on a date. It wouldn't have hurt, except maybe things went terribly wrong and work became awkward. But what were the odds of that? Deep in thought, I hadn't noticed a customer sat her items on the belt.

"Oh, I'm so—" my words slurred, and I paused. Standing in front of me was Maya. Of all the ways I fantasized meeting her again, this wasn't how I imagined it. She looked almost the same as she did when we were younger... well she looked prettier. I didn't know if it was my imagination, but when I saw her, it was like everything slowed down and it was just me and her. Her eyes were beautiful, she had her hair in a bun, I couldn't help staring at her neck, she wore a black tank top and leggings. Her slender frame was mesmerizing, and she hadn't grown an inch.

You have got to be kidding me, I thought. *What are the chances of her being here of all places?*

She stared at me confused.

"I'm sorry, h-how are you?" I stuttered. I needed to calm my heart. I scanned her items as fast as I could. My hands trembled.

"Good," she mumbled. "You?"

"G-great... just great," I whispered, cynically. "So what brings you to New York?"

"I just wanted a change of scenery I guess."

"Yeah, same honestly. I've been here for a few months. I love it."

She didn't respond. She nodded and looked back down.

She was just like she was years ago, very aloof when she spoke to me... but did she even recognize me? Ugh! Why did it have to be that way? Why couldn't it be like my fantasies? Her smiling and hugging me, happy to see me. *Actually remembering me.*

Maybe this is a sign, I thought. While I spent almost 10 years chasing after her, she hadn't thought about me once. Not even spared a bit of remembrance.

I sighed. "Have a great day."

"Thank you," she said, grabbing her bags.

I watched as she left the store. My chest was tight. I guess that was her way of rejecting me. I rung up the last customer in line and logged out of the register. Front End was the last place I should have been. I needed to work on the load to keep my mind busy.

"Hey," I said, calling out to Jessica.

"What's up?" she asked.

"Uh, let's switch. I'm bored working up front."

"Fine with me," she said, walking away. She stopped and turned around. "You okay?"

"Yeah why?"

"Hmm, you just seem a little down."

"A little, but don't worry about it."

"You sure? We can grab some coffee after work and talk about it?"

I smiled. "You know what, sure, let's do that."

"Great." She smiled. "I'll meet you outside."

It was fate. While I thought about if I should ask Jessica out, I ran into Maya who indirectly rejected me. It was fate telling me to give up Maya and go for Jessica. I finished the rest of my shift without a thought about what happened.

After work, I met Jessica outside. She was sitting on a bench, her umbrella in her lap, playing a mobile game.

"Sorry to keep you waiting," I said.

"It's alright."

"You should've waited inside, it's cold and wet."

"I'm okay." She stood up and opened her umbrella. "A little rain doesn't hurt. Besides, the coffee will warm me up."

"I forgot mine," I said, pointing at her umbrella. "Can we share?"

"Yeah, that's fine."

It was all just tactic honestly. I could have easily gone inside and bought one, but what would be the point of going after her, if I didn't pull moves like that?

We walked to Caribbean Coffee. It wasn't that far from Loue's. When we got inside, I motioned for Jessica to go first.

"Hello," the barista said.

"Yeah hi," Jessica responded. "Can I get an iced latte, add caramel but not too much and not a lot of ice. Thanks."

"Did you want any milk?"

"Did I say I wanted it?" Jessica snapped back. "Your tip is banking on you getting my order right. Just get what I said I wanted."

My mouth dropped. *No way she said that.*

I was in so much denial, I assumed I imagined it. Being conscious of what Jessica allegedly did, I was overly nice to compensate it. I made sure to give her a bigger tip too.

Throughout the waiting process, Jesscia continued to make rude comments to the employees. It was kind of a turn off, but I had to remind myself to keep an open mind. I was mentally drained by the time we made it to a table. Never knew I could get so embarrassed in 5 minutes.

"What's been bothering you," Jessica asked.

"Huh? Oh, honestly I can't really remember." There were two reasons why I didn't tell her. One, I didn't want her to know I still had feelings for someone else. And two, I wasn't in the mood to speak to her after what she did.

"That's good." Jessica nodded. "Well I'm glad we were still able to hangout."

"Yeah, me too…"

After a few minutes of conversation, I enjoyed her company again. We all had our flaws, so it was something I was willing to overlook.

Two weeks had passed since I last saw Maya. It felt surreal, like it never happened. I wondered if it was Maya. Logically, I knew it was her, but could that have been why she didn't recognize me? That woman just looked like her. Maybe I was daydreaming? That was only wishful thinking. Searching for some kind of explanation and way to not accept that I was rejected. As much as I wanted to be with Jessica, my heart still desired Maya.

"Another day of front-end?" I complained.

"Deal with it," Loue barked. "Jessica's sick, most likely playing hooky. Hailey's off. It's only two of you here right now."

"Okay, okay," I said, defensively. "I was joking."

Loue looked unamused then walked away.

I sighed. "Man, it's going to be a rough day."

Business was slow, I was grateful but extremely bored. We had one customer every 30 minutes to an hour. As I twiddled my thumbs, the doors opened. I perked up excited to work.

"Hello," I said, looking towards the door.

"Hi," Maya said, grabbing a basket.

My heart sank.

Guess it was her, I thought.

Man, I needed Jessica there to remind me I was after her. I looked at the aisles hoping to catch a glimpse of Maya shopping. I saw her once or twice before she came to check out.

"Did you find everything alright?" I asked.

"Mm-hm." She nodded.

I was impatient. I wanted to hear her voice. "Did you want paper or plastic?"

"Plastic."

I'd forgotten about her one-word replies. She did that especially around strangers or people she didn't want to talk to… I was the former hopefully. I thought about different ways to hear her.

What am I doing? I thought. I was too obsessed with her. *Maya is out of the question. Get it together.*

I rang up her items as quick as I could and watched her leave. I sighed and leaned my head on the register.

"You're sighing a lot today," Loue said. He placed his belongings on the counter and said, "Go on break."

"Okay," I said, signing out of the register.

"Anything you want to talk about?"

I shook my head. "Nah, I'm just dealing with a crisis. I have to fix it on my own."

"If you say so. Just remember, sometimes it's good to figure things out on your own, and sometimes it's best to ask for help."

"I'll remember that."

Over time, it became a biweekly thing, maya shopping every other Tuesday. I made sure I was working front-end those days. I was still interested in Jessica, but that didn't mean I couldn't admire Maya from afar. Only until Jessica and I dated of course. I felt guilty on the days Maya visited. I tried my best to not flirt with Jessica. It was wrong to look at a woman while chasing after another.

"Welcome," I said. I got used to seeing Maya and could talk more casually with her.

She smiled and continued to shop. Man, she had the most beautiful smile, even if it was a "meh" awkward smile. I waited "patiently" for her to bring her items up. She always bought the same items. Off-brand canned food and $1 dinner trays. I wondered if she was shopping elsewhere because that wasn't healthy. None of the canned vegetables had any nutritional value. Maybe that was why she was so skinny? She wasn't eating properly.

If I was dating her, I would've made sure she was eating healthy meals. Was she dating anyone? I really wished she wasn't. *He...or she... would be one lucky bastard and they better be treating her right.*

I must have been a masochist. I kept thinking of things that made me depressed. But why was I blaming myself? It was her fault for being irresistible. If she hadn't moved to New York, I would have been just fine.

Man, time flew by. It was already the holiday season. Couldn't believe I lived in the big city for almost a year. I had a banging hot woman that was interested in me, I had a stressful but fun job that paid well, and I was able to see Maya again.

I hadn't seen Maya in a few weeks, but I assumed she was visiting her family. Which was a good thing. That meant she was adopted and didn't have to deal with Margaret for that long. I wondered if I should go home. My father needed the company but if Jessica didn't have plans, we could have spent Thanksgiving and Christmas together, but what was more important?

Maybe I could spend thanksgiving with dad, and if Jessica's available, Christmas with her, I thought.

As I contemplated what to do, Jessica came up to me. Again, it was fate.

"Do you have plans for thanksgiving?" she asked.

"I was just thinking about what to do," I said, sitting a box down. "I was thinking of spending Thanksgiving with my dad and staying here for Christmas. I'm not sure though."

"It's always good to go home." She nodded. "If you do decide to stay here, we can hang out for Christmas. My family isn't doing much anyways."

"Alright, I'll see about that."

On my break, I called my dad. I just wanted to make sure he was alright. If he wasn't, I would cancel everything to see him.

"Hey dad," I said, as he answered. "Uh, do we have any plans for Thanksgiving?"

"I don't know, do we?"

"That's what I'm asking."

My father was chill, except, he made too many annoying jokes at the wrong time.

"Well, I know you're probably partying it up, so you don't have to worry about me."

"First off, I'm not partying, all I do is work. And secondly, I'm always going to worry about you. This will be the first year we don't spend the holidays together."

"Feels weird, doesn't it?" he asked.

"A little."

"I'm fine if you don't want to. I met a nice lady who will be glad to spend them with me."

"Ha." I laughed. "I see what it is."

"You know it." He laughed.

"I hope you two have a good time. I'll probably see if the girl I'm talking to wants to hang out then."

"Ooh finally moving on from Mira?" He sounded excited.

"Maya dad. And yeah, I hope she'll get my mind away from her."

"Me too, me too," he said. "About damn time."

"Yeah, only thing though is that I ran into Maya again. I don't know if I'm just bound to stay in love with her forever or if I'm just unlucky."

"Don't say that, you're only 22. You'll get over her soon, keep an open mind to finding new love."

"Will do."

"Alright, I'm gonna let you go," he said. "Bye Daniel."

"Bye dad."

I sat at a table staring into space. I flipped my phone in my hands. My life was a disaster…again. It took one look at Maya to send me down the rabbit hole… more like, she dropkicked me down. I wanted her to stop coming to the store so I could move on, or at least long enough for me to catch feelings for Jessica. My father was right, I wouldn't be in love with her forever, but I knew I was going to waste my youth waiting for her.

I ended up spending Thanksgiving alone. I decided not to invite Jessica. She most likely had plans, and we were already planning to spend Christmas together. Well, we talked about it.

Once December hit, Maya was back to shopping at Loue's. I was confident she went to see family. She probably was going to do the same at Christmas. Even if I couldn't spend that time with her, I was happy she had someone to go home to.

I was very wishy-washy about my feelings. I wasn't getting anywhere with Jessica emotionally. All together I was ready to give up on dating. I couldn't focus on Jessica when every time I saw Maya, I became a mess. I needed more time to get over her before dating someone else. If and possibly when, I dated Jessica, I didn't want it to be like my other relationships.

I cancelled the Christmas "date" we had. I told her I was going to work for Christmas. She was clearly pissed but played it off well. And that was fine, I was okay with her losing interest in me. I felt like a dick for not talking to her, but I wanted to put some distance between us. For my sake and hers.

It was Christmas Eve, the store finally settled down after 5 PM. We had an hour before closing. Loue gave those of us who worked a Christmas bonus labeled as a present. He was a great boss and cared about his team. It was peaceful waiting for the store to close. Only one customer was shopping, and they didn't bother us. As I checked them out, only 10 minutes left, Maya entered the store.

"We close in 10," Loue shouted.

"Okay." Maya nodded.

I thought she was spending time with her family. Maybe they're visiting her? I thought.

Loue walked over. "I hate when people come in last minute. I get they need their last-minute items, but we'd like to go home."

"Yeah…" I said. I didn't want to talk bad about Maya, so I left it with that. I was happy to see her. Luckily, Maya didn't take long. She was checking out with 3 minutes to spare.

"Merry Christmas," I said. "Have any plans for tonight and tomorrow?"

She shook her head. "No, just relaxing at home."

"Same. It's always better to enjoy the holidays at home with family."

"Mm-hm, but it's just me."

What? She's going to be alone? What about her family? I thought. *Did something come up and they had to cancel?*

I was sad for her. I hated the fact she was going to be alone. Then it occurred to me, even though she didn't know me, maybe I could invite her to spend it with me. No one wanted to be alone, right? I took a deep breath, but I couldn't get the words out.

Come on, don't be a chicken. Ask her, I thought. I watched as she gathered her bags, but I couldn't speak.

"Merry Christmas," she said, as she left the store.

Damn, I thought. *It really is fate telling me not to go for it.*

I logged off the register and punched out. I sluggishly walked up the stairs to grab my coat. I wasn't sure it was fate as much as it was me fearing rejection. Hearing it, even if it was just hanging out, would crush my heart.

I missed the last bus, the next one wouldn't come for another 2 hours. I had nowhere to wait so I decided to walk home. It wasn't that far of a walk. I'd arrive faster than I would waiting for the bus.

I finally made it to my apartment building. My legs were shivering, and my face felt frozen. I was so cold the heat was painful when I walked inside the building. I saw the elevator opening as someone went inside and shuffled as fast as I could to get in. It was already set to the 6th floor. Must have been one of my neighbors. It was weird, I lived there for almost a year, and never saw any of my neighbors until then. Curious I snuck a peek to see what they looked like.

No fucking shot, I thought.

Standing next to me was Maya. There was no way she lived in the same building as me. She must have decided to visit someone after all. Guess she was the person I saw walking ahead of me in the distance. Man, she was a slow walker.

"Go ahead." I motioned as the doors opened. I felt like a stalker. Naturally, I was being a gentleman letting her go first, but I also wanted to see which apartment she went into. I promise, I wasn't a creep or stalker, I just wanted to know where to avoid. I watched as she walked to 6B. She took her time taking her keys out. I did as well. Was my luck that terrible? The universe was playing a sick trick on me… or maybe I had the best luck?

How did I not know she lived next to me? How long did she live there? It was a nice Christmas present to find out. But at that point, I knew I wasn't going to be able to get over her, not when she was a wall away. I knew every time I left my apartment, I would search for her. She would stay in my head 24/7.

As happy as I was to live next to her, I never saw or heard her leave her apartment and after a few weeks, she stopped showing up at Loue's. I was upset and worried, but I figured she found a better, cheaper store to shop at.

It had been 3 months since I last saw her, and I took the moment I had to go after Jessica. Maya was nowhere to be seen and eventually she would be off my mind

"Hey Jessica," I said, walking to the front.

"What's up," she said, somberly.

"Are you free this weekend?"

"Yeah why?"

"I was just wondering if you wanted to have dinner?"

Jessica perked up. "Sure, what time?"

"How about Saturday at 7?"

"That works."

"Alright, give me your number after work."

"Okay."

After getting her number I went home. I needed to decide on a place to go. She was a rich girl, so it had to be some place fancy, but still cheap. My wallet wouldn't be able to handle much.

Saturday arrived and I met Jessica at L'amour cuisine. She didn't look impressed.

"Have you been here?" I asked.

"Yeah. It's decent, I've had better."

Shit, I thought. Out loud I said, "Oh okay. Sorry, I should have chosen a better restaurant."

"It's alright. You didn't know better."

"Yeah…" I decided to take that as a playful comment.

It was extremely expensive. I was gonna take a huge hit from this. And I knew Jessica was the kind of person that expected her date to pay. And I didn't mind, I just regretted choosing a place she didn't even like.

The date wasn't fun. I realized we didn't have much in common, and I couldn't stand her personality anymore. I was in love with the idea of finding love not with her. She invited me to her place, but it wasn't right to accept when I didn't want to continue dating her.

I stared out the window on the bus ride home. Traffic was bad, we were stuck on the bridge. The water looked pretty, the city lights reflecting off the water was beautiful. My eyes fixated on movement up ahead. It was a person walking on the lower bridge.

Who the hell is crazy enough to walk down here?! I thought sitting up. No one else noticed them. *What are they doing?*

I looked closer and saw Maya. Was she drunk? I hit the stop cord and once the bus crossed the bridge, I ran to her.

A Life: Worth Talking About
A Life: Worth Living

Whoo! Finally, this book is done. If you made it this far, thanks for reading!

I started this book in 2018. The scene towards the beginning of the book when Maya and Daniel are watching movies and she cries, was the catalyst for this book. I didn't cry, but the "Forest Within," (replaced the anime *The Moment You Fall in Love*) sparked the same thought Maya had for me and sure enough I was writing this. It was based in New York because I visited there a week or two after I had this book idea. And the person I stayed at the Airbnb said what Carmen said, and that gave me inspiration. I don't know what led to that sentence, but it was so beautiful I had to give him (V) and his wife (C) a role in this book. But not exactly them of course lol.

The book didn't turn out how I originally envisioned it. It was supposed to be a rom-com where everything she saw in romance novels happened to her. And believe it or not, Daniel was annoying and less suave. Haha. But somewhere along the line it became more serious.

A lot of what was written was based on statistics as well as personal experience. I did a lot of research to make sure what was written was as accurate as possible. But some was also based off my experience with old friends in foster care and how they were treated.

I'm happy I finally finished this book. My first full story novel, the first two were short stories so this means a lot to me.

If you made it through my rambling, I have a few things to share about potential sequels. It's not very likely to come out for a while, other projects and all.

Anna's story: A Life: Worth Loving. Her perspective through this book and what happens in her life.

Makayla's story: A Life: Worth Dreaming. Her perspective through the story and what's happening to her.

A lot of hints were written throughout the book about life events for them. I might do a short stories novel about the side characters, maybe give Daniel a quick story, depends on who's interested in them.

Follow my twitter @AJHughesAuthor and my new Instagram A.J.HughesAuthor and tell me what you think about A Life: Worth Living. Check for my other books and novels to come.

About the Author

A.J. Hughes is the author of *Walk on the Other Side* and *A Day of Rain*.

A.J. Hughes lives in Madison, WI. with her adorable cat Fatty. She loves to read Manga. Her passions are music, writing, learning languages, and art. Her hope is to create amazing novels for readers all over the world to enjoy.